PENGUIN BOOKS

NOVEL WITHOUT A NAME

Duong Thu Huong, one of Vietnam's most popular writers, was born in 1947 in Vietnam. At the age of twenty, she led a Communist Youth Brigade sent to the front during the Vietnam War. Of her volunteer group of forty, she was one of three survivors. During China's 1979 attack on Vietnam, she also became the first woman combatant present on the front lines to chronicle the conflict. A vocal advocate of human rights and democratic political reform, she was expelled from the Communist party in 1989. She was imprisoned without trial for seven months in 1991 for her political beliefs. Duong Thu Huong is the author of four previous novels, including *Paradise of the Blind* (Penguin) which was the first Vietnamese novel ever translated into English and published in the United States. All of her work has been effectively banned by the Vietnamese government. She lives in Hanoi with her two children.

Translators Phan Huy Duong and Nina McPherson live in France.

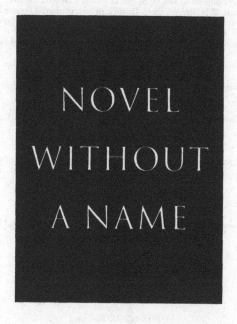

NOVEL WITHOUT A NAME

Duong Thu Huong

Translated from the Vietnamese by Phan Huy Duong and Nina McPherson

PENGUIN BOOKS

PENGUIN BOOKS

Published by the Penguin Group

Penguin Group (USA) Inc., 375 Hudson Street, New York, New York 10014, U.S.A.

Penguin Group (Canada), 90 Eglinton Avenue East, Suite 700, Toronto, Ontario,
Canada M4P 2Y3 (a division of Pearson Penguin Canada Inc.)

Penguin Books Ltd, 80 Strand, London WC2R 0RL, England

Penguin Ireland, 25 St Stephen's Green, Dublin 2, Ireland (a division of Penguin Books Ltd)

Penguin Group (Australia), 250 Camberwell Road, Camberwell, Victoria 3124,
Australia (a division of Pearson Australia Group Pty Ltd)

Penguin Books India Pvt Ltd, 11 Community Centre, Panchsheel Park,
New Delhi – 110 017, India

Penguin Group (NZ), 67 Apollo Drive, Rosedale, North Shore 0632, New Zealand
(a division of Pearson New Zealand Ltd)

Penguin Books (South Africa) (Pty) Ltd, 24 Sturdee Avenue, Rosebank,
Johannesburg 2196, South Africa

Penguin Books Ltd, Registered Offices: 80 Strand, London WC2R 0RL, England

First published in the United States of America
by William Morrow and Company, Inc. 1995
Reprinted by arrangement with William Morrow and Company, Inc.
Published in Penguin Books 1996

20 19 18

THE LIBRARY OF CONGRESS HAS CATALOGUED THE HARDCOVER AS FOLLOWS:
Duong, Thu Huong.
[Tiêu thuyêt vô dê. English]
Novel without a name/Duong Thu Huong;
translated by Phan Huy Duong and Nina McPherson.
p. cm.
ISBN 0-688-12782-7 (hc.)
ISBN 978-0-14-025510-2 (pbk.)
PL4378.9.D759T5413 1995 94–33673

Printed in the United States of America
Set in Bodoni Book
Designed by Liney Li

For my friends who died,
who live on in me

NOVEL WITHOUT A NAME

I listened all night to the wind howl through the Gorge of Lost Souls. Endless moans punctuated by sobs. From time to time it whinnied like a mare in heat, whistling through the broken shafts of the bamboo roof above me, sweeping through the countryside in a macabre symphony of sound.

The flame of our oil lamp flickered weakly. I poked my head from under the covers and blew it out, wishing I too could sink, body and soul, into the night. Against the wall, a dead branch rapped a dull cadence. It was impossible to sleep, so I murmured a prayer. *Dear sisters, you who have lived and died here as human beings: Do not haunt us any longer. Protect us. Fortify our bodies, light the way for our spirits, so*

*that in every battle we may conquer. When victory comes,
when peace comes to our country, we will carry you back to
the land of your ancestors.*

I buried my face in the blankets, trying to block out the
wind. But it seemed to deepen and gather strength, howling
through the Gorge of Lost Souls.

Two weeks earlier we had buried six girls. At dawn I
had gone with Lanh's platoon to gather bamboo shoots.
Shortly after midday we reached the Gorge of Lost Souls. A
swarm of vultures circled in the air above us, diving earth-
ward and rising again toward the sky, their cries shattering
the silence. Lanh stopped suddenly, sniffing. "There must be
a dead animal around here. It stinks!"

It did stink. The farther we advanced, the more the odor
reeked. Someone proposed turning back, but Lanh urged us
on. "It could be a man. Who knows? Maybe one of ours."

"Let's go see," I said.

We moved toward the corner of the forest from which
the horrible odor seemed to emanate. We found six naked
corpses. Women. Their breasts and genitals had been cut off
and strewn on the grass around them. They were northern
girls: We could tell by their scarves made out of parachute
cloth and the lotus-shaped collars of their blouses. They must
have belonged to a group of volunteers or a mobile unit that
lost its way. Perhaps, like us, they had come here to search
for bamboo shoots or vegetables.

The soldiers had raped them before killing them. The corpses were bruised violet. So this was how graceful, girlish bodies rotted, decomposing into swollen old corpses, puffy as dead toads. Maggots swarmed in their wounds, their eyes and mouths. Fat white larvae. They crawled over the corpses in waves, plunging in and out of them in a drunken orgy.

One of the soldiers covered his nose. "Goddamn worms. They're everywhere."

"Let's bury the girls," I said.

Vultures circled and shrieked overhead. The heat was suffocating. Sweat beaded and glistened on our faces. The odor of rotting flesh hung in the air. We gathered the corpses, fighting with the vultures and the maggots for each shred of flesh. We buried them. The girls' pockets were empty; not a single slip of paper, just a few pieces of red and blue yarn, a few betel nuts. The yarn to tie their hair, the betel nuts to clean their teeth. They must have believed they would see their men again . . .

The earth was shallow here, so we had to bury the corpses in a small circular pit. By the time we finished, the maggots had formed a dense mass. Lanh threw an armful of dead leaves over them in a pile and set fire to it. You could hear the maggots crackle. We stood around the blaze, exhausted, bathed in sweat.

We threw the bamboo shoots on the ground and returned to camp. Not a single vegetable. Just a clump of rice mixed with yams, a bit of salt, red chilies, and dried lemongrass. This was our life, our soldier's life. One day there would be nothing left of it.

"Quan, hey, Quan."

Luy's voice was a whine. I didn't move. He continued, "Hey, Quan. Quan, are you asleep already?"

I didn't answer, pretending to be asleep. But then I ended up drifting off. An odd slumber, like a train jerking along its tracks, ready to derail at any moment. A train without passengers, filled with youthful dreams, long letters written in violet ink. Red scarves litter the empty cars. Broken sticks of chalk. A pencil stub. The train rolls on, deaf, mute. Deserted fields spread out along both sides of the tracks as far as the eye can see. I want to scream for the conductor, to pull the emergency cord, to cry out. But I am invisible, paralyzed, formless, featureless. My face dissolves, my voice is smothered by the wind . . .

"Quan, hey, Quan."

A blow against my body. And as if from under water, I rise from the depths of the dream. Glistening waves lap at my body, gently molding me a face. I feel as if I could die of happiness. I have a face again . . .

❖   ❖   ❖

"Quan, brother, wake up."

My arm felt paralyzed; it had fallen asleep. I struggled to pull up my covers. "What is it?"

4

"Quick, get up. I just saw an orangutan."

I wrapped myself more tightly under my covers. I was no longer some diluted substance in the depths of the water; I was lucid, but I didn't dare move. I wanted to wallow in this happiness, the warmth of these blankets; I was still alive, still myself, safe and sound, with my body, all thirty-two teeth, my sweat-damp feet in moldy socks, a belt around my waist.

"Get up, elder brother. We've got all the time in the world to sleep. The orangutan is huge. At least fifty pounds. Get up, quickly!"

I didn't move. Luy pleaded with me. "Please get up. We haven't had fresh meat in so long. Our knees go weak on patrol."

I didn't budge. Luy shook me. "Get up, elder brother. The men will finally be able to eat."

I peeled back the covers. "Why don't you just go by yourself?"

Luy winced. "I don't want to. It's a bit spooky. Come with me. I'll do the shooting. I never miss."

I sat upright. "You asshole. Why are you up so early?"

"I'm hungry. My stomach is screaming at me. Please, put your shoes on, elder brother. It'd be a shame if he got away."

I sighed, exasperated: Luy always called me "elder brother" when he wanted a favor. But I threw on my shoes and jacket and followed him. The forest was covered with a thick fog, and the cold, damp leaves brushed our faces as we walked. I was freezing. We advanced through eerie stands of trees. The shrieks of gibbons echoed in the distance.

"How can you see a monkey in this darkness?" I asked.

Luy laughed. "Chief, you forget that I've got the sharpest eyes in this company. Remember the time I shot those two bucks on the mountain? And the time on Mount Carambola, hunting wild goat? That was my rifle, after all."

I grumbled in acknowledgment.

"Boy, you sure have a short memory!" Luy continued. "It was on Mount Carambola that you first tasted orangutan."

I shuddered. I hadn't forgotten, I just didn't want to remember. But Luy wouldn't let me off so easily. He grinned, squinting at me mischievously: "I do have a good memory, don't I?"

I said nothing and bent down to pull a leech off the rim of my left boot. It was still dark, but I could see blood on the tip of my finger. The blood smell spread through the chill fog, nauseating and sweet like the narcotics used by the Montagnards. Luy had gone on ahead. "The trail is too narrow here. Let me trailblaze. We're going to have a great soup for lunch."

And he was off. The memory of the boiling-hot soup we had eaten at the foot of Mount Carambola came back to me. The soldiers had squatted down in a circle, banging their spoons against their mess tins, their eyes riveted on the steaming pot. Every now and then the cook stirred the clear broth, with its floating grains of puffy cooked rice . . . and tiny orangutan paws . . . like the hands of babies.

"Perfect. It looks perfect."

"Ten minutes more and it'll be ready. It's even more delicious than the famous swallow's-nest soup."

Everyone had congratulated one another. I just stared at the tiny hands spinning in circles on the surface of the soup. We had descended from the apes. The horror of it.

A long time ago, in the markets up north, I had seen some ghastly soups. There was always an immense cauldron perched on three blackened rocks over a searing bed of coals. A muddy gray scum gathered on the soup, pieces of buffalo, pieces of beef, entire livers, spleens, and horse hooves bobbed and floated to the surface.

The soup vendor wore a sooty black smock dripping with grease. His narrow eyes angled toward his temples like blades, his bald head glistened. He fished out huge chunks of the meat with a bamboo spear and placed them on a wooden board, where he hacked them up with a cleaver, the kind that could sever the thickest neck in ancient Annamite executions.

I used to stare furtively at those soups with a mixture of terror and awe. I had been raised in a different culture, in the famished, poverty-stricken Red River Delta. We only ate meat during ceremonies for the dead, or during Tet, the Lunar New Year. In the shadow of these dead souls, we took a little pleasure in existence. The lie extended even to the way the meat was served. We admired those who knew how to make the meat go farther by slicing it into fine strips; we congratulated those who could make rich-looking dishes out of our poor ingredients. To me, this mountain stew was a dish for giants from the depths of the forest, a barbarous dish that reminded me of the ancient legends about the famous inns where highway bandits came to dream to the strains of a Chinese lute.

The horror loomed large in my memory. Just like the horror of the orangutan soup. Orangutans are large apes, and they bear an uncanny resemblance to human beings. Their eyes can laugh maliciously or flare with hate, pain, or bitterness. Most of all, their hands are smooth and white, like the hands of a two-year-old child.

◆　　◆　　◆

There were some real sharpshooters in my company. We often went hunting, and we always brought back lots of game—bucks, bears, polecats, and grouse. But sometimes we would cross uninhabited regions, places where the bombs had scared off all the animals. For months on end we forgot what meat even tasted like. At the foot of Mount Carambola, we killed two wild goats. Then there had been nothing for a long time. For eight weeks all we ate was rice with a bit of salt, red chilies, and root soup. And so the men had begun to hunt monkey.

On the first day out they killed an orangutan. That time, only the five hunters and the cook had dared to taste the soup. But the next time, the number doubled, and the time after that half the company joined the feast. By and by, everyone took part. The whole troop would go off hunting orangutan. Except me.

Soon they weren't just satisfied with the soup. They concocted other delicacies: a kind of monkey salad, minced-monkey dishes. They showered me with invitations to taste their cooking.

"Chief, if you only knew! After you've tasted it, everything else, the venison, all the wild fowl, seem as bland as snail soup. Orangutans are almost human. There's no tastier flesh."

"Aww, forget your inhibitions, Chief. Just try it once. A bowl of orangutan soup must be more nourishing than four ounces of monkey gelatin!"

We lived in a community. Anyone who stood apart stuck out like a nail that everyone—the cowards and the heroes, the vindictive and the tolerant alike—yearned to pry out. They wanted me to submit to the will of the group, if only to demonstrate its power . . .

That night Luy killed an orangutan that weighed almost forty-five pounds. The cooks minced the lean meat and made it into a salad with chilies, lemongrass, and aromatic herbs they had picked in the forest. They used the bones to make soup. I remember coming up to watch. It was cold outside, and the steam rose off the soup in fragrant, milky clouds.

The soldiers had gathered around the cauldron, their eyes gleaming hungrily. Teu, a private from Tien Hai, tugged at my shirttail: "Will you have a bowl of soup with us, Chief?"

I shook my head.

Teu insisted. "It's delicious, much better than venison."

"I don't feel like eating."

"Oh come on, it's not for lack of appetite, you don't have the guts, right?"

Teu had been stirring the soup with a ladle, and he scooped up a hand: "Like a child's, isn't it? It's scary. But I'm telling you, once you taste it, you'll be addicted."

The other soldiers joined in, jeering at me: "Go on, Chief, be a man. Try it, come on, try it."

"Okay, boys, this time we won't let him off. He has to try our orangutan soup."

My cheeks burned. I took the hand from the ladle and bit into it. I spat out a mouthful of tiny joints and bones.

"Bravo! Bravo, Chief!"

Exultant, they started to bang on their bowls and mess tins. I felt my neck, my back, burning. I glared at them and left the cave. The night was pitch-black. I groped my way to a nearby stream. I washed out my mouth several times, stuffing my fingers down my throat, trying to vomit up the hand.

But nothing came up. It was done. I had eaten it; nothing could change that. I shuddered with horror at the thought of it: the taste of human flesh in my mouth. I quickly lit a cigarette. For an instant its flame lit up the darkness. My chest warmed. Curls of smoke lingered, caressing my face. My mind slowly settled.

◆　　◆　　◆

I was five years old.

Of my childhood, I keep the memory of a distant hill, lush and green. Jackfruit and longan trees hang over the worm-eaten roof of a pagoda; a broken roof panel sticks up through the leaves. It is evening. At the foot of the hill, a warm light flickers through the cassava vines.

Mother holds my hand as we climb the hill toward the pagoda. She is pregnant, her enormous belly sways under an ao dai dyed the chestnut color of mangrove bark. She clutches her belly, wincing as she walks. Her face is ashen, drenched in sweat.

"Hold the bottom of the sack tightly or the clothes and the blankets will fall out."

"Yes, Mother," I yell back. I yell to mask my fear. I have never seen my mother's face like this. To me she had always been young and beautiful. She used to rock me in a hammock, toss me in the air. Her laughter was like music. Even now she is inseparable from the memory of the cool water we poured

from a coconut. She loved me; I adored her. When I wrapped my arms around her neck, nothing could frighten me; not even the shadows, the cries, or the gunshots. But now her face is as white as a drowned person's . . .

Her belly is strange and hideous to me, puffed out like a toad's. As she walks, her back curves oddly. I run behind her, out of breath, sweating.

"Quan, quickly, quickly." She suddenly screams. I am paralyzed. She puts her hand on her thigh and lifts her sweat-drenched face to the heavens. "My god, oh my god."

I see the sweat dripping down her neck.

Mother had come to this strange region after my father went off to join the anti-French resistance movement. She had taken refuge in this pagoda, where a Buddhist nun lived, supported by some distant relatives. My paternal grandparents were dead. My maternal grandparents lived somewhere beyond the horizon, where amber rice paddies were smothered in the smoke of war, where the sky was shattered by gunfire between troops sent by the French colonial puppet government and the Viet Minh. All this I had learned from my mother after she stopped working at the market to wait for the birth of her second child.

Back then, Mother took me in her arms murmuring and caressing me. I watched as her belly filled out. Curious, I used to put my hand over her stomach and draw it back whenever I felt something move. Mother would laugh: "That's your baby brother! You feel him moving? There, he just gave a kick. He's even more restless than you were. When you were here you didn't fidget so much."

I didn't understand. But somehow I knew that this warm, round belly held someone precious to me.

"Careful, Quan. Don't drop the satchel."

"Okay, okay."

Suddenly she collapses on the path, burying her face in the sand. I clutch her splayed thighs, whimpering. The back of her ao dai is drenched in sweat. Her hair sticks to her neck, and she rakes the dirt with her fingers, ripping loose clumps of grass from the path. I am trembling, lost.

"Mother, Mother."

She lets out another howl. "Oh, this is killing me."

I cling to her sweaty back. Suddenly, I don't even know why, I whisper to her in a low voice, "Please, Mother, don't go, don't leave me alone."

Mother raises herself, a haggard light flitted through her eyes. Her lips twist weakly, as if to smile. "My child."

Her voice is just a whisper. A smile flits across her contorted face. She lowers her head and crawls again toward the summit. I follow her, hugging the sack of clothes.

I don't remember how we got past the three doors that led inside the pagoda. I only remember the steps. Those high stones. So slippery.

The nun leads us to an abandoned shack at the back

of the garden. The stone steps are covered with weeds and brush. Dust has gathered on the floor of the house, the window ledges, even the wooden altar to the ancestors. It hangs in huge spiderwebs, like in legends filled with monsters.

Mother lies down on an old mat covered with banana leaves and rags. Blood gushes from between her thighs, scarlet as the blood of the buffalo we sacrificed on festival days. I hear a child's cry. I see little hands, and then, kicking at the air, little reddened feet.

The nun's voice booms in my ears: "Your mother has given you a little brother. Go congratulate her instead of trembling like a little quail."

Another voice rings out. "Praise Buddha, isn't he cute! Don't scare him. Come here, child, come see your little brother."

She shoves a tiny red being under my nose. Its face, sticky and puckered, as wrinkled as an old man's, terrifies me. A few hairs stick to its forehead. Its feet kick the air, my face. Mother turns toward me. "Don't be afraid, my son, he's your little brother."

A final ray of sun lights her face; her eyes shine with tenderness. Her face is clear again. I grab the tiny red feet and rub them against my cheeks. "Little brother. Little brother."

The nun and the midwife start to laugh. My mother laughs too. Her teeth sparkle like jade. I always loved my mother's laugh.

I cry out with happiness. "I have a little brother."

My brother also begins to bawl, and I let go of his feet. The midwife places him in a clay basin, and he howls and wiggles, splashing water all around him.

◆　　◆　　◆

My cigarette was half gone. Just beyond its glowing tip stood a dense stand of trees. A chameleon wriggled out of nowhere, a phosphorescent flash. Once more I felt the nausea, the desire to vomit up the orangutan hand. I took another drag on my cigarette and tried to reason with myself: *It has nothing to do with that . . . nothing to do with . . .*

But again I saw my brother's tiny feet kicking at the air. I watched a curl of smoke vanish, took a last drag on my cigarette, and flicked it into the stream. My mouth had a bitter taste. Something had wandered off beyond the horizon.

◆　　◆　　◆

"What are you thinking about, elder brother?" I noticed Luy had again started to use that familiar term with me. He jabbed me in the ribs with his elbow.

"Nothing," I said, exasperated.

"So let's talk. We've been wandering like two lost bears. This is scary."

"Why don't you always call me 'elder brother'? Sometimes you call me 'Chief,' other times 'Commander.' "

Luy laughed insolently. "When I need to flatter, my

tongue naturally reaches for the words 'Chief' and 'Commander.' "

"So that's it. 'Chief,' 'Commander'—you think those words are enough to get me out of bed, to drag me off hunting somewhere, to make me into your little deputy sharpshooter? You bastard."

"Don't be angry. Anyway, I only trick you when it comes down to little things, don't I? Careful—I'll bet you they've planted mines there in those bushes."

Dawn was breaking. Luy had gotten farther and farther ahead of me. His huge shoulders curved inward like bat's wings; he must have been almost six feet tall. His big body demanded fresh meat. For a long time we had lived on nothing but dried shrimp boiled with a few wild vegetables and lichen we scraped off rocks. Luy's skin was greenish. He would gather up all the grains of rice we had dropped from our bowls while eating. He would wolf down the burned, cindery rice crust on the bottom of the cooking pots.

"Ah, if I could just once eat my fill. A huge pot of sticky rice and a big braised ham hock. Or a big plate of rice noodles with lemon-and-shrimp sauce. Hey, Quan, let's see that box of sugar."

It was always the same story with him. Irritated, I snapped back: "Aren't you ashamed, a man your size? You licked it clean a long time ago."

"Not quite, not all of it . . . The other day I just scraped the surface."

"Well, go get it yourself, then. It's in the pack."

He got out the box of sugar and started to scrape it with a spoon. Then he licked it. Finally, he filled it with stream water, shook it, and drank it in one gulp. It was always like that with Luy. Later he wouldn't know what to do to tame his hunger. And at night he would dream of food he wanted to eat and wake up in a cold sweat, desperate.

An only son, Luy had been very spoiled. His mother had a few rice fields and ran her own small business, so she had a bit of money. Luy could easily down eight or nine bowls of rice at each meal.

"Careful, brother Quan, we're starting downhill."

We clutched tree roots and lowered ourselves down the precipice, which was wider and shallower than the Gorge of Lost Souls. Creeper vines with purple, trumpet-shaped flowers, flecked with velvety black patches, coiled around ancient trees. Inside each flower were stamens like octopus tentacles, swollen with pollen. They were translucent, dotted with gluey yellow beads of moisture that gave off a heavy, cloying perfume, a mixture of marsh weed and blood.

"We're here. Wait for me."

"Listen, just sit awhile and enjoy the view. I'll take care of the rest. That orangutan won't get out of here alive. I've been watching him. He's wandering among the trees at the bottom of that ravine. He must be hungry."

I sat down, hunching my shoulders for warmth. Dawn pierced through the fog, making it shimmer with icy silver shards of light. I followed the course of the stream with my eyes. I could see a cave covered with stunted trees, their dark branches stripped of leaves. Their trunks were thick with gnarled bulges, like deformed bodies. Why would orangutans come here to hunt for food?

The anxiety tree bears small, mushy yellow fruits shaped like canaries. It never bears much fruit, but in autumn it is covered with ash-colored flowers that bloom right through the winter, carpeting the earth with their cindery blossoms and giving off their nauseating, morbid scent. No one has ever succeeded in finding three fruits on an anxiety tree in a single season. The best climbers sometimes gather two. Everyone wants to taste the fruit at least once in their life; not just for its smooth, sugary flavor, but out of curiosity. It tastes good at first, but then a strange, drunken sensation comes over you, the heart suddenly beating faster and then slower in strange, irregular rhythms. People feel faint, sink into bizarre dreams. And all at once you feel the fragility of life, the uncertainty of it all, as you give yourself over to a strange expectancy: a yearning for death. Could it be that apes, too, came here in search of this rare intoxication, this anxious desire for death?

Luy suddenly appeared on a large rock. He stood up and waved to me. I looked in the direction he had indicated. I saw a shadow in the branches of the anxiety tree. It looked like a bear waddling around, searching for honey. Luy signaled to me not to move. Hunched over, he sprinted forward and melted into a milky pocket of fog. I waited, arms crossed. The shadow lumbered about, moving back and forth among the branches of the tree. It climbed from branch to branch and, at the peak, stood up.

A shot rang out. A scream echoed off the rock face. Shivers shot up my spine, and I jumped as if under the flick of a whip. This was no animal cry; the howl had reverberated across the rock walls, amplified by the mountain's ravines and crevices, piercing through space like a sliver of bamboo through live flesh.

Luy ran toward me, his face white. "Quan, Quan . . ."

I couldn't meet his eyes. I too was trembling. "What's the matter?"

"I don't know. The orangutan, it screamed like a man. I'm so scared . . . Come with me." Luy fell back, lowering the barrel of his rifle. We moved down into the ravine toward the forest. My feet slipped on the clammy rocks. I staggered; I felt the sweat soaking my back.

The fog, still thick in the brush over our heads, was as cool and opaque as marble. I tripped over a root. A moan suddenly pierced the thicket.

"Chief, chief . . ." Luy grabbed me by the arm, and we rushed into the fog. Two emaciated legs stuck out of the underbrush, a pair of ripped old army boots on the feet. One had a sock on, the other was bare. My heart raced and I ran forward, pulling Luy behind me. The wounded man clutched his stomach. Under his arm was a bloodied parachute, the kind we used to drop flares. His abdomen and the front of his pants were soaked in blood. I recognized him: It was Phien, the shiest of all my soldiers. When he saw us, he raised his head. "Brother Luy, you shot me by mistake."

He smiled. His buck teeth glinted at the edge of his trembling lip. He looked up at me, his voice rasping. "Chief, don't punish me . . . I wanted to gather . . . A few parachutes . . . to . . ."

He choked and his neck fell limply to one side. I put my hand on his heart. It had stopped beating. I yanked out one of his hairs and held it under his nostrils. It didn't move. Luy let out a wail and began to weep, his head glued to Phien's chest, his huge body racked with sobs. "Oh no, oh no."

Phien's eyes remained open, indifferent, emptied of their last rays of joy or pain. Barely a minute before, he had looked up at me patiently, imploring me not to punish him. He must have gotten up early to get this far. For whom had he been looking for parachutes? Why had I known nothing about this? I looked down the list of the combatants in my unit. He was at the very end:

Nguyen Van Phien
Age: 19
Native village: Neo, Gia Vien commune, Ninh Binh province
Height: 5 feet

Traits: pockmarked face, prominent teeth
Character: patient, gentle

You could always find Phien in the worst places, doing the dirtiest work. Whether we were in the middle of the jungle or camped outside a village, he was the one who gathered the wood, who hunted for vegetables. Phien collected cinders, unblocked sewers, even cleaned the camp. The fast-talking young recruits liked to compete with one another over the pretty village girls. And when something went wrong, they sent Phien to make peace. He was a born martyr. No one who had set eyes on him would ever think of doing him any harm.

After our unit had set up camp, Phien would wander around with a two-stringed guitar. Whenever he had a free moment, he would settle under a tree and pluck a few tunes:

> *Oh, I'm climbing on Mount Quan Doc,*
> *I'm sitting at the foot of the banyan tree . . .*

Luy was still sobbing, doubled over. I shouted at him to get up. He looked at me, distraught, his face smeared with blood and tears. Suddenly I was overcome by fury: "What use is crying? They're going to court-martial you and put a bullet through your head."

Luy sat motionless. A blood-red tear fell onto his shirt collar.

"Wipe your face. Even if you do end up in court, I won't have to go looking like this."

Luy fumbled in his pants pocket and pulled out a crumpled swatch of dirty parachute cloth. He smoothed it out and wiped his face mechanically.

"So, what are you going to do?"

He stayed mute.

"No matter what, you'll end up in front of a firing squad. Maybe I should just put a bullet through your head right here."

He nodded and got up. He walked over until he stood face to face with me. "Shoot me. Go ahead, shoot me, elder brother. It's going to end like that anyway."

Luy closed his eyes. I looked over at Phien's corpse and then back at Luy. What a bitch, this life: The survivor had closed his eyes, waiting for a bullet, while the dead man stared wide-eyed into space.

"Go ahead, shoot. It'll be easier that way."

Luy's eyes were still firmly shut. It was now light out and I could see his face clearly. Wrinkles creased the skin on his cheeks and around his eyelids. It was the face of an old man. How could this bastard have aged so quickly? Perhaps I too had aged. After all, you never see your own face. I didn't allow myself to brood on these thoughts. I didn't have time. My arms and body went limp.

"Open your eyes," I said.

He opened them and stared at me.

"Do you really believe that I could turn my gun on you?"

He didn't respond. A green reflection of trees flitted across the surface of his eyes.

"Do you really believe that, you bastard?"

His eyes brimmed with tears; they rolled down his cheeks.

"Only the two of us know about this. Nobody meant this to happen. No one could have seen it coming. Now it's happened and we can't do anything about it. What good would it do to shoot you or throw you in prison for life? And then there's your mother."

Luy heaved a sob. His mother was a widow who lived and breathed for him. If he were to die in combat, she would waste away. If he were convicted, she would hang herself or jump in a river.

I had met her once, on the day of our mobilization. Back then Luy had the rosy cheeks of a young girl. He had walked awkwardly behind a huge woman whose body swam in an ao dai the yellowy color of chicken fat. This was his mother, his guardian angel, his slave, his best friend. An ugly, lonely, elephantine woman. Luy was her only pride, her sole reason for living. I turned back to him now, impatient: "Well?"

Luy was still sobbing. I exploded. "Shut up! I can just see it now: You die and your mother goes and commits suicide. No, I don't want to hear a word about this incident. We're going back to camp. Act as if nothing happened. At noon, before lunch, I'll ask Khiem to call roll. Then we'll make investigations. They'll find Phien just like we found those girls in the Gorge of Lost Souls. Understand?"

"I understand," Luy said, whimpering, "but you'd better just shoot me. How can I go on living after this?"

I grabbed him by the shoulders and shook him hard: "Get a grip on yourself. If this gets out, we'll both be in trouble. What good would that do? We're not traitors. We didn't intend to kill him. You're not the only one I'm making up this little fable for. Do you think I care if they pump you with lead? That's the easy way out. But there's your mother to think of. You understand? I'm doing this for her, not for you. Shut up and stop sniveling. And wipe your face. You look like a ghost."

At noon I asked Khiem to call roll. Everyone was whispering:

"Where has Phien gone to?"

"He's deserted, of course. I'd bet on that."

"That chicken? Impossible."

"Why not? It's always people like that who create scandals."

In Phien's pack they found a large parachute cloth and eight smaller ones from artillery flares. That evening, while Khiem sent out patrols to search for Phien, I was urgently summoned to division headquarters. Luy accompanied me part of the way. The liaison officer had gone off into the bushes to urinate. I asked Luy: "Why did Phien collect all those parachutes? It's crazy."

"Everyone collects parachutes. To make scarves, or just as souvenirs. He thought he could trade them later for real fabric. In his village, a scarf made out of parachute cloth is fashionable."

"How do you know?"

"He told me. He often talked about it, how after the war we wouldn't know how to make a living. So he thought we could trade the parachutes for fabric and make ourselves some clothes. You didn't know, but he was very poor. His parents died and left him with a two-year-old sister to raise. They made a living tending ducks, stealing a bit of paddy rice here and there, fishing in the rice paddies. He adored his sister."

Luy hiccuped.

"The liaison officer is coming back—shut up. If anyone hears about this, they'll shoot me first, you understand?"

Luy fell silent, then left. I followed the liaison officer to division headquarters

✦   ✦   ✦

It wasn't the division commander who received me, but Luong, his deputy. We were childhood friends; we had known each other since the time we used to scamper naked under the stars, when a hibiscus hedge was the only fence between our families' houses. Luong was two years older than me. He was a tall young man with a large, square face and jaw and straight eyebrows. His lips used to be rosy all year long; now, after ten years of war and countless bouts of malaria, they had paled but were still redder than most soldiers'. Tonight Luong had a hesitant air about him. We sat in silence, sipping rice wine and nibbling at a salad of canned sardines and minced wild-banana stalk. After an hour, he invited me to take a bath with him in the stream.

"I washed yesterday. Anyway, in this weather we'd get pneumonia. This is no time to come down with a fever."

Luong lowered his voice. "Come with me anyway, I've got to talk to you."

My heart leapt. Had he already heard about this morning's incident? No. Impossible. He would have had to be clairvoyant. And what clairvoyant would have been crazy enough not to have fled the bombs, the famines, the massacres that plagued this country? Calmer now, I agreed to his request.

It was nightfall when we left camp. After three hundred yards we reached the edge of the forest. The tree tops sparkled in the sunset. Silently we drew long, deep breaths in the breeze that rustled through the forest. Luong led me down a slope strewn with brambles and saffron-colored flowers. The brambles grew right up to the edge of a stream. When we reached the water, Luong motioned to me to sit down.

We sat side by side, smoking silently, for a long time. The stream was dry, but a few puddles of water still glinted in the twilight like mirrors, fading from amber to rose and then violet.

"It's going to be dark soon," I said.

"Yes," muttered Luong, his eyes vacant.

He took two long drags on his cigarette.

"Listen, Quan, don't you miss the village?"

"Of course; who wouldn't?"

"Especially the river. Every time I see a stream like this, my feet go numb. The worst was crossing Phien Bong. Have you ever taken that route?"

"What soldier who has lived in these parts doesn't know that river?"

Luong agreed rather vaguely. "It's really wonderful."

"Well, okay, it's wonderful; but I don't think you brought me all the way here to chat about the village."

He didn't agree or disagree. He just lit another cigarette. "I don't want the other soldiers to hear us. There's a war going on, you know."

"Yeah, war," I snickered.

We had joined the army the same day. Ten years later, Luong was a staff officer. He was three grades higher than me in the army hierarchy. He had never been through the ordeals I had, but he had self-control and he knew how to look out for himself. Back then we were both just young recruits. One day an instructor had slapped him because he had missed a few times at target practice. Furious, I wanted to jump on the guy. But I remember Luong holding me back, telling me to keep quiet. I remember his voice, a demanding, imperious whisper, how I stared at his lowered face, incredulous. The instructor, who was only about ten yards away, continued to swear and hurl insults at him. I still remember his red face, his jutting, belligerent chin, and snub nose, the glint of his gold tooth. That evening, coming back from the local cinema, I found Luong seated facing the wall, tears streaming down his cheeks. On his bed lay a mangled old spoon. In his fury he had twisted it into a knot.

Ten years had gone by. Now he was an officer at division headquarters, deputy to the commander. He had earned the respect and the confidence of his superiors. The officers of his own rank were all jealous of him, and he was even talked about in the lower ranks. Everyone knew that one day Luong would be summoned to army corps headquarters. He was a soldier, a professional, and the first quality the war demanded of a man was self-effacement.

Above the streambed, the sunset had faded to deep violet. In the distance the bushes loomed dense and shadowy. Luong rubbed his chin.

"I asked you to come tonight because of Bien."

"What do you mean?"

He continued to rub his chin pensively. He had a balanced, square jaw, and I remembered how handsome he looked when he had a beard. When he stopped shaving his beard rivaled that of Karl Marx, the god who reigned in our grade-school textbooks, who bolstered our daily morale, inspired our solemn vows. But Luong didn't realize the power that beard gave him, the authority he had wielded over the rest of us. Now, obsessed by something, he rubbed his chin nervously.

"Bien has gone crazy. They came to tell me yesterday."

"What are you talking about?" I cried. "Bien? Crazy? Impossible."

Calmly, Luong continued: "The messenger was sure. Bien is locked up in an infirmary, waiting for someone to decide on his case. If it's true, if he is crazy, he'll be sent to a psychiatric hospital."

"I don't believe it," I said. "If he was ever going to go crazy, it would have happened at Phan Khen, when he almost went out of his mind with malaria."

Luong fell silent. He had learned to conceal his thoughts. But like me, he must have had his doubts about reports of Bien's "madness." We had all been childhood friends, tended the same buffalo in the same fields among the same graves. We had chased crabs together, wrestled with one another, gone to school under the same roof. Our schoolteacher, Bac, who we called "Bac the Madman," had punished each of us in turn, yanking our ears when he got angry. Bien lived three doors down from me, at the edge of the village. He was my age, but he was taller than me by a good head. He weighed 155 pounds and could carry 442 pounds of paddy on a bamboo pole slung over his shoulder.

We had shared the same joy the day of our mobilization, watched the red flags that lit up the courtyard in front of the village committee, read the slogans plastered on the walls:

LONG LIVE THE NEW COMBATANTS FOR OUR COUNTRY!
THE YOUNG PEOPLE OF DONG TIEN VILLAGE UPHOLD ANCESTRAL TRADITION!
LONG LIVE INVINCIBLE MARXISM-LENINISM!

Squads of Young Pioneers banged on drums from dawn until noon. They had recruited the most beautiful girls from our village to honor the combatants. The girls wore pink and blue scarves around their necks, and they sang into the microphones: *"Beloved, depart with your heart at ease, you the one I love."*

We fell in line and stared straight ahead. Behind us, our mothers wept, muffling sobs in their handkerchiefs. Their eyes were red and puffy, but they forced themselves to laugh gaily for the local dignitaries.

"Yes, Uncle, we are very proud that they are going."

"Yes, Uncle, I swear."

And they repeated the slogans: "a plow in one hand, a rifle in the other, we will be worthy of our loved ones at the front.

"Yes, the women of Dong Tien village will do everything to win the Three-Merit Flag."

◆　　◆　　◆

My mother died when I was eight. But I had seen other mothers weeping soundlessly through the night, squatting in their kitchens, in front of their flickering cooking fires. I remembered the crumpled, tear-stained hems of their ao dais, the dirty handkerchiefs they carried. Their swollen eyes. I had seen it all in broad daylight. I had watched all of this while we young recruits, drunk on our youth, envisioned ourselves marching toward a glorious future; we were the elect in a grandiose mission.

This war was not simply another war against foreign aggression; it was also our chance for a resurrection. Vietnam had been chosen by History: After the war, our country would become humanity's paradise. Our people would hold a rank apart. At last we would be respected, honored, revered. We believed this, so we turned away from those tears of weakness.

Ten years had passed. None of us spoke about this anymore. But none of us had forgotten. The deeper we plunged into the war, the more the memory of that first day haunted us. The more we were tortured by the consciousness of our appalling indifference, the more searing the memory of our mothers' tears. We had renounced everything for glory. It was this guilt that bound us to one another as tightly as the memory of our days tending water buffalo together.

Luong interrupted my reverie. "I want you to go find out what's happening with Bien. I've written a letter to Nguyen Van Hao, the division commander, and another to Doan Trong Liet, the political officer. You'll see what the story is when you get there. Do whatever you think is necessary. After you've settled this, use the opportunity to take some leave. West of Quang Binh, as far as Thanh Hoa, you can use the liaison agents. They'll guide you the next step of the way. Once you get to Thanh Hoa, you can take a bus. I've prepared all the papers. Tomorrow I want you to turn over your command to Khue. He's not bad. I think he'll manage in your absence."

I was stunned; he had done me a huge favor by offering me a chance to take home leave. I struggled to regain my composure and answered him in a calm, neutral voice: "It's a long way from Bien's camp to our village. I won't have time to take any leave."

"Go ahead. I'll take care of that. As long as you don't go and desert on me."

I just laughed: "No problem. They'll always be able to use my manpower in some camp."

Luong began to laugh. I heard him rummage in his rucksack for a battery-powered lamp—a luxury in the army —and try it out.

"Hey, Luong . . . why are you giving me leave?" I asked.

"Because of Bien. Okay, so I'm taking advantage of that to hide you."

He got up abruptly and headed back to camp. I followed him in silence. At the edge of the forest, I tugged on his shirt and whispered: "The war . . . It's going to be a long time, isn't it?"

Luong didn't answer. I pleaded with him: "It's just you and me. Tell me."

Luong stood without moving or speaking for a few minutes. Then he turned and started walking away. I followed him, and we plunged into the forest. The air smelled of rotting leaves, and it grew more and more humid. The night engulfed us, broken only by the sudden, aimless cries of birds. I still wanted to call out to him, to put my arm around his shoulder. But I held back. Time had slipped between us; we were no longer little boys, naked and equal. That time had passed, the time for diving headlong into rivers at dusk, for shouting and swimming, for splashing little girls.

◆　　◆　　◆

It took me nineteen days to get through the defense lines. On the twentieth, the liaison agent left me to my own devices.

"Here we are. This is the valley. From here on in you can go it alone. You can count on the locals for whatever you need. I've got to head back to camp; there's a delegation of psychological warfare experts waiting for me. I've got to guide them to our mountain bases. From here to Zone K the trail is really dangerous. Here's a map."

He fumbled in his pocket and produced a piece of crumpled paper; it was just an empty cigarette pack covered with marks and tiny letters.

"Thanks for all your help. Maybe we'll meet again?"

"Sure. I'll pick you up on the way back. I'm too tough and stringy to die. I've already survived three hundred and seventeen bombing raids."

I fished a can of meat out of my knapsack. "This is the last one I've got left. You have it, comrade."

The liaison agent scrutinized it like a connoisseur. "This is a real luxury for an ordinary soldier. Good-bye, comrade."

He stuffed the can in his sack and turned to go. He had a pug nose and puffy red eyes, the kind of face they say brings bad luck. There was something sinister about him. But then he was just a faithful liaison agent, by all appearances a gentle, decent man. God bless him. After all, he had survived 317 bombardments.

✦　　✦　　✦

The sun shone like a ball of fire. The liaison agent disappeared into the forest. I walked toward a strip of grass, an open space of endless green and light. And when I lay down, I let myself go, drifting toward a feeling I had forgotten. At last I was free from the suffocating atmosphere of the forest, its stifling shadows of dense vegetation, its poisonous fragrances that sent shivers up my spine.

Above my head, the sky was an uninterrupted blue. Cloudless. The grass stretched out in front of me as far as the eye could see. O earth, o greenness, o light. The memory of old school lessons came back to me like a shout.

◆　　◆　　◆

Bac the Madman, our instructor, pulls my ear.

"You little idiot. When do we use the interjection? 'Alas, cold is the wind, forlorn is the moon. Gaunt, dejected, my love wanders in a foreign land, down roads carved from the wind and the dust.' That, boys, is the most beautiful verse in Mac Tuyet Lan's play. Memorize it. And here's another example: 'O Vietnam, beautiful country rich with your four thousand years of culture, you await our laboring hands.' That is the first sentence of the reading lesson: Vietnam, my country, understood? No, I'm not going to flunk you—your mother would cry again. Okay, one point. Return to your seat. And study that lesson on interjections . . ."

◆　　◆　　◆

I press my face to the earth. Yes, Master, today I've learned the lesson . . . O happiness! The fog soaked into my clothes. Prickly grasses tickled me, scratching my feet, my legs. I could feel the sun burning into my scalp, my back, the shaved nape of my neck. A delicious warmth washed over my head, my body, in a million droplets of light. I felt my pale skin redden in the sun. The pleasure of it, just being alive. I rolled over. The sky beamed red through my eyelids. My cheeks, my neck, my chest, my arms, everything was gently warmed. The sun flooded me like a tide. I remained a long time like that, without moving, without sleeping, floating in a half-unconscious state. Memories glided across my dazzled eyelids. There were faces, landscapes, murmurings, laughter. They seemed to float in smoke, pierced by a long, thin shaft of light, like a sparkling thread of glass. I had never known happiness. So this was it, just this moment? I had never known freedom. Maybe this was it. Just this instant. Who would ever understand? Words, words are as slippery as eels. Just when you think you grasp them, they slide out of your hands and disappear into the mud. But these grasses, razor-sharp at my side, this blue sky above my head, this was real. I was happy.

I stayed stretched out like that for a long time. The ground beneath me was scorching now; the fog had evaporated and the grass had turned a deeper shade of green. The sound of an airplane rumbled overhead. I didn't care. Why bother running for cover? I thought: Bullets may miss people, but no one dodges a bullet. I got up and looked at the carpet of grass. It had been ten years since I had seen such beauty. What miracle had allowed this patch to survive so many bombings? It was an unreal beauty, like a satin ribbon discarded along the shattered, bumpy road of the war.

Planes howled across the sky. I remained buried in the high grass. The grass protected me; at the very least, its green tenderness soothed my soul. The planes veered toward the southwest, glinting in the sun. A carpet of bombs gushed forth. They tilted toward the ground, gently, calmly. Falling toward the earth, they looked like a cloud of giant termites, their wings sheared off.

The cataclysm lasted about half an hour. Then the forest and the mountain sank back into silence. The sun was dazzling, at its zenith. The ground around me was hot and gave off a dense, steamy vapor. I undid my rucksack, drank a bit of water, ate some dried provisions I had, and returned to the road. The prairie was much vaster than I had imagined. I struggled across what seemed like a sea of grass. At dusk, I reached the footpath through the forest marked "N22" on the map. About three hundred yards down the path I saw a board bearing a cross and the word "Shelter." Map in hand, I walked toward it. After about four hundred paces, the footpath widened into a courtyard paved with wood and sheet metal cannibalized from old trucks. At the back of the courtyard, a small stone staircase led to another shelter hollowed out from the rock. I cupped my hand around my mouth and shouted: "Hey, anyone there?"

In the still air of the forest, my voice echoed, bouncing

lugubriously off the rocks. Another voice responded immediately: "Just a minute . . ."

What luck, I thought. I took off my hat, wiped my face
with my handkerchief, and waited. Ten minutes passed. I
could hear the heavy tread of footsteps. A hulking shadowy
figure approached. Night had already fallen, and I couldn't
make out the features of its face. "Greetings, comrade. I've
come from the third line of the front. Could you offer me
shelter for the night? I'll be off at dawn."

The shadow answered me in a rasping voice: "You could
be a deserter. Show me your papers."

I chuckled: "No, I'm no deserter. I'm on a mission to
Zone K. Here, here are my papers."

The shadow lit a battery-powered lamp. A tiny sliver of
light illuminated my mission order and my army ID card.
Then I saw the face: a flat square, cheeks covered with red
pimples, buck teeth protruding over thick, horsy lips. The
light suddenly went out. A puffy hand stuffed the papers back
into mine. The rasping voice continued: "Follow me, elder
brother."

A woman. It's a woman! I almost said it aloud. She had
turned away from me, guiding me toward the shelter. The
lamp glowed intermittently, sweeping over the crumbling
steps.

"Be careful. The other day a guy from Lao Cai fell and
broke four teeth."

"Thanks, comrade," I murmured.

"Here we are," she said, pulling me through a wooden door. "Wait a minute. That's strange—I'm sure I left the lighter here somewhere. Ah, here it is."

A sudden pop. Light poured out as the woman lit another lamp: It must have burned on a mixture of gasoline and salt, judging from the thick smoke it gave off. I looked around. There was a bed made of munitions crates covered with tenting fabric. Tacked to the wall were a tin can, a tiny mirror decorated with a paper flower, and photos of famous Parisian singers and movie stars.

"It's awfully bright. Won't the planes be able to spot us?"

"Impossible. We're perfectly safe here. As for the gasoline, don't worry about that. I get a steady supply from the truck drivers."

She disappeared toward the back of the shelter and came back with some empty munitions crates.

"What are you doing, comrade?" I asked.

"Your bed. Here you go. Empty crates. We've got as many as you want."

"Thanks, but I've got my hammock."

"A hammock? You might as well go sleep in the forest. As long as you're here, it's silly to sleep in a hammock." She arranged the crates to make a smooth surface, then pulled one of the tent shells off the wall. "Here, stretch this out. I've got to go to the cave to get some wood."

"What cave?" I asked.

"At the back of the shelter. It's a kind of storage space," she answered, shuffling off. The darkness engulfed her massive, bearlike body. I could hear the sound of wood splitting as I spread the tent cloth over the crates. I propped my knapsack and my rifle in a corner of the room, and sat down, stretching out my exhausted legs. A tongue of flame ran down my thighs to the tips of my toes.

The woman reappeared, a bundle of logs in her arms. She knelt by the hearth and the flames cruelly lit up her face. I shuddered; she was hideous. She looked up at me: "I'll put a pot of rice on. You stay here and watch it. I'm going to go take a quick bath in the river, then I'll be back."

I looked at the pitch-black night outside. "At this hour?"

"I'm used to it. I've got to wash."

Just then I noticed that her uniform was stained with something like black mud; she gave off a nauseating, sweaty odor.

"What's that on your clothes? Blood?"

"Yes, it's blood. I've wrestled hand-to-hand with three corpses since noon."

"What do you mean?"

She smiled weakly and then pursed her lips. Her nose twitched slightly as she spoke: "What about it? I'm in charge of N22 Cemetery. My job is to gather corpses in these parts. All the unidentified ones are behind the hill. They're all combatants. Just like the three who were killed by this morning's bombing. I buried them all myself. The cave at the back of this shelter is a stockhouse for their belongings. I pass them along to the army when they come through."

She turned, took the lid off an aluminum pot near the fire, and poured in some water through a hollowed-out bamboo trunk. Then she dipped into an old egg-powder canister and measured out some rice. "Don't wash the rice or it'll lose its bran," she lectured me. "If you catch scurvy, it's all over. You can forget about finding medicine here."

She raised herself off her knees. "You make the rice. Here's the lighter. Use the pinewood for kindling. It lights in a flash. The water will boil in seconds."

She grabbed some clothes from under the bed and rushed outside. I heard the gravel crunch under her feet. I chopped up a plank of pine and lit the fire. I stacked a few logs on it and watched the pot. The water began to boil and slowly evaporate. The rice was cooked by the time she returned. She had changed into clean clothes and rolled her hair into a tight chignon on top of her head. As she wrung out her wet clothes, she shot a glance in my direction: "Spread the coals, otherwise it's going to burn."

I obeyed her mechanically. Meanwhile, she hung her laundry out to dry on a metal wire strung up near the fire. A strange odor filled the room. When I started to sniff, she tossed her head, unfurling her wet hair onto her neck.

"I haven't had soap for three months. Without soap, you'd need a miracle to get rid of the smell of blood. Build up the fire; the smoke will cover the smell. You'll get used to it."

She combed out her hair. Her caressing, feminine gestures jarred with her hulking, wrestler's body. I tossed a few more logs on the fire and kept my eyes fixed on the flames.

The fog had rolled in and a few wisps hovered in the cool darkness. The woman sat down beside me. Her soft, shiny black hair streamed down her back. She placed a tiny pot over the fire and dropped a lump of lard into it. "I want you to taste some vegetables sautéed in MSG. I found them this morning, just before those bastards started bombing us. There's even a can of meat. Just over a pound: enough to really eat your fill." She threw a handful of wild chilies and a bit of salt into the pot and stirred it rapidly, like you stir grilled paddy rice. Then she pulled the pot off the fire: "Put the vegetables in your mess dish."

I obeyed her like a child. She got up abruptly and went off into the cave, returning with a can of meat.

"It's imported from China. 'The Queen of Canned Meat'—you're probably familiar with it. There's no fat."

She placed the empty can by the side of the fire. My heart jumped. I recognized the can I had given to the liaison agent this morning, the knife mark on the lid. Luong had given it to me before my departure. I had wanted to offer it to his soldiers as a treat, but he had stopped me, muttering that it wasn't considered normal to offer such fare to foot soldiers. The knife mark on the lid was from an American penknife I'd borrowed from Luong's aide-de-camp.

"Where did you find this?" I couldn't help asking the obvious question. The woman looked at me, surprised: "They told me I could eat whatever food I found on the . . . I keep a list of the belongings I find in their knapsacks. You've probably never seen anything like it. I'll show you—they're odd, rather funny. Some of them collect dozens of handkerchiefs, underwear, bras for their sweethearts back home. Others carry around stones or acorns with their girl-friend's name carved into them. Every soldier is different. As for the diaries, most of them are in shreds. Anyway, let's eat. I'm hungry."

She pried open the can of meat and pushed it in front of me. She filled a bowl with rice and set it in my hand, just as a wife would do for her husband. Awkwardly, I murmured my thanks.

She didn't answer, just lowered her head and started eating. I realized that she was waiting for something, something more tender, but my tongue froze. I ate with my head lowered. Silence fell between us. Time passed. I heard it passing with the crackle of the flames. Suddenly, she raised her head: "Why are you just eating the vegetables? Are you too good to eat canned meat?"

"I've got stomach problems. For a long time now I've only eaten rice."

"You can't find bamboo shoots back where you come from?"

"Sometimes. But it's rare."

She served me another bowl of rice. Little by little the atmosphere grew less tense.

"You men are so lazy. There are bamboo shoots in every forest. There's never any shortage of vegetables."

"It's true. We male soldiers are useless, not like you."

"You call us she-soldiers, don't you? What a bunch of bastards . . . What's your name, anyway? I didn't catch it."

"Quan. My name is Quan."

"What a lovely name. I'm Vieng. Have another bowl of rice. Or have you had enough? With your appetite, you can't be much of a heavyweight in combat. Even I eat two bowls more than you do."

"Thank you, comrade."

" 'Thank you' this, 'thank you' that—what hypocrisy! You must be from Hanoi."

"I come from the village of Dong Tien."

"You sure don't look like a villager. I'd say you've turned your back on your roots. Here, taste some of this burned-rice juice. It's very refreshing. Leave the bowls and the chopsticks. I'll wash them tomorrow. Let's sleep. I'm exhausted."

She drank her bowl in one gulp, stretched out on the bed, and began to snore almost at once. Her head rested on a little white pillow. One of the red threads had started to come loose. She slept with her mouth open, her teeth pointing toward the sky. I sneaked a sidelong glance at her. She filled me with a mixture of horror, curiosity, and pity. I closed the door and climbed onto my own bed. I sank into sleep, a deep, restful sleep.

I didn't dream. I woke up feeling a weight on my stomach, and I knew instantly that it was her, that she had come to press herself up against me. Her hair brushed over my shoulder, her huge arm circled my stomach. She seemed hesitant. I felt her warm breathing, and from time to time, she shifted and heaved a sigh, murmuring something. I lay totally still, feigning sleep. But all my senses were on alert, as tense as radar before an air attack. I knew that she was watching me, waiting for my slightest movement.

At the foot of the bed the coals still glowed, and the heat comforted me. The light exposed me, and I kept my eyes firmly closed. She shifted violently; I could hear her panting. Suddenly, impatiently, she shook me by the belt. I grumbled, pretending to sleep, and rolled over. That was a mistake: She knew immediately that I was awake. She called my name: "Quan."

I didn't respond. She said my name again: "Quan?" I kept silent. She let go of my belt and sat up in bed. "Quan, why are you so cruel? I'm all alone here. It's terrible. Open your eyes. Listen to me."

I didn't dare open my eyes. I turned over and spoke to her softly: "Comrade Vieng, it's because you're alone here that I want to spare you trouble. If by accident you got . . . it would kill you."

She let out a little cry and threw herself onto me: "There's no risk. If I got pregnant from you, all the better. Quan, come, Quan."

She began to moan. I said, "Comrade Vieng, get hold of yourself. You have to control yourself or you're going to make a fatal mistake."

"No, no," she moaned softly. "But I want to die. Take me, kill me, make me die."

She pulled me against her, lifted me onto her.

I felt paralyzed by a strange sensation. *Just close your eyes*, I said to myself. *Let's get this over with. Close your eyes.* I felt my arms and legs grow numb. Throbbing terror, a fascinating desire. I heard her pant, cry out, "Quan, darling, darling."

I saw her by the red light of the coals, her eyes closed, her large mouth agape, stammering, panting. Nonsense words gushed from her horrible teeth. "Quan, darling, kill me, kill me."

Her cry of agony aroused a morbid feeling in me that entirely drowned my desire; all at once I felt totally lucid. My face burned with shame. I pushed her away and sat up. "Comrade Vieng, we mustn't."

She jumped to my side: "Quan, you think I'm ugly, don't you? Do you want me to put out the fire?" She rushed to the fire, grabbed a log, and proceeded to crush the coals with a hurried, but careful stroke. I stared at her stooped back: "Comrade Vieng . . ." I moved closer to her. "Come sit down. I can explain."

She followed me obediently, gazing up at me with docile, consenting eyes. Each feature of her crude face—her pug nose, her low forehead, her buck teeth—looked neglected, pleaded for pleasure with an expectancy that was as much a female animal's as it was a woman's. Why didn't I have the courage of a To Vu? Stranded on an island during a journey, he had slept with a monkey. Why didn't I have this ancient king's resolve, his compassion? Out of respect for a certain woman's dignity, he had made her a queen, despite the hideousness of her face. These rare men, had they been sages or wild beasts?

"Listen to me, Comrade Vieng." I took her hand to maintain a distance between us, to protect myself. I forced myself to look at her directly, to spare her any shame.

"Please don't be angry with me. I don't want to hurt you, but really, I can't . . ."

She looked at me, her voice quavering, stammering my name.

"Do you understand? I just can't," I repeated.

She gave me a suspicious look. Suddenly, she plunged her hand between my thighs. The investigation was conclusive; she could feel for herself that I was useless. She withdrew her hand and stared at me in silence, her eyes soft, pitying. It was my turn to be pitied. *Saved*, I thought to myself with relief. "Look, please understand me—I didn't mean to . . ." I stammered.

She got up and angrily tossed her head. "It's probably all those chemicals. Those American bastards!" Then she turned toward me. "Go on, try to get some sleep. You've got a long way to go tomorrow."

She returned to her bed, but I couldn't sleep anymore. I added a few logs to the fire, rekindling it. I watched, hypnotized, like an old gibbon staring at the sun.

My relief had evaporated. All I felt now was bitterness. I was innocent, but still sorry for the lie. Despite myself, shame overwhelmed me. It crawled like an invisible fungus growing in my brain, its pale, poisonous shadow seeping slowly into my body. My thoughts jumped about frantically: Was I a coward? Impotent? A man so lacking in virility that he ran from the chance for a wild coupling? Was I selfish, so lacking in humanity that I could not even respond to her as an animal would? I felt enslaved by centuries of prejudice and ignorance. Dreams of purity—outdated values, lost in an existence steeped in mud and blood—or else . . . I didn't dare follow my thoughts. I had rejected a woman who had welcomed me simply and warmly, who had begged me for a moment of happiness, a moment of life, of the life we had all lost a long time ago and that we remembered now only intermittently, in sudden flashes and premonitions. Or was she just too hideous? No, it couldn't have been only that.

She had dragged three corpses in the sunset. She had closed the eyes of three dead men. Alone, she had buried them on the other side of the hill. She lived here, guarding their belongings, keeping watch over their shadows, these mementos of life.

This woman was born of the war. She belonged to it, had been forged by it. It wasn't just because she was ugly that I had rejected her. I had been afraid to face myself, scared of the truth. I was a coward. Ten years of war had gone by. I had known both glory and humiliation, lived through all its sordid games. I had needed to meet her to finally see myself clearly. I had been defeated from the beginning. The eighteen-year-old boy who had thrown himself into army life was still just a boy, wandering, lost out there, somewhere just beyond the horizon. I had never really committed myself to war.

The fire burned brighter and brighter, its light seeping into the corners of the shelter, its gentle warmth enveloping everything. The woman had gone back to sleep; her breathing was regular, rhythmic, and one of her arms lay over her forehead. Pensive, I watched her. With all my heart I wished her luck. Surely, there were men somewhere, truly born of this war, who would bring her the happiness she deserved.

I scribbled a few words of thanks in the notebook that

listed the belongings of the dead. I gathered my own belongings and left. It was 4:32. The night was freezing, pitch-black. I looked the map over carefully, and when I had committed its contours to memory, I headed off, groping my way.

◆   ◆   ◆

Hunger tortured me. My knees trembled; my back was drenched in sweat. For two days, I had walked in circles in a valley covered with red colocassias. It was as if I had wandered into a haunted labyrinth. I had been walking since dawn. Now I realized I had come full circle to my point of departure: a colocassia bush wedged between three large boulders. I rested for half an hour and then struck out in another direction. Two hours later, at noon, I found myself back in front of the same bush. There was no longer any doubt; this wild, chilly gray valley was spirit-haunted . . .

I put my knapsack down on one of the boulders and began to search the brush. Both sides of the path were choked with the violet flowers and silvery leaves of creeper vines. The vines twined around one another chaotically, tougher than any man-made rope, weaving through the dwarf brambles and ferns. I got out my knife and started slashing the brambles that hung overhead. Green snakes might jump out of them in a flash; their venom was always fatal. For a long time all I had seen were brambles and creeper vines. By early afternoon, the north wind had started to howl. It seemed as if

I could hear strains of a bamboo flute. My skin contracted, my hair bristled. Sweat trickled down my back in slow, chilly rivulets.

I pulled myself together. I examined the surrounding vegetation, a dense mass of greenness and silence. I headed north. A hundred paces on, I found myself again in a forest of giant colocassias almost two yards high. Their trunks glinted a strange, iridescent green. At their base, they entwined into one gnarled root the size of a banana-tree trunk. Dwarfed by these plants, anxiety seized me. The wind swelled with their dark, clammy shadows. I slashed with all my strength. The colocassias crashed down. A few paces on, I saw a carefully arranged cluster of large gray stones. I hacked away the colocassias along a rock wall. A house appeared, or more like a room without a roof, sealed off by four rock walls, meticulously layered like a box without a lid, bottomless. In the middle, in a hammock strung between two trees, lay a human skeleton. It looked as if it was sleeping there. The bones, intact, shone an immaculate white.

So it was you, companion, who held me back here, I murmured to myself in prayer. The dead man's face was frozen in a toothy grin; his teeth were shiny, straight. These were the teeth of a young man. Like me, he must have wandered for days and days in this surreal valley shrouded in fog, choked with vegetation.

His strength waning, his hope fading, he must have

made one final effort to preserve his body from the animals, to leave it intact, if only in the shape of some distant memory, in the form his parents had given him. He must have been handsome, a stronger, more determined man than I. Otherwise, dying of hunger like that, he would never have been able to build such a tomb. A blade of ice ran down my spine: *Companion, I know how desolate this region is, how horrible it is to molder in this wretched place. We've been condemned to the same gallows. On the day of our departure, who knows what destiny awaits us.*

The fog rolled across the ground, seeped into my armpits, crawled up my neck. I heard, as if in a dream, the strains of a flute. It was a song from the countryside, an evening song:

> *The moon has risen over the hillside*
> *River water glistens, eternal*
> *Slowly, the water buffaloes return from the fields*

Never had this old music sounded so beautiful to me. The dead man still laughed. The arm and leg bones were well aligned. I remembered the plaster skeleton at our high school. The supervisor in his white jacket used to shoot us threatening looks through his round glasses and say: "Watch it—it is forbidden to touch it. Look carefully and remember the placement of the bones. The skull bone, the hands, the feet. Quan, stop fidgeting! The sixth form already broke one of the femurs like that last year."

That was the first time I had ever seen a human skeleton. This was the second. The plaster skeleton had been fragile; this one looked more resilient. Our parents had given birth to quality products. I gazed at the skeleton stretched out on the hammock, tried to imagine a young man slowly losing consciousness. How he must have felt his blood thicken like glue, fading from red to gray, then moldering, stinking of death, his breath going chill. Surely, in that instant of fevered agony, he had seen his life file past him like the images of a dream. Dreams of peace, of hatred, of childhood, of love . . . This had been his last supper, his last solace on this earth. Then the bloodied pus clogged his arteries and the dreams had flickered out.

And then the feast for the animals. First, vultures, then crows. Next ants, insects, worms. Finally, the rain. It would dissolve the corpse into a liquid fertilizer. The colocassia flowers would grow more lushly, nourished by this flesh that had been the pride and masterpiece of creation. The immaculate skeleton looked at me, laughing, as if to say, "So, I'm still whole. Magnificent, isn't it, companion?" The nylon hammock was still in perfect shape. Our civilization of plastics has worked miracles for this century.

Brother, in any case, solitude is your lot. I still have things to do. A young man is waiting for me. They say he's crazy. If they put him in a psychiatric camp, he's finished. I still have a father, a younger brother who's just been mobilized. I don't know whether he's dead or alive. You lived as a man, may you now die as one, and accept my prayer.

I felt lighter. The deceased soul must have heard me. But my own limbs remained paralyzed, stiff with cold. I slapped them.

No, there is still something more, some unfulfilled wish . . . a man who had created such a dignified agony must surely have left behind a few relics. I squatted down and pulled back the grass. I cut away the vines. A small tombstone appeared under the hammock, directly under the skull. I tossed the stones to the side one by one. The knife sliced easily into the earth. I dug a hole about a half a yard wide, imagining the dimensions of a knapsack. About twenty-five inches deeper I cut into nylon. I widened the hole and pulled out the knapsack. It had been tightly bound with nylon cord. Impossible to unknot. I cut the cord and opened the sack. It only appeared after three layers of nylon. Though intact, it exuded the odor of musty cloth. A machine gun, plus two and a half boxes of ammunition. The cartridges weren't rusty. I opened the knapsack and jumped back. A fine gray vapor. I heard the chant of bamboo:

The river water glistens eternally
The kite string has broken
Wind, O wind, go blow on the other side of the hill

As if a young man were playing the flute at sunset, out on the dikes. I opened the knapsack and pulled out a card with handwriting on it: "To the Comrade Who Finds This Sack: Please bring it back to my mother, Madame Dao Thi Lo, 68 years old, Em Mo Hamlet, Phung Commune. Thanks."

Inside were three uniforms, one for autumn and winter, two for spring and summer. Amid the clothes was a rare, precious variety of bamboo flute, with a silky patina. At the bottom, a diary. It was a soldier's war journal, stained, dog-eared. Stuck to the first page, a photo of a country girl, not so young, sort of pretty. On the next page, one of a young man, barely twenty years old, clad in army uniform, laughing, his face sparkling with optimism.

I had an almost identical photo. It was taken on the day of my enlistment . . . The air vibrated with the frenetic beating of drums; the space around us was resplendent with red flags. Drunk with hope, we scoured the horizon for our own image, yearning for the moment we would leave for the front. Over there, rising out of the smoke, were the faces of heroes, proud, happy, their uniforms dripping with medals.

I sat down on the ground and plunged my hands into the dank fabric of the soldier's uniform. Hunger gnawed at me, I could see stars. A cloud of fireflies swirled in front of my face in a sickening display of fireworks. I let my head drop onto my knees, closed my eyes, forced myself to think of something important, joyful, tender. But the same images kept coming back: a plate piled high with sticky rice, a ham hock braised in water, a basket of rice noodles with a bowl of shrimp sauce. To eat! Luy's obsession had become my own.

My stomach churned. Hunger, like an open wound in every cell, nerve, and muscle in my body. Now it twisted into spasms and I doubled over, gasping. I found myself suddenly crumpled on the ground. I pulled some of the dead man's shirts over my head and fell asleep. Like a tide, time gently slipped away from me, evaporating, slowly, silently, in a wisp of smoke. I slipped in and out of consciousness. A hand caressed my cheek . . . I opened my eyes, saw myself stretched out, my head on the dead man's sack, nestled in his sweater, drenched in fog. My sack at my feet. Above, motionless in the hammock, the skeleton slumbered.

The sun had risen. Its warmth on my cheeks. A tender caress of life. I contemplated the vines, translucent in the dawn, the luminous clouds. A strange desire overcame me. Under the quivering red light, my body warmed. The blood flooded back into my chest. My heart pounded with nostalgia and anxiety, as if it would soon stop beating forever. Suddenly I felt it, how much I wanted life. I didn't know what would happen to me, but I wanted to live.

I pulled myself up, felt my strength rushing back. To live, to still be alive. I raised myself. My head hit the top of the dead man's skull in a flash of pain. *Oh, brother, your skull is so hard!* I winced and gathered my belongings. The dead man's diary fell open on the ground. I deciphered a few halting words: "Mother." And the same cry howled through me. The whole valley seemed to sway and pitch, the echo of it reverberating toward the horizon. The sun was drowned out behind a curtain of fog and tears. "Mother, I'm dying. I'm never coming back. There will be no one to repair the thatch roof."

I scanned the tortured lines in the dead man's diary. Here we were, the skeleton and I. Two single young men. In our hearts, we both worshipped the same female image, the only woman we had ever known: Mother. We had remained children.

I saw my mother's smile, her long, flowing hair. A memory of a familiar mixture of perfume and sweat overwhelmed me. I slipped the diary in among the clothes and rolled the bamboo flute up in a handkerchief. Gently, I placed it in my own knapsack. I tied the dead man's sack onto mine with a nylon string. The machine gun and the cartridges shone on the plastic sheet. I took them, too. *Who was the bastard who invented this thing?* I thought to myself. The machine gun was as heavy as the granite mortars we used to pound food. They said it only weighed fifteen pounds, but it felt like a hundred. And that wasn't counting the ammunition. I would never make it, not even by sucking ginseng root for strength.

I hurled the machine gun into the bushes at my right and kicked the cartridge boxes aside to the left. In a few months, the colocassias would swallow them all. A new forest of flowers would bloom over the decomposing remains, suckled on blood and rotting flesh. They would cover the earth again with their pale, icy blooms, echoing the wind of death through the valley.

Good-bye, brother.

I gazed at the glistening skeleton in the hammock, its straight, flawless teeth. The skull no longer grinned at me; it looked almost tearful.

Resign yourself. That's life; in the end, we will all be separated. I'll bring your belongings to your mother. If by some misfortune she has left us, I'll visit her tomb, light incense, and read your diary to her from beginning to end. I won't skip a word. At least her soul will taste this sweetness, this solace. We sons are good for nothing. We make them suffer in this life and then console their ghosts.

I put my cap back on and left. I walked well into the afternoon. When I left the valley, I stumbled into a vast region of rolling hills covered with brambles and camphor trees. The wind from Laos blew here, dry, searing, sucking the body of all sweat and saliva. There wasn't a drop of water, not a grain of rice. I walked on, staggering through low drifts of clouds. I lost count of the hills I climbed. As the sun dipped behind a crest of hills, I could just make out the "A" shape of a bunker. I didn't even have the strength left to shout out. I ran toward its mouth and collapsed there.

◆   ◆   ◆

"Uncle bo doi, uncle."

A tiny voice echoed over and over in my ear, soft, tender, lapping at me, washing over me like ocean waves.

"Wake up, uncle."

The voice was insistent, quivering, as if on the edge of tears. I struggled, painfully, to open my eyes. All I wanted was to sleep.

"Uncle, oh, uncle."

I tried to move, and as I shifted, I opened my eyes a crack. The light was blinding. I closed them. A few seconds later I slowly opened them. Two tiny, glittering black eyes watched me attentively. A patch of sun illuminated a cheek, one fine hair. Only after a long time could I make out a face: small, alert, a bit severe. Seeing me completely awake, conscious, the little girl said: "You frightened me."

Her voice still quivered. I wanted to ask her questions, but my tongue stuck to my jaw. Somehow she sensed this: "I've been trying to wake you up since noon. My voice went hoarse. You were as still as a dead person . . . The worst is over now. I want you to eat some rice porridge."

She climbed down from the wooden plank where I lay, scampered toward the inside of the shelter, and reappeared clutching a chipped bowl and an old spoon without a handle. A thin curl of steam rose from the bowl. She climbed back up on the plank and perched the bowl by my side. Propping my head against her thigh, she fed me, spoonful after spoonful of thick, warm porridge. It smelt of bran and young paddy rice. The grains were marrowy, only half open. They crunched between my teeth, scraping my swollen throat as they went down. I remembered my mother saying: "White rice is like mother's milk." I forced myself to swallow.

"One more try, uncle, one more try."

The little girl seemed to sense my confusion. She consoled me: "You're very, very sick. With such a high fever, your saliva is as thin as river water. But you have to eat to get well. This porridge is made from young paddy. It's very good for you."

My shrunken stomach must have already digested some of the porridge; I suddenly felt more lucid. The little girl noticed that I had started to swallow more easily, and she fed me more rapidly. "Eat a few more spoonfuls. Keep trying, it's almost finished."

I could hear her scraping the bowl with her spoon. It must have been almost clean. The little girl wiped my mouth with the hem of her shirt, then climbed down, carrying away the bowl and spoon. I heard her rummaging at the back of the shelter. In the time it takes to roll a cigarette, she was back. Thick steam rose from an earthenware bowl in her hands.

"Uncle, try to drink this bowl of honeyed tea before you go to sleep. Tip your head back, just like that, yes."

The drink exhaled the earthy smell of honey and leaves. People here gathered herbs along the hillside as a substitute for tea. We soldiers used the same leaves for camouflage. The hot, sugary drink spread a feeling of tenderness through me. I closed my eyes, felt the softness of her thigh under my head. My clothes had a fresh, dry scent of the sun. Even from beneath my closed lids, I could sense her eyes, attentive, anxious, following the movement of the spoon. I imagined she must have looked like a young mother, my second mother.

"That's right. Sleep now."

She wiped my mouth with the hem of her shirt and then, climbing over my legs, pulled out a cover made of parachute cloth.

"Sleep well. Don't roll around or the covers will slip off. Grandfather is very busy these days. He doesn't have time to clean up the shelter."

She covered me with the parachute cloth, tucking it carefully around my feet, under my stomach. I couldn't speak yet. She touched my forehead, then slipped down into the underground part of the shelter. Now she was in full view; she couldn't have been more than six years old. She wore flowered trousers patched with a swath of black cloth. Her shirt was a faded blue. With her coppery skin and fine lips, she looked like a young mother in miniature. She seemed relieved that she had nursed me back to health. She pulled a shard of mirror from her pocket and began to brush her hair with a comb made from aircraft metal. I watched her tiny

hand flick back and forth, her girlish gestures. The tips of her
inky black hair turned up, slightly reddened by the sun, re-
minding me of one of the cherubs around the Virgin Mary. A
church bell chimed somewhere in the distance.

The old priest wore a flowing gray tunic. The day before
my little brother was born he took us to a monastery where
the father superior was a friend of my maternal grandparents.
Once, when we had needed to borrow money, he helped us
contact them in Hanoi. That was a long time ago. I still remember the pretty face of the child-god; so like the face of
the child who had just saved me. Images past and present
jumbled inside my head. I lost consciousness.

◆   ◆   ◆

*A peaceful dream followed by the bloodiest of nightmares.
Rearing up from the horizon, a tidal wave drowns everything:
mountains, forests, streams, towns, villages; the eastern front,
the western front; the soldiers fighting in the name of nation-
alism; and us, the revolutionary army in the name of social-
ism; the sparrows and the larks; the rabbits, foxes, vultures,
maggots, and ants . . . This churning black tide that demol-
ishes all borders, the mountains crowned with stars, the sun-
drenched peaks, the church spires, the vast libraries piled up
with all the ideologies, manifestos, and polemics by all the
balding, bearded geniuses, with all their resolutions adhered
to by all the herds of dreamy, militant sheep. Everything.*

Then the silence grins a wide, arrogant smile. A black tide gushes forth, bursting into an endless spray of green flotsam. Dazzling, the sun beats down on the macabre beauty of a world drenched in blue tears that rain from some distant planet. Everything is over. Finished. There is no one left. Absolute equality: nature's final gift.

But now, bobbing at the edge of the charred horizon, a few shabby rafts. From all sides, like dots piercing the leaden gray, desperate people appear. They cling to the edges of their rafts. I am one of them. We swarm like maggots onto fragile Noah's Arks made of bamboo. We are naked, drenched to the bone. Some of us have wizened skulls; others are hairy, bearded; they paddle, goatlike, in the river. Nothing but men, without a thread on them, miserable, awkward in their nakedness . . .

In the middle of this herd, my little angel appears in her faded blue shirt and patched flowered pants, her black hair singed red by the sun. She fishes the naked men out of the water, one by one, like drowned mice. She bathes them in an earthenware basin. Buffeted by the bloody tide, the men have become wretched creatures. Docile, they float in the basin. Just like they did on the day of their birth.

◆   ◆   ◆

"Grandfather, you're back!"

I woke suddenly and sat up. An old man stood in the

middle of the underground shelter, his back to me. The little girl had wrapped her arms around him. "Where were you all night? I was so worried. Why do you always go away like that?"

She started to cry as if she had been beaten for no reason. The old man caressed her tenderly. "Come now, come, it's nothing. Forgive me."

The little girl cried more loudly, drawing deep breathless sobs, her back shaking. The old man sat down and took her head in his hands, kissing it and sniffing her hair. "Come now, please. Listen. I went to Uncle Kien's. Aunt Kien and his children were killed by mortar fire. I had to stay and help with the burial. Then I stopped by Aunt Huong's to give a few pounds of rice to the kids. And after that I went into the forest to look for honey. Look, I brought back a whole beehive. There are lots of larvae. Later, we're going to have a feast."

The little girl still sobbed, her face curled into the old man's shoulder. He stroked her gently, seeming to measure each gesture, as if afraid to use hands accustomed to heavy work on such a fragile face. I closed my eyes, feigning sleep.

"Don't cry anymore, my child, okay?"

She sniffed.

"Have you eaten?"

"I ate some rice soup."

"Why not some cooked rice? There's still some left."

She shook her head.

"Oh, I see. You've made some rice porridge for the soldier, the bo doi . . . he's sick?"

"Yes."

"How's he now?"

"Last night I went to pick vegetables from the garden to make soup. When I got back, I found him keeled over near the banana tree. I called to him for a long time, but he didn't answer. Then I went to Auntie Lai's. She helped me drag him into the bunker. She massaged his head and then she went back to nurse Lanh. I decided to keep him here. When you didn't come back, I left the light on all night. I called him, pulled his hair. But he didn't move at all."

"Are you frightened?"

"Yes, that he'll die. You never come back from death. Just like my father."

"Yes."

"He didn't open his eyes or cry out. I didn't dare sleep."

"Good, very good, my child. You did the right thing. You're very good. I love you more than anything."

Then I heard the little girl and the old man tidy the bunker, make preparations for a meal. My guardian angel had become a spoiled child again. She ate the bee larvae and the honey. She let the old man comb and weave her hair into two long braids. Now and then she let out a yelp: "No, not like that."

The old man murmured to her, "Ssh, quiet. You're going to wake up the bo doi. Listen . . ."

I was awakened at twilight by the flickering flame of the oil lamp. The old man fed me rice porridge flavored with honey. He forced me to swallow a bowl of sticky, black liquid, a traditional medicine made of herbs and leaves. I was bathed in sweat, but I felt lighter, like after a steam bath. Then he brought over a small, chipped earthen stove filled with coals.

"Later, when your clothes are dry, you'll be able to think more clearly, my son. Do you feel a bit cooler now?"

I yielded to his attentions. The bunker had warmed up. I felt as if a warm breeze caressed my skin. I dreamed. Something peaceful.

When I woke up the next morning I was in a shelter, surrounded by people. The floor was a sea of parachutes and tarpaulins for tanks. The others were beginning to wake up too. Covers were thrown off; to my left were three young girls from the volunteer brigades, and on my right two veteran liaison agents. Further down in the bunker, the old man and the little girl were still asleep. The air was steamy. A suffocating animal heat. Everyone sat up. The young girls combed their hair and fussed with their clothes, unashamedly, in front of the old combatants. The liaison agents chatted and joked continuously. They would never expect anything to come of this encounter, but the mere presence of women and men together in such close quarters gave life a certain softness.

Bombs rumbled in the distance, back there, near the front. The old man brought us a stew made of potatoes and beans.

"Eat your fill, my children. You've got a long road ahead of you."

My little guardian angel reappeared carrying a motley assortment of bowls made of porcelain, stoneware, Chinese aluminum, some even fashioned out of B-52 debris. Previous bombings had shattered almost all the cooking utensils made of glass and porcelain. Every family dreamed of having a soldier's tin mess kit and a dozen enameled iron bowls. The young women teased the old soldiers as they served them:

"Bon appétit, elder brothers. Eat your fill. May your legs be swift! It's a long way from here to the next outpost."

"Bon appetite, little sisters. May you be our stronghold, our citadel in the struggle! After victory is ours, we'll be back. Will there be chicken at the banquet for our return?"

"First come back victorious. Then we'll see about filling you up with nice plump frogs."

They laughed as they ate, slapping each other on the back after each joke. When they finally got up to thank their host, their voices faded against the rumble of bombs somewhere to the west.

"Good-bye, elder brothers, may you be victorious."

"Good-bye, good-bye."

"Are you angry with us? We were just teasing."

"No, of course not!"

A strange hand, warm, fleshy, grazed my forehead and placed a package at my side. "Grandfather, good-bye now. I'm leaving a can of milk for the sick soldier. Tell him we wish him all the best. I hope he regains his strength soon."

Now one of the girls spoke up: "Grandfather, yesterday I slept by his side. Now that's fate for you: the handsome Chu Dong Tu appears in the tent of the beautiful Tien Dung. Tell him to remember my name. Tell him that on victory day he should come see me in Nga Mi village with plenty of areca and betel nuts for the engagement party!"

The women left. Their laughter echoed in the distance. All day I drifted in and out of sleep. As I hovered on the edge of consciousness, a clear young laugh rippled through my brain. That evening my fever broke.

The next morning I bid farewell to my host and prepared to leave. The old man grabbed hold of my sack.

"You can't go yet, my son."

"Grandfather, I've got to get to Zone K. It's very urgent."

"To get there on foot, you'd need the strength of a water buffalo. You don't realize how far it is. I know this region. We used to go by horse. Sometimes the horse collapsed and died on the way."

"But it's urgent. There's no time . . ."

The old man spoke sternly: "This war still has a long way to go. You should watch your health. You're a soldier of the people."

I said nothing. He continued: "Stay another few days. I'll build up your strength. Yesterday I traded a bottle of honey for a chicken. We're going to make a nice soup. Tomorrow I'll go catch some fish in the stream. We'll grill them. Fish with shrimp sauce—nothing like it to give you your strength back. After that you'll be ready to make it to Zone K."

He disappeared into the back of the bunker in search of something. He reappeared with a battered, old cage. A young hen with a tiny crimson crest cocked her head at me haughtily. She had probably never laid an egg. I stretched out on the wooden plank that had been my bed. My head resting on my palms, I examined the bunker's roof beams. On the main beam, in a furrow, I spotted a nest of fleas. Sated, they slept soundly. The war was a paradise for them. They lived well, always satisfied. We offered them unlimited blood. This was a meager tax compared to the tributes the bombs claimed from us.

Absently, I glanced up. It was beautiful out. The sky was an even, cloudless expanse of blue. I felt the urge to gather my strength, to take to the road.

No doubt, at that moment, Luong was thinking of me.

◆　　◆　　◆

The map the liaison agent had given me was too sketchy. I would never have been able to arrive at Zone K if I hadn't met a young Van Kieu man named Te Chieng. He was spreading out soggy letters at the edge of a stream when I met him. "What's happened?" I asked.

"I slipped. My mail sack is soaked. Where's the bo doi going?"

"Zone K."

"Let's go together. I'm bringing their mail."

"How many miles off is it?"

"What's a mile?"

"Uh, how many days' walk, one or two?"

"Is the bo doi as fast as a horse? A good horse would take three days and three nights."

We left together. We crossed two forests and forded a wide stream. That night we took refuge in a tiny cave just big enough for the two of us. The next morning I was jolted awake by a tide of pale-red light. I sat up in shock; the air around me looked as if it had been suffused with blood. I clapped my hand on Chieng's back, but the young Van Kieu just rolled over, covering his head under his arm. "Let's sleep a bit more. I'm tired. I can't walk yet." And he fell back asleep. I curled up next to him; somehow the warmth of his wild body reassured me. This dazzling space, this horrible magnificence dizzied me. We had been sleeping in a minuscule hole on a pile of rocks. Beyond this stretched a few dozen yards of underbrush. Then nothing but sand as red as blood all the way to the horizon. A savage expanse of scarlet sand. A desert of congealed blood. The dawn was flushed red, flooding the air with a surreal color.

The wind howled around us, kicking up the dust in swirling blood-red tornadoes that jostled and chased one another, reeling helter-skelter in the icy light. Everything was awash in somber, distant music, murmuring in endless, droning prayer, bewitching chants. Like a curse that time had carried from century to century in a symphony of innocent blood, raining down, drenching the earth. As if this blood had bred the tortured vegetation, these scarlet blooms where macabre butterflies alighted, the reincarnations of lost souls.

"Chieng, Chieng!" I thumped the young Van Kieu, who finally sat up, rubbing his red-rimmed eyes. "The sun is high already," I said.

"It will be like that all day," he grumbled. "No hope of shelter from it."

Chieng knew the region, so he was calm. I was terrified. It seemed to me that I could see mournful ghosts wandering on the horizon, pulled along by the whirling eddies of red dust. This anxious, pulsating wind, was it waiting for someone? Me? It was possible. Here you could feel the icy breath of ancient massacres, the chilled bodies that had rotted over the centuries, whose souls still seemed to haunt the place.

"Why is the bo doi so pale? Is he sick?"

"I don't feel well."

"Should I give the bo doi some medicine?"

"No, thanks."

How proud we were of our youth! Ten years ago, the day we left for the front, I had never imagined this. All we had wanted was to be able to sing songs of glory. Who cared about mortars, machine guns, mines, bayonets, daggers? Anything was good for killing, as long as it brought us glory. We pulled the trigger, we shot, we hacked away, intoxicated by hatred; we demanded equality with our hatred.

Here I am, twenty-eight years old, temples graying, trampling through fields of glory, soil consecrated by my ancestors. A few centuries ago, perhaps one of my ancestors even passed through here, straw hat on his head, a musket slung over his shoulder, a saber in hand, belting out a song of glory, drinking to victory from an earthenware bowl, proclaiming his happiness, his pride.

Without even bothering to move out of earshot, the young Van Kieu urinated noisily. "Come on. Let's go," he said.

I shouldered my knapsack and followed him in silence. With each step I carefully plunged my boot into the sand to keep my footing. Space whirled around me. I reeled, gasping for breath. The blood-colored sand seemed to spew forth from the horizon, shooting up into the sky. The thinnest clouds were tinted violet. Here and there, a few cacti poked out of the sand, the dew nestled in their flowers glinting scarlet, as if they were gorged with blood.

I thought of my youth, how it had ticked by in long, merciless years of pain. Why this fate, why had it been reserved for me?

In front of me, Chieng suddenly froze: "Look, bo doi. How beautiful. There, behind the dune." He pointed. In the middle of the brush, behind a slope of sand, I could just make out a Cham temple.

◆　　◆　　◆

When I arrived in Zone K, neither the general of the Nguyen Van Hao division nor the political commissar Doan Trong Liet was there to greet me. I had exhausted myself for nothing trying to keep Luong's two letters of introduction dry. They had all left Zone K twelve days earlier to attend an important army corps conference. I was received by Commander Dao Tien, a small, corpulent man with slitty eyes and a pompous, booming voice. Over fifty and balding. He read Luong's two letters and said, "The three of us are like brothers. Look into the case yourself and come up with a solution. And don't worry—whatever Comrades Hao and Liet want to do, I'll go along with."

I was impatient, anxious to see Bien, but I couldn't rush my host, the commander, who held me back when I tried to leave. "Nine days on the road isn't so easy. Rest awhile here first. He's not going to fly away," he said, laughing raucously. His mischievous eyes made him look more like a young prankster than a fifty-year-old man. I resigned myself to staying and went off toward the division guest barracks. I hadn't even raised the mosquito net when he came into the room.

"Would you like some tea?"

"Yes, thank you."

"I brought along some tea from the high plateaux. It makes a nice black liquid, sort of like grilled-rice broth. We'll make do with it." He steeped the tea in a mess tin, then poured it into two tiny enameled iron bowls.

"Here, take some."

"Yes, I will, thank you."

" 'Thank you' for this, 'thank you' for that. How affected, especially at your age. You're from Hanoi?"

"No, Dong Tien village."

"Well, you certainly act like someone from the capital."

"Only on the surface. It fools people."

"Apparently. But like they say, the inside comes from the same barrel. My instincts are seldom wrong; I'm known for it in the division."

I smiled. "Well then, here's to your powers of observation."

He laughed. "How old are you, comrade?"

"Twenty-eight."

"The year of the Monkey. Just like my little brother. He's a bo doi, too."

"Oh, so you have some shared memories. That must be nice."

"Not really. He always wanted to be a doctor. I had to give him a real lecture to convince him to join the army."

"Doctors are useful to society, too. You can be a man without being a soldier, you know. In my unit, for example, there's this guy named Huong. A first-rate combatant, a real professional killer, but—"

Dao Tien dismissed me with a flick of his hand:

"Enough. Enough. I know that argument by heart. My brother drove me crazy with it. Young people today really lack judgment, can't see further than the tip of their own nose. They're out for their own interests, never the glory of the Party."

Old bastard, he's going to drone on with the old sermon. I laughed dryly. "Yeah, and the rest of us, we young people, we're so ignorant, so uneducated. Go ahead, I'm listening."

The commander looked at me inquisitively: "Don't joke with me. I know them well, our young soldiers."

I sipped a bit of the blackish tea to calm myself. "I'm wide awake now. Really, I'm all ears. After all, who can pretend to know everything? Everybody has their own particular blind spots. My generation, we joined the army as soon as we reached the age to do our patriotic duty. The blood in our veins is Vietnamese. As long as a foreign invader remains on our soil, we'll fight. That's the way it was for the Tran dynasty against the Mongols, and the same for the Le dynasty against the Ming Chinese invaders."

He nodded his head. He rolled himself a cigarette out of black tobacco grown by the Van Kieu. It oozed a thick goo, like bear's bile. If you weren't used to it, a single puff could knock you out. He rolled the cigarette, deftly licking the edge of the paper. Pride and satisfaction shone on his face.

"That's true, but it's only half the truth. You're still young; you neglect your political studies. Our ancestors were brave, but they were not as fortunate as we are; history didn't entrust them with the same mission. I totally agree with you: The Tran and the Le families, the Nguyen, they all fought glorious battles, but they were just defensive wars to protect the country. We're doing something greater. Our victory won't be just that of a tiny country against the imperialists. It will also be Marxism's victory. Only Marxism can help us to build communism on earth, to realize the dream."

"Yes, I remember now—a paradise for mankind."

Dao Tien cut me off, irritated: "You never took the courses or followed the education campaigns, did you?"

"Of course I did. How would I know how to detect the enemy or test the soil? Or how to handle artillery? That was what really interested us. We seem to have forgotten the rest."

Dao Tien's tiny eyes squinted. "What do you mean? You're a commander and you got out of ideological study?"

"Yes, and our unit fights well. Not only that, we get special treatment. We're spared the political lectures. Between battles, we usually pass the time playing cards, or hunting. It staves off boredom."

Dao Tien sighed. "How odd."

"Your little brother is probably like me. At our age, you know, we have a tendency to forget things. It's nothing unusual."

He knit his eyebrows together: "But ideology is fundamental. You can't forget ideology."

"Amnesia doesn't have an ideology."

He interrupted me and snapped: "Comrade, you've totally missed the point!"

"Yes, perhaps."

We both fell silent. The gas lamp sputtered. A feeling of sadness.

Why tease this old man? He's not mean. He treats me well. Tomorrow he'll be the one to take care of Bien's situation.

Outside, an owl screeched, its cry echoed in the night's vague murmurs. For no particular reason, I decided to break the silence. "Your black tea is very good."

"Yes, it's the best of the black teas. But of course it can't compare with the Thai Nguyen tea you get up north."

"Of course, Thai Nguyen tea is really something."

I imagined the limpid, lemon-yellow tea being poured into a jade cup. I had seen this magnificent ritual for the first time at a friend's house in Hanoi. We became close at the time of the Great Dispersion, during the bombings, when the cities were evacuated. He had come to live in my aunt Huyen's village. Thai Nguyen, the high plateaux: the areca palms on the crests of the hills straining toward the sun; the paths padded with fresh hay that gave off the warm, musky scent of ripe paddy. We had come from the same province in the north, my hometown. Turning now to Dao Tien, I asked: "What was your brother's name?"

"Dao Khanh. When he was born, my father decided to name him Dao 'Precious' Khanh. But my brother dropped the Precious. What a joker!"

"What division is he in?"

"Z.702. Apparently they're moving toward Three Oaks Valley."

My heart leapt: "What division did you say it was?"

"Z.702. Odd designation, isn't it? That goes with my brother's character. Like they say, to every cooking pot its cover."

I said nothing. Z.702, Z.702 . . . There was no mistake: It was a number that had haunted us for some time now. Three months earlier we had fallen into an ambush. The enemy had been better equipped than we were and had three times our numbers. The battle raged from dawn until midnight. We had too many wounded. There was no hope of beating a retreat if we had to carry them. We fended off the attacks, fighting with the energy of despair, driven only by the idea that we might be able to inflict an equivalent number of losses. For each of our lives, the enemy would have to pay with six or seven of their own. They might be superior in numbers and weaponry, but those well-fed boys couldn't possibly have the drive of those ready to fight until death. To die. To accept death. That was the first quality necessary to the combatant in any army that had fixed its sights on glory.

Darkness had been total. Still, the enemy artillery rained down on us relentlessly. No other army in the world could have had our capacity for suffering, for resisting, for perseverance.

"Give me a sip of water," I remember the voice murmuring in my ear.

It had been Phien's.

"The water bottle's on my ass."

Phien pulled it over toward him and took a long, noisy swig.

"Hey, Quan, we're right on target."

"How do you know?"

"All you have to do is listen to their hiccups. I'm the ears for this whole unit. You know that. How do *you* know where they are?"

"Smell."

"Smell?"

"My rising sign is the dog. I can smell everything. Come on, get back to your position. Soon it's going to be—"

A mortar exploded right next to me. We flattened ourselves against the ground, heads covered. A hail of gunfire followed. By two o'clock that same morning, the enemy fire had subsided. Though they had plenty of ammunition, perhaps they had begun to feel the weight of their dead.

We took stock of our troops, our wounded. Thai didn't say a word. Nor did I, but I felt proud. The art of equilibrium in extermination is the supreme art of war. One of ours for seven of theirs. The enemy weighed next to nothing in our rate of exchange. Whoever found a way to regain equilibrium was the real victor.

"God, I'd love a cigarette," Thai whispered, his voice raspy.

"Wait a bit."

"You've got a will of steel."

I didn't answer. I had taken advantage of the lull to sleep a bit. My back wedged up against an embankment, a rifle between my legs, I had drifted off. I had always been able to sleep like that, through all of our battles. Five minutes. Seven minutes. A quarter of an hour. The tension evaporated. All you had to do was abstract the situation and to let yourself float for a few moments to imagine the most beautiful dreams. In those moments, I felt alive again. I dreamed of a green rice field, the one near the village temple, a patch we kept for the best paddy plants. In the evening we went there to play soccer. The fragrance of young paddy plants soaks right through me; I can still see the mud-spattered stalks . . .

All at once a spray of machine-gun fire erupted to the

south, spreading toward the Valley of the Pregnant Cow. Another round of steady gunfire. Thai screamed: "Those dogs—they've got reinforcements!"

I sat up: "Calm down."

"There are a lot of them. Let's open up right now and scare them off. All cats are gray at night. If we let them get any closer, by dawn they'll know that there are only a few of us. They'll pound us to dust." We both let loose with our machine guns. Thai thumped me on the back:

"Aim carefully. Down the line of men. They'll snap and fall like straw."

Another burst of gunfire. A bizarre, half-formed thought tormented me, I didn't really know what. I just stared at the tracers that ripped through the night.

"Quan . . ."

I wheeled around: "Who is it? Oh, it's you, Phien."

He panted: "Quan, stop—I think we've made a mistake!"

My heart froze. In a flash a realization shot through my brain. I suddenly knew what had gripped me earlier.

"Why?" I screamed. But inside, I already knew. Phien answered, his voice quavering, "Those are our troops, our weapons. Listen—there's only the sound of our weapons. Not a single mortar."

We didn't have mortars, ever. Suddenly, I began screaming over and over again at them to cease fire.

Thai stopped shooting first. Then the others. Everyone waited silently for some explanation. I swallowed, then said, "Perhaps those are our reinforcements."

No one spoke. I heard Thai's foot crush a tin can.

Then Luy broke the silence, his voice halting:

"So that's why I felt so bad. My hand was shaking."

Thai asked: "What do we do now? Wait for dawn?"

We knew there would be no hope for us once their helicopters brought them reinforcements.

"What's your decision?"

"We reopen fire. To the west. They know we don't have any mortars. If we can tell what they have just by listening, they can do the same with us. They'll follow and focus their attacks on our targets. Once they start to do that, we have to get out of here fast. We'll head south, down Pregnant Cow Gorge. Every man carries one injured or dead."

Perhaps in that instant experience had made me lucid, helped me see clearly. A few minutes later, after we had opened fire, we were joined by a steady fusillade from the south. Thousands of tracer flashes arcing toward the enemy. They put up only a feeble response. From time to time the flash of a few solitary mortars. A machine gun sputtered in bursts, and then petered out. One hour and twenty-five minutes later, there was no response at all.

We took a head count, gathered our wounded, and retreated. It was almost dawn when we met our reinforcements in the forest a half mile inside Pregnant Cow Gorge. Division Z.702—the darkest of all my memories.

❖   ❖   ❖

I stared at Commander Dao Tien. I tried to remember the faces of the dead and wounded to recall if among them there had been one who resembled him.

Twenty-eight years old. Born in the year of the Monkey. Perhaps he had died that horrible night. After the battle every face had been smeared with mud, dust, smoke, and blood. In death they had all looked alike.

Suddenly Dao Tien asked me: "I just got the latest bulletin from the front. Have you read it?"

"Yes," I lied. There was a time when I read the news bulletins from the front regularly. Once, by coincidence, at Camp 88, I had picked up off the ground an old issue of *Nhan Dan*, the Communist Party daily. The issue was celebrating the glorious victories on the B3 front during the Tet offensive. The year of the Monkey, 1968. We had been there. I had buried with my own hands countless numbers of my companions, had dragged away from the line of fire little Hoang's corpse, one of the many angels lost in the war. All he had left was one arm, one leg, and a diary filled with gilded dreams.

I remember ripping the Party newspaper into shreds and throwing them into a stream. I never told anyone, of course. It was then that I realized that lies are common currency among men, and that the most virtuous are those who have no scruples about resorting to them. Since then, I've stopped reading newspapers, let alone bulletins from the front. I understood how those who didn't know this still felt joy, just as I understand their lust for victories, their fervor for drawing lines between true and false. Blindness gave them such extraordinary energy.

Dao Tien yawned noisily. "Let's get some sleep. We'll settle Bien's case tomorrow. Do you need the light?"

"You can leave it on."

"Remember to turn it out, then. To save gas."

❖   ❖   ❖

It was Dao Tien who woke me up the following morning. Apparently he had been bored and was looking for company. He invited me to lunch: rice and a plate of green papaya fried in shrimp sauce. He even served me a dessert: two slices of sweet potato.

"Do you smoke? I still have a pack of Dien Biens left."

I nodded and took one.

Dao Tien lit my cigarette. He must not have done that for just anyone. I spoke to him calmly: "Please excuse me for what I said yesterday. We footsoldiers, you know, can be a bit vulgar."

Dao Tien shook his head. "You don't think much of me, do you, comrade? You are the country's future. It's our duty to boost the morale and forge the spirit of the generations who will succeed us. We have no right to look down on the young. On the contrary, we should love them."

"Yes."

Dao Tien continued in a solemn voice. "Take my brother, for example. By the time he understood, by the time he learned to distinguish true from false, when he decided to drop out of college to join the army, we were immediately reconciled. We both knew we would never amount to anything if we didn't participate in our country's noble mission."

"Yes," I said blankly, watching a grasshopper slice through the air.

Participate in the Noble Mission! Reserve a seat at the glorious banquet of the Future! The squares of sticky rice and the slabs of roast meat we ate at village banquets had been transfigured into the glorious banquet of History. But it was still the same ambition. That was ten years ago.

I had never known such intoxication, even in the arms of my first woman.

That was during a campaign in Nghe An, a tiny mountain village in central Vietnam. The girls in that region were really easy. They would walk right up, rubbing their breasts and thighs against us. At night, we could smell their scent in the hills. A cool breeze swayed the carpet of damp grass, rippling through the groves of myrtle. One of them had pressed herself to me, wrapped her arms around me, murmuring nonsensically.

I didn't understand a word. This sudden encounter with

another human being hadn't weighed very heavily on my heart. I preferred more solemn phrases. Months and years had passed. Months and years wallowing in mud and carnage. The blood and the filth had filed words down, gnawed through them just as they had rotted through the soles of our soldier's shoes. I had had my dose of glory and adulation.

I stared vacantly at the space in front of me, not knowing what I was searching for. A grasshopper jumped on my neck; I felt its spines sink into my skin. With a brutal gesture, I flicked him off. Dao Tien laughed: "Are there a lot of grasshoppers where you come from?"

"Quite a few."

"Where I come from as well. When I was little, I remember my elder sister was really fond of fried grasshoppers. I was horrified by the dish. My mother used to tease me: 'A commoner's son with princely tastes . . .' No one dares say that, but that doesn't stop you from thinking it. Who doesn't dream of becoming a mandarin someday, of getting the best place at the village banquet?"

"Yes."

Dao Tien glanced at his watch and gestured to me: "Let's go. At this hour, the medics will all be there." He started out first. I followed. We walked past a long lane of shacks, over a hill, finally arriving at a small, isolated hut in the middle of a field.

"This is the division infirmary?" I asked.

"Yes. At first, we wanted to set it up next to the camp. Fortunately the political officer decided to put it here. Otherwise we would have had problems."

"Problems? Why?"

"Why? The ones that come down with malaria have crazy fits—they strip naked, scream and dance around. As for Bien, he's truly crazy."

"Have there been deaths?"

"Oh, yes. Several from bacterial infections and malaria. We didn't even have time to transfer them behind the lines. So we just wrote up reports. We buried them over there."

I glanced in the direction his finger was pointing. A few mounds of earth poked out from a thicket of brambles and wild grass. Gravestones fashioned out of pieces of iron or sheet metal were planted on each mound. Barbed wire had been spread between the cemetery and the infirmary. The infirmary was also circled by barbed wire twisted into all kinds of spirals and rectangles; it looked like a strategic hamlet. Empty tin cans had been hung on top of the wire fences. It was a bizarre sight; you couldn't tell whether it was a prison or some sort of joke.

"What are all the tin cans for?"

"To alert us to deserters. The crazy ones crash right up against the barbed wire and make the cans clatter. That's when the nurses know to intervene."

I didn't ask any more questions. I followed him in silence to the entrance, a rather flimsy wooden door. Dao Tien slid his hand through a crack, lifted the latch, and closed the door behind us. We walked toward the last shack. That's where Bien was locked up. You could smell the stench of excrement and urine from ten yards away. The cell had been made out of wood slats. There was just one tiny, unshuttered window. I walked up to it and peered in.

Crouched in a corner, naked, filthy, his head slumped over his knees, was a young man. He heard the noise and sat up. Sun was shining from behind me; he probably couldn't even make out my face. His eyes were dull, expressionless. His face was emaciated, ravaged, and his cheekbones stuck out at angles. His hair was spiky, like a hedgehog's. Even against his bulky frame, his head looked enormous. He sat in a pile of filth and excrement, surrounded by pools of milky, rancid urine. A torn calendar. An old tin can filled with water. It was Bien, all right, the childhood friend Luong and I had both known. I tried to fight my nausea. "Bien?" I called to him.

I turned to one side, letting the sunlight expose my face. Bien straightened and sat up. He had seen me. A flash of recognition shot through his dull eyes. In that moment, I saw all the emotions of a normal man in him. But he slumped immediately back down. His head on his knees, he let out a series of abrupt sobs. Then he began to sing:

> *The moon shone over the tea garden*
> *In an old tumbledown house, we lived together*
> *For the silkworms, I gather mulberry leaves*
> *For you, I endure this bitterness*

And then he screamed: "Attack! Let's go, brothers, attack! First company, follow me. Bayonets fixed and aim carefully. Let's go—hand-to-hand combat." Then he jumped up. He banged his forehead against the wall. Blood streamed through his hair.

Dao Tien spoke: "The nails. He always aims for the nails—but that's nothing compared to what he used to do. Before we locked him up, he'd jump onto barbed-wire fences and roll in it. Every day, he would try it again. We'd pull him off covered in blood. The others turned their heads. They couldn't bear to look at him."

"Let's go," I said, pulling his hand.

"He should be in a straitjacket. Don't you think?"

"Even crazy people have their moments of lucidity. I'll talk to him. Then he'll recognize me."

"You were his neighbor?"

"Yes."

"Were there other cases of madness in his family?"

"No. Or maybe—I'm not so sure. It seems to me there was one on the mother's side."

"Try to remember. I'm sure there was. If not on the father's side, then the mother's."

"Yes. Possibly."

"No, not possibly. *Absolutely.* Let me tell you a story. A man used to live across from me. Not just anyone, a high school teacher. He was a serious, distinguished man. An honest wife, polite kids. In short, a very dignified family. One day he got a fever and went mad. He crawled through the streets stark naked, on all fours, barking like a dog. The village dogs would bark back as he passed. The whole village was terrified. They said it was because of his elder brother, a magistrate whose hands were smeared with blood. As for me, I'm a materialist, I didn't believe in all that superstition, so I investigated the case. Well, it turned out to be hereditary, on the mother's side."

"You're probably right," I said. "That's probably also the case with Bien."

"At first I was suspicious. I thought he was faking it."

"Why?"

"He was in perfect health, as full of energy as the next man. Oh, once in a while he seemed moody, but that was all. One night, for no apparent reason, he went into the stables. A cow kicked him and knocked him unconscious. They carried him to the infirmary. The next morning, he went mad. It was bitter cold. He stripped naked and danced around outside. Sometimes he would wave a piece of rag, shouting,

'Plant the flag on the fortress!' Other times he'd club himself with a stick. The comrades were full of theories. Some thought he was crazy; others said he was just faking it because he was ashamed."

"Ashamed of what?" I asked.

Dao Tien smiled. "Well now *that's* a story. Why, all of a sudden, did he start prowling around in the stables? That's the supply section's business. Every time we take stock, we slaughter a few cattle and throw a banquet for the soldiers. There aren't any calves, so there isn't any milking to do on the sly. We thought he was just too hot-blooded. He'd been here for more than four years, and since there was never any chance to meet girls, he went to the stables . . ."

"That's ridiculous."

"You don't believe me? Well, it's happened before. In Hac Mon, the village next to mine, there was a half-breed kid about seventeen years old. His mother was raped by a Moroccan during a police raid by the French Foreign Legion. The kid was about six feet tall with curly hair, dark skin, and shiny white teeth. No one dared go near him except his mother. As if that wasn't enough, he was a bit strange. All the women and girls in the village avoided him like a wild animal. One day, the boys who watched the water buffaloes came running back to the village. The men armed themselves with knives and sticks and ran to the cemetery where the kids used to graze the buffaloes. They saw that crazy boy fucking a cow. Some of the people wanted to beat him up. But my uncle, who practiced traditional medicine and was a soldier —a sergeant—told them to leave him alone. He said that otherwise the boy would end up committing some sexual crime. If he did, then the village tutelary spirit would abandon the temple and bring down misery and unhappiness on us all."

"That's a terrible story," I said.

The commander just shook his head: "But it's true. I've lived a bit longer than you have. I've seen a lot of things. That's the least you can say; that I've certainly seen a few things in my day."

"But Bien is no Moroccan half-breed."

The commander laughed in agreement: "I know, I know, no argument there. I had some doubts at first, but when I saw him rush into the barbed wire like a mayfly into a fire, I realized that he was really crazy. Crazy for good."

"Incredible. Ah, yes, now I remember. Bien did have a crazy aunt—she used to walk along the dikes with nothing on but a skirt made of banana leaves. I was just a kid. She had disappeared by the time I grew up. She must be dead by now."

A moment of silence. Then I said, pensively: "It's a shame Bien didn't take after his father. On that side, they were all hardy folks who slaved away all year round. They never skipped a day of work."

Dao Tien shook his head. "Who can control fate?" he said, clucking his tongue.

At that moment, he had a tenderness about him, an earnestness. I was surprised that I had been able to convince him so easily. We got up and walked away, crossing a patch of brambles dotted with purple flowers. A bramble caught the leg of Dao Tien's pants. He bent over to pull it off. His back had started to hunch over with age. I noticed that fat had begun to pad his thighs. He had the pale skin of someone who had lived for too long in the shadows of the jungle. I wondered how long it had been since he had seen his wife, his children. Did he ever question all this, did he ever feel desire? Or was he just a machine propelled toward the future, driven by promises of fame and glory?

"The weather here is really awful."

Dao Tien nodded: "Yes, it changes all the time. Never gives us any warning. We've had a lot of men die of fever."

"Let's go eat. And you should rest. At your age, you shouldn't take risks with your health. I'll go see him alone this afternoon."

We ate. More rice, more green papayas sautéed in wild chilies and shrimp sauce. Nothing for dessert. No more sweet potato. Instead, I told war stories. It was clear to me that Dao Tien was bored; he kept groping for topics of conversation. Here, because he was a leader, he didn't have the chance to joke around with subordinates and ordinary soldiers. I left him, somewhat touched, and went back to my room in the guest house. It was 12:03 by my watch. I collapsed on the bed. I still had an hour and fifty-seven minutes to wait. Then I could go back to the infirmary.

The stench of excrement and stale urine . . . rivulets of blood trickling down that filthy, emaciated face. I never dreamed I'd find Bien in such a state. He had been part of my life, part of a time when it was still beautiful.

✦ ✦ ✦

Harvest time. The autumn wind whistles through the clear white clouds. We stretch out on a pile of fresh straw. We are talking. About love, of course.

Hey, Bien, why did you leave little Hien?

I didn't. It was Luong who put me up to it. He forced me to do it.

But Hien was the one who told me.

It's not true.

You say I'm lying?

No, not you. Her—it's her fault.

What are you talking about?

She was always so stuck up.

She says she loves you.

Funny sort of love.

✦ ✦ ✦

Hien had a sister named Hoa, who I had a crush on. I knew both her and Hien well. They were shy, delicate, virginal. It was obvious to me that Bien's passion was a little too much for Hien.

Bien was the biggest boy in the village. He could carry a hundred baskets of paddy a day, and carry them running. That was more than a hundredweight each time. At dawn, he ate five bowls of rice. At noon he needed eight or nine, and the same every evening. Sometimes, late at night, we would go walking together. He never went to sleep without first stuffing himself with a few bowls of mung beans or half a basket of sweet potatoes. His body looked as if it had been sculpted from ironwood. Rosy lips, perfectly aligned teeth, a head of hair so thick that a single tuft could fill your fist. He was the spitting image of his father and mother.

Mr. Buu and Madame Nhan were a truly unusual match, a couple known throughout the region. They both had wrestler's bodies. Mr. Buu had black hair, a thick beard and coppery skin, and eyes as oblique as those of a general in a Chinese opera. Madame Nhan had white skin, long hair, a booming voice, lips as fleshy as ripe plums. They both worked constantly. Money seemed to spring from their fingers. With one onion harvest they could earn as much as if they had slaved for ten years in the rice paddies. Then they switched from growing onions to tomatoes and earned two sacks of silver in a single season. But just when the whole region had turned to growing tomatoes and onions, they switched to distilling alcohol and raising pigs. It was dizzying to try to keep up with them!

And that wasn't all. They had raised sixteen children together, all of them healthy. They were so openly affectionate in public that it stupefied people. No one had ever seen a couple so amorous, so affectionate at their age. A gallon of wine for him, a bowl of sticky rice for her, they could just sit there and whisper sweet nothings to each other. Sometimes, in the middle of banquets, in front of all their relatives, they would fondle each other, giggling and boozing away together.

The villagers were accustomed to living in misery and shadow. No one even dared kill a chicken in public. ("Those bastards, why, they go and kill a chicken and it's not even a festival day!") In the villages, you had to wait for Tet or the temple ceremonies to flaunt a new ao dai. ("That bitch goes and gussies herself up like a grasshopper. Red, green, all those bright colors, and at the height of the working season!")

Young lovers met on moonless nights, in the bushes, at the edge of the rice fields, where they could tumble to their hearts' content in the cow dung and the nettles; but if you dared to make eyes at a woman in the light of day, they would hurl insults at you. And so, for no real reason, the villagers hated the Buu couple. Hated but feared them; they were afraid of Mr. Buu's arms, as thick as plowshares, which kept everyone at a distance. One day, a woman couldn't help herself and insulted him as he passed her on the road: "Dirty old goat!"

Mr. Buu turned on her threateningly: "Old goat? Precisely. Up until now, I've never felt like fucking anyone but my wife. But now I think I'd like to fuck you, you whore. Let's see if you're wide or narrow." Before she could blink he had pulled the drawstring that held up her pants and ripped off her shirt. Then he turned to the crowd that had gathered around them: "Ladies and gentlemen, you all heard this whore call me an old goat. Please be my witnesses before her husband."

Then he threw the woman to the ground. She cupped her hands over her crotch and kicked her legs in the air like a frog, screaming, "Oh heaven and earth! Save me! Save me!" The crowd tried to calm Mr. Buu: "Come, come, her tongue got the best of her." "That's enough as a lesson, big brother. They'll avoid you like the plague after this. Take pity on her, please." It was as if they themselves were begging for mercy.

Mr. Buu planted his foot on the woman's wrinkled, sunburned stomach. "You're leathery and ugly as an old frog. Who'd want to screw you? From now on, watch your mouth. Next time, that's what's going to get fucked. Understand?"

And he left. The villagers were green with fright. From then on they held their tongues. And later on, many of them had to ask the Buu couple to lend them some rice or a bit of money. In the end, everyone had to accept the Buus' scandalous way of life.

Bien was Mr. Buu's eldest son. His strapping body couldn't be satisfied by the kind of platonic love I had with Hoa: a few amorous glances, an exchange of letters, innocent chats about village events, our rice paddies, the irrigation work. In the end, Bien dumped Hien for Vinh, a girl from the village of Xuan Vien.

At the time, I remember being with Luong and Bien and a few other village boys and saying, "You don't know it yet, but I know what the story is. Bien's after little Vinh."

"Who, the *cheo* singer from Xuan Vien village?"

"The very same."

Luong laughed. "You're not afraid of anything, are you?"

One boy chuckled loudly: "You're a fool, Bien. That woman from Xuan Vien is Vuong's castoff. Last year, they were together for the whole harvest season. I used to see them going at it every night when I went fishing."

Another guy clucked his tongue: "Firsthand, secondhand, who cares as long as she's pretty?"

"Pretty?" someone protested. "Our girls are a thousand times prettier than the ones from Xuan Vien village. You must be blind—that bitch isn't worth the trouble."

Luong cut in: "Very funny. Each to his own. First find a woman, then we'll see about you."

Bien didn't say a word. He was a gentle person and hated to argue. He was always ready to help others and never refused a favor, even if it meant hard labor. But in conversation he was at a total loss; he couldn't even talk back to a twelve-year-old kid. He was a dynamo, always bubbling over with ideas, which was unusual in our repressive, backward society. That was what we liked about him.

I remember one night when under a full moon the three of us stretched out on the grass at the edge of the lake, a cool breeze blowing above us. We had fooled around the whole evening after a day of net fishing. We kept part of the catch for the market, but the rest was for dinner. I had given my little brother a few dong and sent him back to the village to buy special "button" tea wrapped in banana leaves and a basket of rice. Now, side by side, we watched the translucent, shifting purple of the sky, drunk on its immensity. A few stars twinkled like the fish scales that clung to our nets. Next to us, the embers glowed, blossoming into incandescent flowers.

Bien suddenly spoke up: "Hey, Luong, do you ever think about the gods?"

"No, why?"

"I just pictured something incredible. The gods are giants, right?"

"I don't know. According to the ancients, they're about two or three times as big as human beings."

"Not two or three times—thousands of times."

"Where do you get that?"

"Stands to reason," said Bien, and he started to cackle, delighted with himself. When we asked him why, he hooted, choked with laughter, tears in his eyes.

"You idiot. Shut up," I grumbled.

But Luong pestered him: "Tell us."

"Well," said Bien, "like the saying goes: Nu Oa's cunt is as wide as a three-acre rice paddy, and Tu Tuong's cock is fourteen times as long as a bamboo pole. It's obvious that the gods must be hundreds of times as big as we are."

"Hmm, possibly," Luong mumbled dreamily.

"There's no doubt about it. So I imagined this fantastic scene," said Bien.

"Yeah, what's that?"

"Just imagine her and him. My God, the sky would explode with fireworks and thunder; the earth would be drowned in the flood!"

I was dumbfounded. I never thought a decent fellow like Bien would come up with a fantasy like that. Luong laughed and then said slowly: "So you're not satisfied fucking your little *cheo* singer? You also need to fantasize about wild sex between Nu Oa and Tu Tuong to get you going? You're too much."

Bien laughed and sat up. "Luong, I'm hungry." He turned toward me and gave my shoulder a punch. "Hey, Quan, let's have that carp."

I looked over at the fire and at the two-pound carp. It was still wriggling. I wrapped the carp in a banana leaf and then in mud before stuffing it under the coals. When I pulled it out, the dried mud was white and crumbly. I broke the crust of dirt and opened the banana leaf. The scales fell off to reveal the fish's magnificent, fragrant white flesh . . .

◆   ◆   ◆

I opened my eyes. It was already two o'clock. I must have fallen asleep. I got up and headed for the infirmary. The medics had already seen me with Commander Dao Tien, so they let me wander freely around the premises. I walked right up to the main door and clicked open the lock. The stench of excrement stung my nostrils. Bien sat bolt upright. He looked as if he wanted to jump on me. "Quiet!" I said, articulating each syllable.

He sat motionless, silent. I continued to speak, but in a low voice. "The holes you made in your skull this morning haven't healed yet. You may have the strength of a water buffalo, but your heart is no bottomless pit."

He stared at the ground in silence.

"Let's get out of here," I said. "I can't stand the smell of your shit much longer."

He glanced around.

"I'm alone. Let's go," I said.

He followed me out of the stinking room. Dumbfounded,

a few medics craned their necks in our direction. No doubt they took me for some fancy psychiatrist.

We walked for a long time. The infirmary was more than two miles away from the stream. The water level in the stream didn't even reach the chest of an average-sized man, but it was clear and rushing. "Go wash yourself," I said to Bien.

I fished a piece of soap and a clean pair of trunks out of my pocket. "And hurry up. Your commander may be along any second."

Bien slid into the water. He washed himself in silence. The soap suds stuck to his mud-encrusted hair, floating on the water in a scum like the froth on crab soup. His body was covered with scars. How many times had he rolled in that barbed wire? His ribs stuck out from his emaciated torso. This wasn't the young man I had known. He was so thin now.

We scamper through the courtyard, naked. We are waiting for our uniforms. We look at each other, laughing. The muscles on Bien's chest and back flex. We look like huge field rats.

I turned back to Bien: "Scrub your neck well. It's black with filth." Obedient, Bien scrubbed his neck, shoulders, and ribs. The filth flaked off in waves in the soap suds.

"When did they stop bringing you here to bathe?"

"Two months ago."

Suddenly Bien shot a glance over my shoulder. Commander Dao Tien was swaggering toward us. I had guessed as much.

"Keep the crazy look," I whispered to Bien.

He nodded. Calmly, I rose to greet the commander. He must have slept well; he looked cheerful.

"Extraordinary! How did you get him down here?"

"Oh, even madmen have their moments of lucidity. A few years ago I read a book on mental illness. I know how to speak to them at the right moment, just before they slip back into the madness."

"Careful. Bien's a powerful guy. When he has one of his fits, five of our men aren't enough to control him."

"With crazies, I find it's better to use cunning than force."

Dao Tien laughed. "You're a clever one. Just like my younger brother. People born under the sign of the Monkey are all like that. A difficult life, but always clear-headed."

"Nevertheless, I brought along this rope to tie him up. Just in case. In about a half hour he'll fall back into the madness."

I got out a piece of parachute cord and waded into the stream. I guided Bien back to the bank, got him to put on the pair of clean shorts, and then bound his wrists. Bien stared at me with dull, mournful eyes. From time to time, he smiled idiotically.

While we walked back to the division guest house I asked Dao Tien if he had any sleeping pills for Bien.

"It won't work," the commander responded. "The medics once tried to give him a whole bottle, but it had no effect."

I cut him off sharply: "It does when you combine it with psychological therapy."

Dao Tien said nothing more and went to get the medication. I was amazed at his credulousness: the few pretentious words I had picked up in my reading had had the desired effect!

That evening, at dinner, I used all my oratorical talents to impress Dao Tien. I proposed all sorts of solutions: Bien could be cured by moving him to an environment totally different from the one in which he had developed his madness; that it was better to have Bien discharged if he was truly incurable, or at least have him transferred to a unit specialized in psychiatric treatment.

Dao Tien was totally accommodating. "Whatever you think is best, comrade. I'll do everything I can to facilitate things."

"Thank you, comrade."

Then he laughed loudly: "Bien must have ancestors buried in the dragon's mouth to deserve a friend like you."

"You know, we were comrades in arms, childhood friends. We used to go swimming together. We were even recruited the same day," I said.

"That doesn't mean you have to love him," scoffed Dao Tien. "Why, I had a friend—we were recruited the same day as well. You know, you'll probably accuse me of being a pes-

simist if I say it, but, well, one day we were surrounded, and
he took off with all the food. He left me alone, hiding in a
stand of bamboo."

I laughed. "You know as well as I do: Even silk has a
rough side."

Dao Tien sighed. "Yes, I know . . . and yet I don't
know."

I put my hand on his shoulder. I liked his candor, even
his sentimentality. Perhaps he had always dreamed of true
friendship.

"A man like you," I said softly, "sooner or later, you'll
find the friend you deserve. Heaven has eyes . . . I'm going
up north to resolve Bien's case. Can I bring anything to your
family?"

His eyes lit up: "You wouldn't mind, comrade?"

"Of course not."

"Tonight, I'll sit down and write. I'll give you the letter
before you go. We'll see each other before then."

He got up and left suddenly. The next day Dao Tien
handed me a thick envelope. He must have been up all night.
Along with the envelope, he gave me a comb made out of
aircraft metal for his daughter, a scarf of parachute netting
for his wife, and an American ballpoint pen with three different colors for his son. The soldiers made me a ball of com-
pressed sticky rice and a mixture of salt and crushed peanuts.
No doubt that was on orders from Dao Tien.

Dao Tien accompanied me for about half a mile. When he shook my hand, I noticed his eyes were moist.

"You will go see my wife?"

"Don't worry, comrade."

"Travel safely."

He turned on his heel and left, his head lowered. He had an air of doggedness about him; of someone who was born to persevere, to just carry on. I watched him, and when he was far enough away I spoke to Bien: "Let's go."

We set off in silence and walked for a long time. The hills were barren; the sad little base camps that had once jutted out above the brambles were gone. Now there were only sparse fields cultivated by locals, shriveled fields of stunted manioc with stalks as frail as chopsticks. An hour later, we arrived at the edge of the jungle. When I was sure there was no one spying on us, I untied Bien. The cord had left violet traces on his wrists. I put my arms around him and wept. Tears—it had been a long time, a very long time. Not since my mother's death.

◆　　◆　　◆

The village cemetery is littered with tombstones old and new; rotted wooden gravestones, brambles infested with the macabre kind of grasshopper that haunts cemeteries. I hide behind a bush, under an old tree at the edge of the cemetery, to weep. I cradle my head in my hands. People come to look for me. Busy with all the funeral preparations, they finally abandon their search. I weep for all the other times, for my orphaned childhood, for the woman I had loved most in the world. I cry until I have no tears left, until the sun fades and fireflies begin to flash, starlike, out of the brambles. Finally I return to the village.

That was twenty years ago. I was eight years old.

◆　　◆　　◆

Now I wept again, and I felt Bien's tears wet my shoulder. He tried to choke back his sobs. A long, wet silence . . .

"Sit down," I finally said.

We sat cross-legged on a bed of moss and leaves that glistened like fish. Bien's face was streaked with tears and red dust.

"What are you going to do now?" I asked.

Bien said nothing.

"Do you know why I came for you?" I continued. "It was on Luong's orders."

Bien frowned: "Those bastards. Hao and Liet probably told him about me."

"I said, what are you going to do now?"

He lowered his head, wiping his face on his shirtsleeve.

"Go back to the village and get married," I said. "The little *cheo* singer probably didn't hold her breath waiting for you. But we don't exactly have a shortage of young women at the moment. You can have three of them in one night and no one will cry scandal."

Bien shook his head. But I continued, trying to encourage him: "I'll get you a medical certificate. You can be discharged on grounds of psychological instability."

He shook his head again. I persisted: "Are you afraid of what others will think? Of their contempt? As far as that goes, only deserters are considered disgraceful. But for you, sick and wasted like this . . . maybe it's not exactly glory, but at least you could lead a normal life. The woman you marry will understand; she'll probably love you all the more for it."

"No. I couldn't stand it," replied Bien.

"Why?" I cried, exasperated.

"Go back to the village? Now? What would I say? I couldn't . . ." Bien stammered. He lowered his head. A vein on his forehead swelled, traced a pulsating line to his temples. His skin, now pockmarked with holes and scars, had aged. Bags had begun to form under his eyes.

"Why say anything? All you have to do is work hard and keep your mouth shut. There's nothing to say."

"But I've thought about this constantly . . . it's impossible."

I fell silent. I understood. A cock will fight to death over a single crowing. We had both been mobilized the same day. Luong was already a commander, a staff officer. Despite my

impossible temperament, I had been a captain for three years
now. Bien was still a sergeant. Now, with a mental illness on
top of it all, he didn't have a prayer of leaving the front and
returning to the village with any honor. The rumors would
be awful. No doubt, somewhere in his young peasant's heart
he still dreamed of glory. He couldn't let go of the struggle.
Bien would rather hide in some godforsaken hole, in this immense battlefield until V-day—until he could march with the
rest of us under the triumphal arch.

He dreamed of returning to the village, of decorating his
obscure, colorless life with trophies of victory.

"Okay," I said. "I'll have you sent to Huc's unit, M.035.
They're in charge of special missions."

He lifted his head. "Special missions?"

"I don't know anything about it. They only mentioned
it vaguely. But I've known Lieutenant Huc for a long time.
I'll take you to Zone F right away. We'll take care of the
formalities once we're there."

"Well, now that I'm safe . . . Let's get out the rice, I'm
starving."

I unpacked some rations. As I watched him devour
them, I felt something like regret. After we ate, I would have
to leave him and go on my way. For a moment I saw him as
he used to be, the rosy-cheeked boy who could hoist a hundred baskets of paddy rice onto his back, who fantasized
about lovemaking among the gods. A dream. Our youth.

❖　❖　❖

Torrential rain as I cross the Thanh plain. Like a white curtain of tears. Mother has come back to me in this shower of tenderness. The villagers stare at me, dumbfounded. I plod barechested through the driving rain. I am drenched to the bone, to the soul.

❖　❖　❖

Homecoming: the return to the native village. Showers of tenderness. The same dream haunted our days as soldiers. *Native soil.* These two words expressed everything we had lived for, cherished, adored. I didn't share these emotions. Mother had been dead for years. My father had always been a stranger to me.

I still remember the day that I went with her to the pagoda. The pain that threw her to the ground. Her hair matted with dust and grass. Her sweat-drenched back. Her stomach bloated out like a frog. Her cries: "Where have you gone? Why did you leave us here in this misery?" I knew that she was calling to a man. My father.

From then on I had waited for him with all my five-year-old soul. Waiting was a mixture of curiosity, jealousy, and pride. I suspected that she loved this man I called "father" more than she loved me. When I quarreled with other children in the village, I would often threaten them, my fist raised, saying: "You wait and see. When my father comes back, you'll see what happens." I used to slap my thigh and say: "My father carries a pistol right here. A six-shooter. Bang, bang! And he'll get you all, your parents, your sisters." Quang, my brother, was barely a year old then. He would cling to my trousers and imitate me, saying, "Bang, bang."

Quang was a year and a half old when the war against the French came to an end. Our village was in the Liberated Zone. Feast after feast, celebration after celebration . . . We all danced feverishly around bonfires, singing: *"May friendship bloom between Vietnam, China, and the USSR! With each passing day Imperialism shudders more violently, faced with the love that unites the workers!"*

He came back one night, the man I had waited for. It was dark out. I saw the silhouette of a bo doi carrying a backpack. He had a cap made out of cloth. He stank of tobacco and sweat. Seeing him, my mother shrieked and ran into her room, weeping. The bo doi followed her.

"Don't cry, please don't cry."

I squeezed my little brother's hand. We stood in front of the door and watched, wide-eyed. A moment later, she emerged.

"Quan, Quan . . . bring your little brother. Come greet your father . . . come on, greet him."

She turned on the light. The bo doi held little Quang in his arm. With the other, he grabbed me by the shoulder. "Come, come to Papa."

He still stank of sweat and tobacco. I wriggled out of his

grasp. He looked me over and laughed. "Do I scare you? It's nothing. I was busy fighting the foreign invaders. Come over here; we've got to get to know each other."

At that moment, he looked friendly.

That same evening, our house was filled with visitors. My mother prepared green tea and five plates of nougat candy. The bo doi was back. The laughter lasted long into the night. Their friends were still chattering noisily when my brother and I drifted off to sleep.

A few days later, I saw my mother crying again. But these were no longer tears of joy. It was evening. My parents sat facing each other across the table. My father banged the table with his cigarette lighter. His face was twisted with rage.

Mother wiped away tears as she spoke: "But the road was so long. There were so many enemy soldiers prowling around. That's why I had to ask him to come with me."

My father banged the table again violently: "That's enough. Shut up."

Mother broke down, sobbing: "What have I done to deserve this injustice?" Quang, who was cradled in her arms, woke up. She tried to console him even as she wiped away her own tears. I saw my father frown and wince. His brow was furrowed, his lips trembled. I slid over to her side, latching onto her shirt. She pulled my head up to hers and kissed me. I felt her tears wet my face.

"What have we done to deserve this unhappiness? You

were gone. We lived alone, in misery, without any money. Now that peace has come you start quarreling with us?"

I didn't know what to say. I caressed her damp cheeks. My father, furious, stormed out into the courtyard. The love I had begun to feel for him suddenly vanished. He was nothing but a brute, a cruel, hateful presence.

They fought more and more often. She cried a lot. In the end, she stopped sobbing aloud and wept in silence. Sometimes I would watch her, the tears streaming down her cheeks, as she weeded the courtyard, as she started the cooking fire or stirred the rice. She stared into the distance, her eyes distraught, pained. I felt helpless. I wasn't even seven years old.

The following year she died of typhoid fever. They said she had worked too hard. I never believed that. Alive in my memory was a beautiful, engaging woman with a clear laugh. A woman whose face was stoical and radiant even in the most miserable of times. She had loved us, given us strength and faith in life. Her love had seemed inexhaustible. The more she gave, the more she had.

She had begun to die that day my father had frowned and banged the table. A long, slow, painful death, a vale of tears that lasted eighteen months.

Afterward my father lived like a shadow. He raised us and looked after us like any other father, but without much tenderness. He must have sensed that inside me, his eldest son, there was a kernel of hate. I obeyed him. I never contradicted him. But I never looked him in the eye.

Three years later he married a thirty-four-year-old woman who was as plump as a sausage. There didn't seem to be much love between them. It lasted five years. They had never had children together, so my stepmother left for the city. I was sixteen at the time.

Later, the people in my village told me what had really happened between my parents. They said my father had been out of his mind with jealousy.

Mother was seven months pregnant with my little brother when it all started. She didn't know how to make money to feed us. She left me with neighbors and took the risk of going to the occupied zone to seek help from her relatives. The road was long and dangerous. There weren't any bandits, but the place was swarming with roughneck soldiers. She asked her cousin Quyen, who lived at the other end of the village, to accompany her. He was just a poor orphan, but he was intelligent and could wield a club against attackers if it came to that. He agreed to go with her to the occupied zone, where she was able to get money from her relatives. When she returned to the village, she rewarded Quyen by giving him three baskets of paddy.

"A woman alone with two kids, one still nursing and the other still in her womb, incapable of working in the fields, has enough trouble just surviving. Where on earth would she have found the energy to cheat on her husband? It was Old

Han, your father's cousin, who spread those rumors. It was his way of getting back at your mother because she had refused to lend him some paddy rice." The rumors and the stories trickled insidiously, like a steady drizzle through a thatch roof. Later in life, I learned that all the petty treacheries and crimes between people happen like that, seeping into relationships as easily as rain passes through straw.

I was eighteen years old when I enlisted. My father asked me: "Before you leave, did you remember to light a few sticks of incense in front of your mother's tomb?" The rage broke inside of me. "No," I responded. He was livid. He picked up a shovel and went out to weed the garden. I watched his hunched back and asked myself: *What ill wind had blown my mother into the arms of this man, this calamity?*

Mother was from Hanoi. My grandfather had been a schoolteacher and my grandmother an embroiderer. My brother and I both bore a terrible resemblance to my father; whenever I saw a boy who looked like his mother, I was consumed with envy. One night I went to the cemetery with incense and flowers. Will-o'-the-wisps glittered in the night, dancing in the wind, twirling in the sky, and then wandering back to earth. I placed the flowers on her tomb and lit the sticks of incense. They flickered like embers. I watched the grass shiver in the purple glow of their light. I was overcome by the urge to bury my face again in her hair, to breathe in its scent of herbs and lemongrass.

I got up to go home, but was startled by a shadow just

a few feet away from me. Someone had been watching me, waiting behind one of the wild pineapple bushes. I kept my silence. My father kept his. We separated at dawn. Drumbeats echoed through the village.

◆　　◆　　◆

By the time I arrived at our village, it was nightfall. I took off my cap and headed for my father's house, praying no one would recognize me. My stomach churned. Fortunately the streets were deserted. The children had already brought in the water buffalo and the women were feverishly preparing the evening meal.

The house was dark. My father hadn't lit the lamps yet. I tossed my knapsack at the foot of an areca palm and ran to the outhouse in the garden. Everything was as I had left it: the garden path, the trees. As I climbed the steps of the outhouse, I felt, for a moment, like the ten-year-old child I had been. After relieving myself, I went to the well and drew some water to wash down the outhouse. I heard my father grumble: "Is that Si's girl, is that you washing up?"

I said nothing, continuing to draw water. The pail clanked at the bottom of the well.

"Bitch! Do you have to make such a racket? You're going to smash the well's coping!"

From the frailty of his voice I could tell that my father had grown feeble. Before he would never have grumbled like that; he would have just marched into the courtyard and slapped her. I washed my face, picked up my rucksack, and went into the house.

My father was eating in the darkness.

"Father? Are you having dinner?" I asked.

He turned toward me and was silent for a moment before he spoke: "Is that you, Quan? You're back?"

"Yes, I just got here." My voice seemed to echo through the house. "Why don't you have a light on?"

"What for? A few silkworm grubs and soup? It's not worth attracting the mosquitoes."

I sat down at the low table. I felt the night invade my eyes, the bitterness unfurl in my soul. Still, he was my father.

While mother was alive, she was the one who made sure we got by. She received support from her family, tended the garden, the rice fields, even ran a small business with her friends. After her death, the house fell into ruin. My father had neither the strength nor motivation to do much. He only went to work in the fields when he saw the neighbors go; he planted potatoes when he noticed them plant theirs. The only way he didn't starve was by imitating his neighbors. This obstinacy, this perseverance reminded me of a water buffalo. Still, he was my father . . .

"You're so funny. Light for living and music for dying." I spoke with irritation in my voice. He stayed seated, silent. After a long pause, he replied: "There's been no kerosene in the house for several days. I still haven't gotten my retirement pension."

I suddenly realized that he was living off the meager pension allocated to cadres who had taken part in the anti-French resistance.

"How much do they give you?" I asked.

"Enough for about one and a half gallons of kerosene."

"You finish your meal. I'll go borrow a lantern from the neighbors."

I hurriedly combed my hair, jumped over the hedgerow, and entered Luong's family's house. I arrived in the middle of their dinner. Six or seven people were huddled around a huge tray. Above their heads, a lamp, suspended from three wires, cast its light. The light seemed so warm, so totally different from the harsh neon of the streets. Seeing me, Luong's father ordered his children to bring me a bowl and chopsticks and a glass of rice wine. His wife, who was moved to see me, spun feverishly about, chattering and laughing. I had to recount my journey home in minute detail. The whole family stared at me, hanging on my every word.

Luong was their eldest child, and he was respected by everyone—his parents, his brothers and sisters. Despite his absence, he was still the soul of the family. I began by telling them his news . . .

The neighbors arrived. Word of my return spread from mouth to mouth. Ten minutes later, the whole village was there. My father had also come. He stayed seated outside, on the veranda, with Si and her mother. Luong's father lit more kerosene lamps, illuminating the entire house and veranda. A crowd gathered around me, plying me with questions.

And I talked, about the eastern front, the western front, the strategic regions, A, B, C, the ultra-secret region X. I talked about what I knew, about what I had heard, about what I imagined. The war seemed to engulf the vastness of the earth. And just as vast, in its image, the reckless destiny of men . . . The men of this village had been scattered across all the fronts. They were all over the country.

It was half past midnight by the time the villagers left. I found myself alone with Luong's father in the middle of the courtyard. "Your father is reverting to childhood," he told me. "He doesn't do anything anymore. He spends all day watching the palm trees, or wandering in the cemetery."

"What's happened to him? Last year, Quang wrote to tell me that he was doing well, that he was still working in the rice paddies."

Luong's father flinched and looked up at me. I shuddered. He lowered his head, took out a match, and began to clean his water pipe. I waited in silence. He ended up telling me.

"You probably didn't hear about it, being at the front. Your brother is dead . . . We received the notification in May."

It was over. I heard myself laugh, coldly. I got up. "Lend me your lantern," I said. I took it from him and headed toward the door. He accompanied me to the bamboo hedgerow between our two houses.

"Tomorrow I'll come by to see you," he said.

I placed the lamp on the family altar and knelt down before it, clasping my knees in my arms. I stared at the flame, distraught, mesmerized by its flickering, my mind reeling.

It's over. It's really over.

I repeated it again and again. A dull sound resonated inside me. My hands, I realized, were trembling, then my arms and legs; my whole body seemed to shudder as if stricken by a raging fever. My mother's horrific childbirth cry pierced through me. An earthenware basin. Water splashing. Two little red legs that kicked and kicked . . . Why was he kicking? He was dead now, swept away like a rag in the dust of the roads.

I heard my father snoring. I saw his sunken chin, his white beard. The tip of his nose shone in the light. He snored even more loudly now, his bony shoulders rising and falling in rhythm with his breathing. His face faded into the shadows. A peaceful sleep. A yellow flame danced tirelessly, playfully casting waves of lukewarm light across the empty room. The ancestors' altar seemed huge, barren, dusty. Shadowy silhouettes rose from the copper candlesticks, the censor, and a sprig of dirty paper flowers that had been eaten away by flames and cockroaches. I stared at the lantern, at its borrowed light.

The snoring became louder. I shook more and more violently. The soldiers, the commanders, they all called me "Quan the Impassive." They were proud of me and yet they feared me. My superiors both respected and despised me. Danger, hunger, thirst, bravado—I had had my fill of everything, had sated myself. But I had never trembled like this. Terrified, I felt my whole body ready to snap, to pounce, to commit some irreparable crime. What, I didn't know. I lowered myself to the ground. I stared at my hands, my feet. They no longer seemed to belong to me; I couldn't seem to control them anymore.

More snoring. This time it was finished between us; the scales had tipped. I jumped up from the low table. "Papa."

He let out a few indistinguishable grunts. I shook his shoulders violently: "Papa, wake up."

I don't know why I acted that way. It seemed I would go crazy if I didn't. I felt the urge to run naked through the fields, to take a hatchet and hack down the areca palms in our garden, destroy the walls, block up the well. Perhaps by instinct, I spoke to him: "Wake up, Papa, answer me."

He got up and rubbed his eyes. They were red. He was one of those men who was totally devastated by sleep. The other old men didn't sleep like this. Even if they only slept a few hours, they remained lucid, as if, nearing the end of their

existence, their vital forces strained to record every signal of
life before the final separation . . .

My father yawned a few times: "Pass me the water
pipe."

I brought it. He drew a long puff: "What's the matter?"

I stared at him. I could have been staring at a stone wall.
An indifference, an ancient deprivation. My hands and legs
still trembled. I forced myself to stay calm: "Where is my
brother's death certificate?"

For a moment he sat motionless. Then he raised himself,
walked toward the ancestors' altar, pulled an envelope out
from under the left candlestick, and handed it to me. "Here."

The envelope was so light it felt empty. It was made out
of rough brown paper smeared with glue and dust. My father
sat down and picked up his water pipe.

"You've smoked enough . . . First answer my questions!" I snapped at him.

He tossed the matches on the table: "Go ahead. What
do you want to know?"

I felt my gut twist: "How can you be so indifferent?"

He frowned: "And how, according to you, should I be?"

I said nothing. He would never understand me. We
would always be strangers to each other. Like two ponds in
the same field with no canal to link them. Quang was dead.
The last link between us had been severed.

"I think you must know why Quang enlisted," I said.

"And you, do you know why you enlisted?"

"To do my duty for the country."

"So you don't think he could have thought the same?" he grumbled.

"Our family hadn't shed its share of blood for the Resistance. I'm the eldest. It was my duty to leave. But for him it was different. He was brilliant, had won second prize in the provincial mathematics competition. He wanted to study computer science. I wrote you a letter about that . . ."

Exasperated, my father spoke: "What letter? I don't remember any letter."

"You know very well what letter."

"Oh, so you accuse me of lying?"

"I got a letter from Quang. He told me he wanted to study computer science, but that you had urged him to enlist. He said you told him, 'In times of war, the future belongs to the combatants.' You even attended the Party meeting that decided to mobilize him. That's a fact. I was in Ta Cheng when the letter arrived."

My father stared fixedly at the water pipe.

He said nothing, but I kept talking: "I wrote him immediately. Perhaps the communication links were cut . . . He left."

He continued to stare at the water pipe, his left hand fumbling for a match.

"So few people had a memory like his. He could have

become . . ." Suddenly, I could no longer speak. Words choked in my throat. It was useless to speak to my father. I wandered into the courtyard. The palms in the hedgerow cast a tender, melancholy shadow. I sat down on a stone. My brother . . . I saw him again, as he had been during our worst days: a tiny shadow clinging to my neck. We used to walk like that at the edge of the road, under the guava trees, across the temple square. Why had he obeyed this crude, brutish father? He who had been so alive, who had kicked so violently in that earthenware bowl on the day of his birth.

It's over. It's all too late. My letter must have been abandoned somewhere along a road cut off by a flood. Or perhaps it was rotting in the corner of some guard post, or been lost after the death of a liaison agent. Too late for the dream I had of rebuilding our family, our lineage. My little brother had been intelligent. There would have been a place for him in a society at peace. His fate had been sealed the second my father raised his hand at that Party cell meeting: "I promise to convince my boys to enlist." The whole family thrown into the game of war! So that is how it had happened. From the depths of his ignorance, my father's ambition had overcome him: He too had wanted to reserve his place at the victory banquet . . .

A rooster announced the first dawn watch; another answered him in the distance. Then all the roosters in the village sang. A bluish star throbbed in the sky, spreading a soft glow.

The memory of my mother tortured me. The palm hedgerow reminded me of her. On evenings like this, in a courtyard strewn with palm flowers, she used to bathe me in an earthenware basin, the water scented with grapefruit flowers. Everything would have been different if she were still alive. After I enlisted, Quang would have stayed at home. In a mother's heart, there is no glory worth the life of a child, no ideal higher than the desire to give happiness. But this village was ruled by the authority of the father. "In times of war, the future belongs to the combatants!" My father had won. The rooster crowed again, announcing the second dawn watch. The chant spread from hamlet to hamlet. The blue star had vanished. A wisp of smoke had seeped into the wind. I felt my pain subside, the urge to destroy myself ebb away. Perhaps there was still something left. I was alone. After all I had lost, I needed to find something.

◆　◆　◆

The next morning, Bien's mother brought over a basket of presents: sticky rice, bananas, hemp, and paddy-rice cakes.

I had slept an hour when my father woke me: "Madame Buu is here. With a basket."

My eyes stung. I heard Madame Buu shout from the courtyard: "Is Quan awake? I've brought him some gifts."

I wanted to fall back asleep, but I forced myself to get up and welcome her: "Oh my, Madame Buu, why these are

presents worthy of a marriage proposal. It's too bad I'm not
a young virgin!"

She laughed. "It's nothing really . . . Just some sticky
rice and bananas for your breakfast. As for the hemp and
paddy cakes, I took advantage of the occasion to order some
for Thoa's wedding. It's the day after tomorrow. You're both
invited."

I was stunned: "What? She's getting married?"

"Well, of course. She's eighteen years old. Only seventeen if you don't count the first year in the belly, the Western
way. But since her fiancé's family is in a hurry, I've agreed
to the marriage."

"That's frightening. When Bien and I left, she was still
hanging around my neck, asking me to play ponies."

Madame Buu nodded in agreement. "Yes, it *is* frightening. The months, the years, it all goes so fast. Look at yourself in the mirror; you'll see. You've got crow's feet at your
temples. So are you getting married this time? I'll give you a
hundred areca nuts."

I laughed: "You'd do better to think about marrying off
Bien. Who knows if he won't come running home on leave
one of these days?"

"No problem. All he has to do is set foot here and it's
as good as done."

"You mean Vinh, the *cheo* singer from Xuan Vien village?" I asked.

She pursed her lips in exasperation: "You must be

dreaming! You young people—she's been married for eight years. She already has four children."

"So many?" I laughed.

"Four children in eight years? What's so extraordinary about that? All you have to do is look at her. She's like a hen with those wide hips and stubby legs. She'll have twenty kids before she stops. But don't you regret anything. You just come home and you'll have four or five of your own in a flash. But let's not go on about all that. I'm anxious to hear about Bien. He stopped writing a long time ago."

"I just saw him. Eleven days ago," I said.

Madame Buu's face lit up: "Really? What luck! Did he send any message with you?"

"He didn't have time to write. He asked me to send all of you his best wishes. He hopes you're all well."

She flushed, already on the edge of tears: "He hopes *we're* well! So the ones who go climbing trees are worrying about those left on the ground! It's us who should wish him well. We don't know when he'll fall, if he'll get out of this alive."

She started to cry, wiping her nose with a handkerchief. I joked with her. I described our soldier's life. It was hard, of course, but it had its joyful moments. We had enough to eat, clothes on our backs; sometimes performing troupes even came to the front just to entertain us. In brief, I told her about the most pleasant aspects.

Madame Buu seemed relieved. She arranged her cakes

on the table. "Well, I've got to go to the market. Come by this evening and have a drink with my husband. He insists, you must come." She said good-bye to my father, picked up her basket, and was off. I fell back asleep. When I woke up it was six o'clock in the evening. Like someone who had been drowning, I drew a deep breath of country air. The familiar smell of my childhood: a mixture of herbs and leaves, fruit, dung, mud, animals.

"Do you want to eat? I'll make a meal," my father asked me.

"I promised to go by and see Mr. Buu," I said.

"In that case I'll go visit old Mr. Chan, get a taste of their curdled blood and tripe soup. They're slaughtering a pig at their house today."

"Fine."

"Padlock the door before you leave and bring the key over to me at Mr. Chan's house."

"What is there left to lock up here?"

"There have been a lot of burglaries lately. They even steal crockery, pots and pans."

"Okay. I'm going. Lock up and keep the key on you." I left. I heard my father struggle with the padlock on the door. We walked a stretch of the road together in silence. My father turned off in the direction of the venerable Mr. Chan's house while I continued along the road.

Bien's family's house was one of the most luxurious in

the village. Five steps led up to his veranda, which was paved with stones and covered with a roof supported by pillars. The central building had two stories. The perimeter of the roof, above the terrace, was decorated with lively, intricate carvings and designs. The meal was served in a huge, well-lit room.

"Well you certainly took your time. I was about to send Thoa over to get you," Madame Buu scolded me.

I laughed. "I fell asleep."

Half hidden behind a pillar, a girl with rosy cheeks and sparkling brown eyes stared at me. "How you've changed, Quang."

I hadn't even recognized her. It was Thoa, Bien's little sister. Madame Buu saved me from my embarrassment. "This is Thoa . . . Have you welcomed Quan yet?"

Instead of greeting me, she stuck out her tongue. I burst out laughing: "What's this? Still behaving like a teenager two days away from your wedding?"

Thoa blushed and cooed: "Joking is one thing, getting married is another, no? Someone wants to marry me, so I've agreed to be married."

On this note, Bien's father appeared: "Come in, Quan." He turned to his daughter and scolded her: "You cheeky one! You dare mock Elder Brother Quan?"

Thoa winked at me and ran off. She had become a beautiful young woman. Mr. Buu led me toward the dinner table. There were only three of us. The children ate at a separate table. Madame Buu served rice wine in tiny porcelain cups. "This wine was steeped with special herbs. It's rich in minerals. Really builds up your strength. Have some. It'll do you good."

Mr. Buu gave her a look. "It'd do you some good too, wouldn't it?"

They looked at each other with complicity and started to laugh. Now I understood why the other village women were jealous of Madame Buu. The fact that she was still there, drinking with her husband, while in every other house in the village a woman's place was in the kitchen. That alone was enough to fuel resentment.

It was a day at the end of the lunar month. Madame Buu had killed two ducks and prepared two plates of curdled blood. She had stewed one duck with lotus seeds and steamed another, which we ate with a mixture of salt and crushed garlic. The ducks weighed at least seven pounds each. The tray was piled with aromatic herbs. If it hadn't been for the rustic ceramic cups and the peasant crockery, it would have looked like a feast described in one of the Chinese classics.

"Let's eat with our hands," said Mr. Buu. "My wife prefers to serve it this way. It's a waste of time cutting the meat in chunks. And besides, you lose all the juice. Go ahead, bon appétit. Don't be polite." He ripped off a duck thigh, dipped it in the salt mixture, and began to eat.

We sat there for a long time, discussing the problems of

the village and the country. He didn't ask a single question about his own son. He had sixteen children, six boys and ten girls. Bien was the eldest, and on the day of his birth, Mr. Buu had killed a pig of more than a hundredweight to fete the relatives. I had been away from the village for so long that the stories he recounted seemed like ancient legends. We were chatting happily when the secretary of the communal Party section, a man named Ly, arrived: "Hello, everyone. Welcome, our heroic combatant, back from the front."

Madame Buu rose to greet him: "Hello, Mr. Ly, please come have a drink with us."

At the low table, Mr. Buu sat as still as a buddha. "Please, come join us, Mr. Ly."

I saw Mr. Ly's face cloud over for an instant. He seemed unhappy. But then his face lit up in a smile. "My, what a joy!"

"Have a drink," I said.

"No offense, but I've got an important meeting at the Party section. Quan, it's been ten years since you've been gone. Now that you're back, I'd like you to speak with the Party members, then with the villagers."

"But I never learned how to speak before public gatherings," I said. "We soldiers, we only know how to fight."

Mr. Ly took a sip of wine, yanked off a piece of duck, and started to laugh: "That's exactly why it would be interesting. Party cadres just repeat the same old speeches. Speak, the people will believe you. Speak to us about your victories. It will inspire the people for the next harvest season." He paused to chew his duck.

"Today I've already accepted Mr. Buu's invitation," I said. "We've just barely lifted our cups . . . I haven't even had time to give him news. Bien and I were childhood friends, you know."

Mr. Ly nodded his head. "I know, I know. Well, I'll set a time for you tomorrow evening, then?"

"Please, you must understand, I only know how to fight. I can't make speeches," I said.

Mr. Ly emptied his cup and waved his hand at me. "Don't worry. We'll discuss the main points beforehand. The important thing is to understand the Party line."

"Wouldn't it be better to have me start by saluting the country, and then you speak?" I suggested.

Mr. Ly hesitated: "I'll think about it."

Mr. Buu ripped off a big piece of the duck and placed it in Mr. Ly's bowl: "Please, taste some of this. Don't be polite."

Madame Buu filled his cup with wine. "I steeped the alcohol with herbs rich in vitamins and minerals."

The couple sat motionless, watching as the Party secretary dined. Uneasy, I started to drink with him. We had nothing more to say to each other. He wolfed down the piece of duck, wiped his mouth, and got up to leave: "Please excuse me, I've got some important business. The Party standing committee is waiting for me. Think about it, Quan, and we'll come up with a plan." He turned and walked across the courtyard to leave. Madame Buu ran along to accompany him to the door. "Have a good meeting, Mr. Ly."

The Party secretary's silhouette disappeared into the shadows. The day of our enlistment, he had made an epic speech to boost our morale. At the time, I remember thinking it was masterful. Now it seemed a bit weak. Ten years had gone by.

Mr. Buu poured more wine into his wife's cup and laughed derisively: "Never have the little despots conducted themselves so shamelessly."

"Never mind. Let's not ruin the evening," said Madame Buu.

But Mr. Buu continued: "Before, out of every ten of them you could find at least seven who were honest, civilized. Even during the worst intrigues, at least they feared public disgrace. Now the ones who hold the reins are all ignoramuses who never even learned the most basic morals. They study their Marxism-Leninism, and then come and pillage our vegetable gardens and rice fields with Marx's blessing. In the name of class struggle, they seduce other men's women."

Madame Buu yanked his shirt sleeve: "Please, now don't you go looking for trouble. After all, they're the ones in power. We can't do anything about that." She ripped off a duck wing and placed it in her husband's bowl: "This one's nice and juicy. Taste it and see."

We talked about the fields and the harvest. At the end of the meal, Bao, the youngest boy, appeared: "Papa, is it my turn or yours to take over watching the ducks from Binh tonight?"

"It's my turn. You kids go do your homework and don't stay up too late." Mr. Buu turned to me. "It's been a long time since you've seen the village. Come and sleep in the fields with me. We can talk all we want there." Then he turned toward Madame Buu: "Make us some tea and pack it in the padded wicker tea caddy. And how about a bottle of rice wine and some grilled squid?"

Madame Buu rose from the low table. "It'll be ready in a moment."

We had reached the fields half an hour later. I could just make out the pointed A-frame roof of the thatched hut when I heard an adolescent's voice: "Is that you, Papa?"

"Yes, it's me. Are you hungry, son?"

"A little bit. Who's that with you?"

"It's Quan. Don't you recognize him?"

A shadow bounded from the hut, and someone hugged me: "Is that you, Quan?"

I stood without moving in his warm, sturdy arms. Like my brother's arms. I lifted the boy's face and recognized Binh, who was just a year older than his sister Thoa. "My, you've grown!"

He laughed sheepishly: "Have you seen my brother Bien?"

"Yes."

"How is he?"

"Oh, like me, a bit older than you," I said, and then jokingly I added: "You are forbidden to watch the ducks . . . No stealing duck eggs!"

Binh laughed a deep, throaty laugh. Back then, Bien and I liked to steal duck eggs. We sold them at the district market to buy ourselves candies, brilliantine for our hair, and special creams for our pimples. We would give Binh a few dong from our take, and he used the money to buy rubber bands to make slingshots.

"Go on home and get some dinner," said Mr. Buu.

"I'm going. But tomorrow you're going to spend the day with me, Quan. At least a day."

I watched him run off along the dikes and disappear into the night. It was cold and humid. We sat in the tent, listening to the herons sparring in the marshes, staring at the horizon as it dissolved behind the clouds and the mist that rose off the water. We drank in silence for a long time.

"How is Bien?"

I said nothing.

"Look, I know something's wrong. Otherwise he would have written us. Be honest with me. What's happened to him?"

"There's no need to worry. He's alive."

"I'm not like the other fathers. I never urged my children to enlist, to 'nourish the earth with your body or return glorious.' I'm not selfish, and I'm no coward either. Also, I never encouraged them to desert. As long as the country is occupied, whatever it costs me, I let them go."

I nodded.

"Yesterday morning, my wife told me what you told her. I didn't say anything. You were right not to have spoken about it with a mother. Women are like children; they prefer lies to bitterness. But, Quan, I'm his father."

In the starlight I could just make out his earnest, determined face. His eyes were sunk in shadow, but I could feel them coldly fixed on the night. Faced with a father like this, I had no choice. I emptied my cup of tea and began to tell the story . . .

The night passed. The silence of the fields was broken only by the rustle of the wind through the marsh grass. From time to time the ducks squawked inside their pen. I didn't recognize my own voice anymore. So indifferent, like a stranger's voice. Like a machine that ticked out a soulless story, relating pain in the monotonous tones of prayer. As I told the story, I sank deeper and deeper into memory. I was five years old; I watched a horizon in flames, sputtering with gunfire; then I was twenty-five, wallowing in blood and mud in the bottom of gorges. And all this time there was the me that had lived, and somewhere else a me that stood and

watched, dazed, as life ebbed away in torment. This me had
waited, agonized.

Mr. Buu swallowed. "He didn't say anything more?"

"No. He's suffering, though."

"Why doesn't he let them discharge him?"

"He doesn't want to. He's afraid that the village will
hold him in contempt."

"Of course, he wants to spare us the disgrace. Who
doesn't fear the contempt of others? How long has he been
shut up in that place?"

"According to the deputy division commander, for six
years."

"Poor boy, at the height of youth . . . Quan, you know,
we country folk have gagged ourselves, our stomachs and our
mouths, even our penises. But when it comes to the generals,
they know how to take advantage of a situation. Wherever
they go, whether it's north or south, they make sure they
have plenty of women. In the old days they had concubines;
now they call them 'mission comrades.' It's still the same
thing."

"Yes."

"And no one dares *say* it. Even I don't, and I'm the most
rebellious person in the village. I brought you out here to
speak freely. For so long, it's just been misery, suffering, and
more suffering. How many have died since the great De
Tham, Phan, and Nguyen Thai Hoc—how many lives were

sacrificed to gain independence? The colonialists had only just left Vietnamese soil and these little yellow despots already had a foothold!"

"Yes."

"Well, keep this between the two of us, Quan. Don't breathe a word—to anyone. These days relatives spy against relatives, like jackals. Even their faces have changed. These aren't human faces anymore."

A wild duck let out a solitary cry and plunged into the water. The pond broke into silvery circles. A light mist floated over from the fields. I shivered: "Will the cold season come early this year?"

Buu nodded. "Yes. And it's going to be very cold. The harvest will suffer from these salty fogs."

I said nothing for a moment and then: "I miss my mother."

"I understand. You haven't had much luck. She was so beautiful, so dignified. A hell of a fate." Buu sighed.

The fog obscured my vision.

"Why don't you get married? My wife and I could help you arrange it."

I shook my head. "I've got to go back again."

"No one knows when the war will be over . . . Don't wait."

"It won't lead to anything. Just a lot of suffering for the woman."

"That's ridiculous. You can't think like that. An unwanted woman suffers as much as a woman who waits! Get married, give her a child. You'll have an heir and she'll have a baby to love. There's joy for both parties."

Again, I shook my head. "I can't.

"Who did you used to court, back then?"

"Ah . . . Miss Hoa."

"I remember her, little Hoa, Hien's elder sister, Mr. Tien's daughter. Well, that's impossible. I advise you to forget about that one."

"She's married?"

"Oh no, that would have been too happy. Three suitors came forward. The old idiot Tien turned his nose up at them all and demanded outrageous gifts. Last year, the village Party committee drafted her. Poor girl. By the end of the year, she was pregnant. No one wanted to claim the child. She refused to denounce the father. Shamed, her parents threw her out. She's taken refuge in an old hut over there, on that barren hill, near the farms, at the river's edge." I shuddered.

"You're cold?" said Mr. Buu. "Let's drink. That'll warm us up." He got out the bottle of rice wine and spread out the grilled squid on a plate. The oil lamp hanging from the roof of the hut gave off a pallid light. He filled the two cups and we emptied them in one gulp. Even as my brain froze over, the alcohol licked through me like a tongue of fire, warming my body. I imagined a solitary hut on the hillside. Below us the river flowed on, deserted.

◆　　◆　　◆

We often talked about the ideal woman. I don't know if Hoa was mine. But she was the one I had loved all throughout my youth. Compared to the other girls in the village, she was pretty.

Mr. and Mrs. Tien didn't have a male heir, just two girls. So Hoa had been extremely spoiled. Even though they were peasants, the two sisters never went to the fields to graze cattle or cut hay. Sometimes they would help their mother by gathering duckweed to feed the pigs, or go fishing in the pond with their girlfriends.

Mr. Tien had taught Hoa how to play the mandolin. I still remember the song: "From the forests and the fields, across the huge, open spaces." I remembered her ebony hair flowing over her cheeks as she played. Her skin was as soft as silk and glowed the burnished red of a ripe guava. I was one class ahead of Hoa at school. The village boys liked to tease me about her. ("That Quan, he'll marry Hoa and they'll give birth to chameleons.") I don't know who taught them to chant like that. I was afraid of listening to it. In our imagination, the chameleon was a horrible monster. I fought about it with the other boys. I'd plead with them, but they never spared me. One day, the boy who headed up the pack called over to me: "Hey, Quan, you want us to stop?"

"Yes."

He laughed, baring his teeth.

"Well then, later, when little Hoa walks by here, you just throw a piece of cow dung at her, okay?"

I was dumbstruck. The boy curled his lips and said: "You heard me. If you're not in love with her, then throw a big wad of dung at her back. Otherwise we're going to sing you all sorts of songs. We'll even do drawings of you two on the temple walls."

The temple courtyard. The vast square where everyone in the village, young and old, went every day. I broke out in a cold sweat.

The whole pack of boys hid behind a grove of banana trees. Hoa approached. She was probably returning a cooking pot to some neighbor. She sung to herself softly, watching a couple of *chich choe* birds cooing softly in the bamboo hedge. Crouched behind me, the leader of the pack pushed his knee into my rear. "Go ahead! Now!"

I blushed. I no longer know whether it was from fear or shame. I plunged my hand into the pile of fresh dung near the banana tree and flung it at Hoa. The dung hit her full in the chest, spattering her white blouse, her shoulders and neck. The whole pack of boys jumped up, hysterical. I stood there, stupefied, staring at her. She let out a terrible scream and looked toward the banana trees, where the boys were laughing. She had recognized me. Her eyes met mine for a second. Then she burst into tears and ran off.

Even now, the memory of that look makes my cheeks burn. The shame of it has stayed with me, from my youth to this day, a sad wind that whistles through my memory. In spite of this, we loved each other. Hoa was shy; I was always a bit of a timid boy myself. After all, I was poor, I had lost my mother.

I'll always remember the night we crossed the rice fields together just before I enlisted.

"You'll write to me often?"

"Of course."

"You're going to travel all over. You'll meet other women. You'll forget me."

"No. You're all I have."

She turned away from me. She laughed. Then she tripped and as I reached to grab her, she brought me down with her. I fell onto her. It was dark out. The moon hadn't risen. The stars were hidden behind clouds, but I saw her face under mine, felt her chest tremble. I felt dizzy, panicked; our two bodies had never been this close before. Frantic, I felt desire rising in me. I had become a man. Her flesh was there in front of me, like a fruit dangled in front of my mouth. I had heard all about Bien's adventures with Vinh. This was my chance to become a man once and for all. "No, please." Hoa stammered. I felt her hand braced against my chest, her lips on mine. We stopped to breathe, and she spoke to me in a clear, firm voice. "No, we're not married. My parents would throw me out if . . ." My flesh twisted as I imagined a young woman, pregnant, her hat under her arm, walking painfully along the road. I was leaving. They would disown her, cast her out—the woman I loved. A fierce pain shot through my heart. I embraced her. I both desired and pitied her.

"When . . . when—will we get married?" she stammered breathlessly. I held her shoulders.

"Yes, we'll get married."

Hoa curled her head onto my chest. Tenderness overcame me. I pulled her up. "I'll come back on leave as soon as possible. We'll get married very simply, according to the Party's new custom."

I caressed her arms: "You'll wait?"

She nodded. "I'll wait for you."

❖ ❖ ❖

Ten years had passed. *I'll wait for you.* It was just the murmuring of a wave at the bottom of the sea. Now I walked toward the hillside. In the end, the girl I had loved had been cast out, but not for having loved me . . .

All that day I had avoided everyone, planning how I could find time that evening. I had chosen the moment carefully. It was a moonless night, just a few pale stars. I moved furtively along a path that wound through the rice fields, following the curve of the dikes. The perfumes of my childhood floated all around me; Crickets chirped feebly. Nothing was like it used to be. The insecticides the farmers used had depopulated the countryside just as the bombs had killed something in our souls, the divine inspiration that had once filled our lives. I didn't hear the sawing of grasshopper wings anymore. There wouldn't be another chance to chase emerald-green praying mantises. That joy wouldn't come again. Even the night birds had left these fields for other skies.

I rolled up my pants to cross the canal. On the other side was the field that bordered the hamlet. Back then, there had only been a few huts here. Now there were about twenty houses. Dogs barked behind the scruffy bamboo hedgerows. The fragrance of cactus flowers wafted through the air. I was afraid I would meet someone I knew, so I went around the hamlet.

A half-hour later I arrived at the foot of some barren hills. There were only a few weeds and brambles. I had never set foot here. A path cut across vegetable gardens of eggplant, chilies, and pineapple bushes. By now my eyes had grown accustomed to the darkness. I groped my way along the path, crossed a mound, and arrived at the foot of a hill shaped like an overturned bowl. Below the river flowed on, silently winding like a mirror of pewter. Its beauty was terrifying, bewitching. From time to time a fish jumped out of the water.

I climbed the hill. I was sure I would find Hoa here. I had spotted her hut from the summit. It rose silently out of the night. Not a single light. Not a sound. I threw a pebble, hoping to hear a dog bark. But there was none. Had she gone somewhere else to hide?

I wondered, and yet at the same time I was sure I would find her there, in that miserable hut. With her bloated belly, she couldn't really flee. She didn't have the right papers, couldn't possibly get a resident permit anywhere else. She didn't have any money. Everything had chained her to this place.

I tripped over a stake in the ground. A cord ran from it in the direction of the hut. She was preparing for the monsoon. I stepped over furrows of manioc that reached my calves and crossed a tiny courtyard paved with a few broken bricks to arrive at a rickety door.

"Hoa, it's me," I called softly. In that silence my voice echoed across the hills. No answer. I called again, frantic. The echoes were drowned in the space around me. I was surrounded by silence and night. I had never heard such loneliness in my own voice. I stepped closer to the door. "Hoa, answer me."

A tiny, sharp voice replied: "What have you come for?"

I stood paralyzed for a second. Then I entered, moving toward the voice. "Hoa?" Like a blind man, I grasped at the air with my hands. Suddenly I heard her say: "Get out of here."

Her voice was feeble but harsh. I stopped. Silence. I rushed in the direction of the voice, a dry, vulgar voice, a voice nothing like the girl I had loved. Then I saw a silhouette stretched out in a corner. I stepped forward. My hand brushed against a warm, bloated stomach.

The woman screamed. She pushed my hand aside and burst into sobs. I sat down slowly on the edge of the bamboo bed. I slid my fingers along the smooth strips. I put my arm around her thighs, murmuring to her: "Hoa, calm down."

The woman sobbed in jagged waves, over and over, inconsolably. I stretched out beside her, embraced her feverish, trembling body. Her damp hair stuck to my face. It had the vinegary, sour smell of sweat. Silently I caressed her face, her tiny neck, her slight shoulders. I avoided touching her bloated stomach. It wouldn't be long now.

I waited until she had shed all her tears, emptied herself of the pain of the last ten years. Time ticked by in the shrill moaning of insects, in the river's low rumblings. I wiped away her tears.

She still sobbed, but began to breathe more regularly. I tried to console her. "Please don't cry. We aren't children anymore. I was eighteen years old when I left. Now I'm twenty-nine. My hair is even starting to go gray."

She buried her face in my neck and plunged her hand into my hair. I stroked her hand. "You too, you're going to be twenty-seven. The wise men say that at the age of thirty you rebuild your life."

She shook her head. I continued: "We aren't children

anymore." She shook her head again, continuing to silently stroke my hair.

"It's not our fault . . . Not your fault. Or mine. What's important is that I love you." I took her hands. She began to sob again, her whole body shuddering. She held me. Her hands burned. "Don't cry. Listen to me." I stuttered something. I couldn't speak clearly anymore. I held this woman in my arms. She felt so close to me, and yet so strange. I loved her, feared her. It was terrifying. These feelings grew, crystallizing inside me.

I hugged her to me, pressing her face against my cheek, mixing her hair in mine, my chest touching hers. If only I could fill the hole of the last ten years, bury the past. Our mouths searched for each other. A hallucinatory kiss that tasted of tears. I felt my flesh melt with yearning for her, my mind twist frantically, as if trying to rekindle the memory of desire. The fields, the smell of grass, the first emotion, the expectancy of marriage . . .

Through my painful delirium, something like a flash of light. My spirit sank, my mind scattered, and I opened myself to the night that grew ever more dense, ever more deep, ever more unfathomable. A night that erased all thought, all feeling, all memory, leaving only this wave of desire. I shut my eyes violently.

A rooster crowed at dawn, shattering the silence. Hoa still slept peacefully. I got up and went out. A crescent moon hung in the sky like an evil finger. I fumbled for a few crushed cigarettes in the bottom of my shirt pocket, straightened them one by one, and began to smoke. The smell of the smoke calmed me. I watched the white puffs float up and dissolve in the night. It was serene, but the purple clouds on the horizon reminded me of the blood and smoke of battlefields.

This familiar landscape, the breathing of this woman had frozen my mind. I took a long drag on my cigarette and gazed dreamily at the sky. I remembered the fields where we had kissed each other for the first time. The grandiose vision of our marriage: white cushions embroidered with silver-winged doves . . .

But I had learned about women on a hill in central Vietnam, from a woman in heat, round as a sausage, slick with sweat.

And Hoa? Who had it been for her? I didn't have the heart to ask her the name of the father of her child.

Never. We never forget anything, never lose anything, never exchange anything, never undo what has been. There is no way back to the source, to the place where the pure, clear water once gushed forth. The river had cut across the countryside, the towns, dragging refuse and mud in its wake.

What would I do the following day? Would I come back here, furtively, at nightfall! I could avoid everyone, but I couldn't escape my own conscience. Tomorrow I wouldn't love her as I did now. This swollen belly reminded me of another man. The beautiful dream that once bound us to each other had died.

Luong's father had organized a banquet for my departure. It was also an occasion to inform the entire village of Luong's imminent promotion. Relatives, neighbors, everyone bustled about noisily. It was a sumptuous feast. Seven side dishes, three main dishes, four soups, not to mention the sticky rice stained red with rose-apple juice. Just like a real city banquet.

"May the gods protect the Huong family! Luong will be a general one day!"

"I told you. With each new generation, the Le family produces geniuses, ministers in times of peace, marshals in times of war. All you need is one line like the Le family to bring honor to the entire village."

"When Luong comes back, you'll have to slaughter a cow. I'll be in charge of bribing the provincial authorities to give us some electricity. We'll light ten hundred-watt bulbs. It'll dazzle you all!"

Bien's father was seated in a corner, his face somber, listening in silence. All around, wine flowed freely. Glasses were raised and lowered, people nibbled at the dishes. Faces flushed red as if burned by the sun. General. Commander. Captain. The talk of stripes and stars flitted from mouth to mouth, endlessly, in a dream of grandeur. Mr. Buu hadn't

eaten. He munched a few peanuts. They had forgotten him.
At another banquet, he would have been at the center . . .

◆   ◆   ◆

If only human beings had a guide to help them cultivate their
rice fields, to raise their domestic animals; if only they had
an elder to help them, to teach them to love their wives, to
understand and guide their children; if only they sought a
friend to teach them the art of life, how to savor the taste of
a wine, to admire a flame in the cold of winter.

If, if. But that day still hadn't come.

◆   ◆   ◆

Mr. Buu sat hunched in his corner, listening in silence. I
thought of the fields, shrouded in fog, where we had spoken.
I felt the sadness seep into me with the wine, engulfing me.
Someone thumped me on the shoulder.

"Come on, Quan, you've got to leave tomorrow. Have a
good time! A little enthusiasm, for goodness sake!"

I turned around. Mr. Ly was laughing, his lips oily with
food. "Oh, hello, Comrade Ly," I said.

He settled himself down next to me. "Move over a
bit . . . On behalf of all of you, I empty my glass to this officer
of the People's Army. May he bring honor and glory to Dong
Tien village!"

"Oh, I never made that promise."

Mr. Ly swerved around. "What do you mean?"

I laughed. "I don't have Luong's qualities. I'm not . . ."

"You should forge your own will to conquer," Ly broke in. "We Vietnamese have a long tradition of heroism. And now, on top of it, we're armed with the dialectical materialism of Marxist thought. Who can beat us?"

"You're absolutely right. Let's eat."

"I've already eaten. They made us a special tray. I just came to chat with you, to thank you for your contribution to yesterday's meeting."

"It's nothing, really."

"Oh, but yes, you and the men from the front, here among us in flesh and blood, speaking to us about your experiences . . . Thanks to you, our propaganda campaign was a real success. Why, after that meeting, twenty-eight young men volunteered for service. At Ha hamlet, they were only able to recruit seven, even though they have twice our population."

Luong's father personally served tea to everyone. It was a Thai tea that his wife had scented with lotus blossoms. Exquisite. All around me, the clicking of chopsticks against bowls. I excused myself. Luong's mother told me that she would bring me a letter and a few gifts to carry back to her son that same evening.

◆   ◆   ◆

The banquet only ended toward midnight. I slipped off into the hills to visit Hoa. Seated in the courtyard, she was waiting for me, her long hair flowing down her back. I gave her some money to help with the birth. She wept.

"Don't cry. I've shed tears, seen tears. Tears from soldiers who've seen death too many times. I want you to stop crying so that I can have just one moment of peace."

Instead, she broke into sobs, as if she had been beaten unjustly. I stood motionless, furious. Who could ever understand a woman? "Listen," I said calmly. "It's no use—"

She jumped up and ran into the hut. I heard her throw herself onto the bed. I rushed toward her in the darkness, and ran face-first into a pillar. Something like a shard of ice cut into my skull. From the depths of my pain, a wave of rage overcame me. I felt it rise in me, the fever of combat, the hatred, the irrepressible desire to kill, to annihilate, like a fire sweeping through my body, my brain. I grabbed the central pillar to break away from it. Suddenly, I imagined the hut collapsing, a pregnant woman wandering among the ruins. Tomorrow I would be gone. I stopped, terrified, unable to control the urge to destroy that had ravished me. My hands twisted, greedy for carnage. To snap a neck, to plunge a bayonet into flesh, to turn a hail of machine-gun fire on someone . . . on everything that reminded me of this life, of everything I had lost, of all the invisible forces that had ransacked and trampled my existence.

"My god, my god," Hoa moaned. She was still sobbing. I stared at the woman, my eyes bulging. I felt my body tense like a guitar string. Just a bit tighter and it would snap.

It's over. There's nothing left. Painfully the idea crawled inside me, dislocating my muscles. My murderous rage had subsided, suddenly snuffed out. My dreams too. I couldn't offer a single word of consolation or encouragement. I couldn't even sit down beside her. I couldn't do anything more. I was barren, emptied, beaten. An abandoned train station. A lone rock in the middle of the ocean.

I left the hut. No good-byes. No promises. When I left, it was the middle of the night. Dogs barked somewhere in the distance.

❖   ❖   ❖

I dream: A radiant young man leads me through a field of roses. The sun rises. A few wisps of fog still chasing some crazy dream. The air is fragrant. Roses bloom, opening passionately all the way to the horizon. We walk silently, obstinately.

"Quan! Get up! Quickly! You're going to miss the train!"

❖   ❖   ❖

I had to fight to find myself a seat on the train to Thanh Hoa. The huge feet of a merchant woman dangled just above my head. She had hung her hammock across the compartment and was sprawled out, mouth open and snoring, oblivious to the to-and-fro of the other passengers.

A train seat in wartime, like a bowl of rice in the time of famine. Poor, filthy, miserable, the train stopped at each station for just five minutes. People scrambled on, shoving and pushing, trampling everything in sight—clothes, rubbish, the gravel strewn on the floor. People walked right over suitcases, rucksacks, baskets filled with dried goods, the backs and feet of other passengers. Everyone fought for a seat. A seat anywhere. On a bench. On the floor. The corners of the compartments reeked of urine. A nauseating odor that made you gag. The seats, made out of slats of wood, were nicked and gashed, patched with tar. Sometimes there were still a few panes of dusty, soot-covered glass left in the windows. Sometimes there was nothing. Seen from outside, the train looked as if it were covered with green-colored moss, the color of camouflage. An emaciated old man with dark, sunburned skin pushed me against a partition: "Excuse me."

He sat down, flinging his huge sack made out of jute onto my thigh. "I hope you don't mind," he said.

"I'll be glad to help you find a place for this, because we've got a long way to go and I'm not going to be able to stand the weight of this sack you've got here."

He winced: "Bowls. It's all bowls. They'll break if I put them on the floor."

"Well, we'll have to find a solution," I said.

He shook his head furiously. "Oh, please . . . They're going to break. Back where I come from the bombs have shattered everything. Even the bowls and plates. People eat out of coconut shells now!"

I weakened. "Don't worry. I'll find a way."

I started to negotiate the situation with the other merchants in the compartment. Finally they agreed to wedge the sack between their rush baskets and a bag of dried manioc.

The old man beamed with joy. For an instant the whiteness of his teeth lit up his dark, bony face. "What luck!" He sighed, fished a piece of dry, stale bread out of his satchel, and broke it in two. He offered me half: "Have a piece!"

I shook my head. "Thanks anyway, I've already eaten."

The old man started to eat, his face still beaming. The stale bread had traces of mold on it. I stared at his neck bulging with ligaments and swollen veins, at his dry, gnarled hands, as twisted as roots. At the front we had often been tortured by a hunger that blanched men's stares, that melted their bones. Sometimes the supply division would suddenly shower us with food. But here, behind the lines, people lived with a kind of hunger that raged without ceasefire, that went on and on: the hunger for protein.

The old man sensed that I had been staring at him. "I still have more in my satchel. Want some?"

"No thanks," I said cheerfully. "I was looking at the birthmark on your neck. My father has one just like it."

The man chuckled loudly. Then he reached down,

painstakingly gathered the crumbs of bread that had fallen onto his thighs, and popped them in his mouth. His meal finished, he folded his arms over his stomach and fell asleep. It wasn't long before he was snoring regularly.

The train siren howled for a long time, but the train didn't move. The merchant woman stretched out in the hammock was talking to herself in a dream. "Pay me right now . . . I don't give credit . . . Who knows if you're going to be there, at the next market day, or if the bombs will have cut off your right to residence . . . Pay me now!"

Her shrill, indignant voice amused everyone.

The howl of the train siren again. A ticket collector entered our compartment. "Step aside, please, compatriots, step aside . . ."

Passengers grudgingly pressed up against the walls to open a passage. They weren't pleased. Just the same, the ticket collector's company uniform, his kepi, and the fake leather sack he had slung over his thigh, all this gave his stooped little body a certain authority. Two men, well-nourished, even a bit plump, followed behind him. The shorter one wore gold-rimmed spectacles; the taller man's were as thick as the bottom of a glass.

"Come on, squeeze in a bit, let us by."

The ticket collector moved toward the seat across from me. Two young men—who knows at which station they had boarded—were already seated there. They had been sleeping back-to-back under their rattan hats when I got on. They were soldiers. The ticket collector thumped them on the shoulders. "Get up, get up."

They woke up and looked around, dazed, rubbing their eyes, which were red with sleep. Seeing the ticket collector, they immediately sat up straight. "Your tickets, please," he said icily.

The two young people squeezed their hats to their stomachs and glanced nervously at each other. They were scared. "Ah, yes, comrade, it's just that—"

"Your tickets, please," repeated the ticket collector.

The two older men who had followed him watched the scene. Suddenly they both spoke up at once: "Never mind. Drop it, never mind."

"Follow me," said the ticket collector. "We'll settle this at the booking office." He turned and bowed respectfully to the two older men. "Will these seats be all right, comrades?"

The smaller man nodded. "Very good."

"If you need anything, I'm at the booking office. At your service."

The smaller man with the gold-rimmed spectacles nodded again. "Yes, just perfect."

"Will you excuse me now?" said the ticket collector. Bowing so low to speak respectfully to the little man, the ticket collector looked like a real hunchback.

"That's just fine," said the little man, exasperated. "I'll

call you if necessary." The ticket collector bowed his head again and left.

The two men didn't have any bulky luggage, just a small travel case, probably for food. No one dared sit on the same seat with them. The two men were fat, their skin as pale as crickets left too long in a matchbox. They sat like masters in the middle of the crowd. The other passengers only gave them sidelong glances, frightened, fawning looks. Even the merchants with their sharp tongues didn't dare chatter in their vulgar slang. Everyone was stiff, frozen, paralyzed by some invisible force. The siren screeched again. The train lurched forward and set off. The two men leaned back, their heads against the seat, and looked at each other. The short man with the gold-rimmed glasses started to laugh loudly. "You see? I told you so . . ."

The taller man nodded, silently, as if waiting. The little one continued: "Life isn't as sad and gloomy as it is in your literature, your articles. All you have to do is board a train for a few minutes to see that."

"I followed you onto this freight train to see with my own eyes," said the big myopic one. "My wife was against the idea. She said 'Watch it! If you bring any cockroaches back, I'm kicking you out!' "

His shorter companion burst out laughing. "Ah, the wife, a husband's unofficial enemy! Ha ha ha. But we can't live without 'em. Now let's get back to the point."

"The content or the form?"

"Precisely—I don't need to cite any essays or testimony. Here, in front of your very eyes, you had a perfect example. Don't forget it: Those two young tricksters called the ticket collector 'Comrade.' The ticket collector addressed us the same way. In reality, though, the first case was a relationship between delinquents and an agent of the law. The second case, now that was a relationship between masters and servants. If the Party is the faithful servant of the peple, as Ho Chi Minh says, then the ticket collector is just a servant's servant. Is that clear? So the word 'Comrade' can mean many things. From a linguistic point of view, it's a lie. From a historical point of view, it's an adaptation. And from a practical angle, well, it's just a leader's trick."

The tall, myopic one adjusted his eyeglasses and shook his head.

"In a civilized society, we should try to make the form correspond to the substance."

The fat little guy glanced up at him. "You're so naive!" he snorted. "We don't always need to have a civilized society."

"I don't follow you."

" 'I don't follow you, I don't follow you,' " huffed the little fat man. "Stop repeating that. You're over fifty, aren't you? Civilization is a long, difficult journey, and we don't have much time. Life is short. We've got to find another way."

The tall, myopic man wrinkled his nose. "What barbaric ideas."

The short fat one laughed: "That's exactly what being in power is all about. You're just like a woman. Oversensitive."

"I am like I am."

"Have you ever seen an ostrich? Faced with danger, they hide their heads in the sand. They think sand can make reality disappear."

"But you and I, we went off to fight for an ideal."

The short fat one nodded, determined to continue: "That's right. That's the indisputable truth." Then he burst out laughing. Buck teeth stained yellow from tobacco. A flat pug nose with nostrils that flared out into two gaping black holes. Undoubtedly the most valuable thing about this man was his gold-rimmed glasses. The most seductive thing about him seemed to be a mixture of certainty and insolence that seems to come naturally to all veteran bastards. He continued: "You, me, and many others, we abandoned everything for an ideal. That came with our seventeen-year-old consciences. Once you're over fifty, they're just a bunch of moldy old memories. That ideal, well, the kids need it. And it's all we need to turn them into monks, soldiers, or cops. And it worked, whether it was the revolutionary uniform or the Nationalist police cap."

"I know that's what a lot of people think, but—"

The short one cut him off: "Words are like everything else in life: They're born, they live, they age, they die."

"So when you and I left the city of Quang Tri to join the Party, what was born and what died?"

"Look, we were fifteen years old at the time. We were young. The revolution was also young, fresh. We sang our way from one battle to the next. 'The Comrades' Chant'—how did that go again? Oh, yeah: 'You come from a land steeped in salt and bile, and I from a village where the plow is worn down by the stones . . .' Lovely lyrics, eh? Words that flowered and bore fruit. Now they're starting to fade. That's the universal law. Revolution, like love, blooms and then withers. But revolution rots much faster than love, 'comrade.' The less it's true, the more we need to believe in it. That's the art of governing. Spreading the word, now that's you intellectuals' job. We pay you for it."

The little man tossed his head back and guffawed. He lit a cigarette. The large, myopic one spoke up hesitantly: "There is some truth in what you say, but—" The little one cut him off again: "But it's tough to hear it, isn't it?" He snickered again, beaming with some perverse sense of pleasure. This conversation was just a pretext. The large myopic one lit a cigarette. They both puffed and exhaled indulgently. They sat in silence for a long time. In the whole compartment only a few men and I seemed interested in their conversation. The vendors were all sound asleep, mouths agape. I listened to the train wheels shuttle along the track, a sad, monotonous click-clack. Suddenly, the little fat man blurted out: "Did you bring the beer?"

"Yes. You're thirsty already?"

"Nah. We'll drink it later."

The large myopic one smiled: "We take the freight train to see how the masses live, and you bring along canned food?"

The little fat one laughed accommodatingly: "I've got a weak stomach. Our people's food is one of the most unhygienic on the planet. In the West, running water is cleaner than our country's bottled mineral water."

"Now there's a contradiction," the large myopic one quipped sarcastically. "You want to enjoy all the comforts of civilization without lifting a finger to build it!"

"Building a civilization is difficult. But guaranteeing a small number of people a civilized existence, why, there's nothing easier. Like I say, civilization is a long, hard road, and—on top of it all—at the end you have to share power. For a people as primitive as ours, using a religion to guide them through some shortcuts to glory is a hundred times easier than trying to civilize them."

The large myopic one squinted. "But isn't that a bit cynical? What are you saying?"

The little man shrieked with laughter. "What truth *isn't* cynical? Put yourself in a king's place. You'd rather show off your finery on a podium at a military parade than rack your brain trying to figure out how to create a new strain of rice or a new manufacturing process. There's where it all leads, the civilization you're dreaming of. It forces kings to grope along, fawning over a bunch of capricious, arrogant intellectual. Don't you see? All you need to do is mount a podium perched above a sea of rippling banners. Bayonets sparkling around you. Cannons booming. Now that's the ultimate pleasure: the gratification of power. Money. Love. Why, next to it, they're nothing. So we need a religion."

"But for years I've heard you quote Marx: 'Religion is the opium of the people.' "

The little fat one was even more amused. "You're being funny. I'm a professor. When I mount the podium, I give the lecture I'm asked to deliver. The students need this food just as much as they need to learn the word 'ideal' by heart. We're not followers. You shouldn't be so dogmatic. If religion is an opiate, then nobody needs that opiate as much as we do!"

His traveling companion just shook his head. "So you've come to this."

The little man gaped at his friend, perplexed. "Perhaps you're still just a schoolboy, after all. That's what I like about you. So you think we're atheists? No way! We demolished the temples and emptied the pagodas so we could hang up portraits of Marx, enthrone a new divinity for the masses. Remember the army's ideological rectification campaigns? With

the cadres from 1952 to 1953? Were those really any different from confessions in church? We invented sins. We tortured ourselves. We repented in exchange for a pure soul,
hoping it would bring us one step closer to the Supreme Being.
Today, it's the same story."

The little man stopped, coughing and wheezing. His
companion said nothing. They both started to smoke again.
The little one exhaled a few puffs of smoke, squinted, and
looked over at his friend: "Have you ever really read Marx's
biography?"

"Nah, just the preface in *The Holy Family*."

"Of course—naturally! To canonize Marx they had to
erase the real person. Me, I've visited the house where he was
born. I've signed countless visitor's books in museums de-
voted to him. I even placed a wreath of flowers on his tomb
in England."

He paused for a moment and leaned toward his friend,
an ironic twinkle in his eye. His gold-rimmed glasses glinted
under his thin eyebrows: "Obviously, a great man can't be
judged on the basis of his private life. But just for a laugh,
do you know what kind of a man Karl Marx was in real life?
Well, he was a debauched little drawf. As a student, he hung
out in brothels. He particularly liked gypsy girls. As for his
mature years, everybody knows that he got his own maid
pregnant. It was only when he died that his wife Jenny for-
gave him and adopted the bastard kid. Ha ha ha ha! Ha ha

ha!" The two men doubled over laughing. They wiped their eyes with their handkerchiefs and got out their cigarettes again.

I sat without moving. A chill ran up my spine. My mind spun. I saw myself walking over a bridge; then, suddenly, balanced on a rope over a chasm. Furtively I glanced in the direction of the man with the gold-rimmed glasses, watched how he puffed and sucked at his cigarette, inhaling the smoke through thinly drawn lips. The self-satisfied air about him. The contemptuous smile. He had spoken the truth.

I see a magician who by sleight-of-hand transforms a piece of wax into a figurine. He blows on it. The marionette becomes a grandiose, majestic genie. Billions of men prostrate themselves and begin to pray. Billions of eyes opened wide in fear and adoration. Billions of lives wait for the signal to jump into the fire, into hell . . . I am one of them, they are my kin, all those who are dear to me. And seated behind this curtain, I see this little man, this dwarf magician with his pug nose, grinning, puffing on a cigarette . . .

"Attention!" The authoritarian voice made me jump. I wheeled around. A military officer wearing a red armband stood in front of the two men. He spoke carefully, weighing each of his words: "We have a report that you just insulted Karl Marx, our venerable leader, that you slandered our socialist government."

The small, fat man jumped to his feet, his chest puffed out. "Who? Who dared claim such a thing?" he shrieked again.

There was nothing mocking about him now; he looked hard, ruthless. "Who?" he shrieked.

The officer glanced behind him; the informer had obviously stepped out of sight. "It was someone. That's certain . . . someone reported it," stammered the officer.

The little fat man got out what looked like a red notebook and shoved it in the officer's face: "Read this." It was small, a bit dog-eared at the edges. I recognized a diplomatic passport, the kind issued to high-ranking dignitaries. Wide-eyed, his hands shaking, the guard took this precious symbol of power. He flipped through it quickly and blanched. The little man just smiled and grabbed the passport out of the guard's large, peasant hands.

"It's we who are in charge of introducing Marxist thought to Vietnam. *We* are the ones who teach the people— to which you belong—just what Marxist ideology is all about. When it comes to defending Marxist thought, that's *our* business, not yours. Is that clear?"

The young man lowered his eyes. Beads of sweat had formed at his temples. The little man continued: "This time I'm willing to forget this ever happened. But if you continue to behave so inconsiderately, I'll have you sent to you know where."

The young man just stood there, his eyes riveted to the ground.

"Go on, get out of here," snapped the little fat man. And then he stalked off, chest puffed out, hands gathered behind his back, his face red with anger. The guard walked off down the corridor, staggering his way between the passengers who had gathered around to watch the scene. Only when he reached the door to the compartment did he dare raise his head. Then he was out of sight.

The little fat man sat down. The anger, the hardness of his face had vanished. He turned toward his companion and winked at him maliciously: "Well? Did you see that? A nation of imbeciles. They need a religion to guide them and a whip to educate them."

◆   ◆   ◆

Four thirty-eight already! It had been hours since I'd gotten off the train at Thanh Hoa. Time had flown. The back of my shirt was drenched in sweat. I still couldn't see any signs indicating the way to the Special Unit M.035.

I studied the map they had given me at Base F a second time. Arrows. Crosses. Tiny lines and dots. A map so detailed, so meticulously drawn. So useless. *Impossible to make out anything. I'm going to have to climb a tree and try to sleep on an empty stomach.*

I folded the map back into my pocket and set off. *Too*

bad. There's no choice. I'll have to guess my way. The map doesn't correspond to anything, anyway. Praying to my mother's soul to guide my steps, I walked quickly, letting my feet guide me, as if ghosts were at my heels.

A half-hour later I spotted a sign about two feet wide and one foot tall. Written on it in a deliberate handwriting was: SPECIAL UNIT M.035. 545 YARDS. A majestic arrow had been painted beside the words.

The sign had been written in coal tar. I stopped and wiped the sweat off my face. The wind rose. My body cooled; a feeling of happiness swept over me, as if I had fallen into a stream after a long march in the dry season. I picked up my knapsack and set off again, already dreaming of a hot meal and the shade of a roof over my head. I used to fight in the same unit as Huc. He would probably want to cook me his favorite dishes: a salad made from wild bananas, a sour soup made from canned meat and flavored with tamarind seed, barbecued mountain goat or deer. God, that Huc was a fantastic hunter.

I still remembered that time of brotherhood. We had looked after each other; he fed me all day with game. At night, while I slept like a rock, he went hunting. At dawn, sometimes even before I had time to get out from under my covers, he would be there, seated at the edge of my bed. His body gave off the chill of the mountain, the smell of leaves, fog, even the musk of the animal he had carried on his shoulders, whose fur still clung to him. All the others teased him, claiming that he had fallen in love with me. Nobody knew that I had once saved him from the political officer's harassment.

Huc was brave and stupid. In battle he fought selflessly, but in normal company he could be rough and vulgar. He was as fine a cook as he was a hunter. He concocted exquisite dishes with wild fowl and forest plants. Salads made out of banana trunk, colocassia roots, and bindweed. He even dared make them from young manioc and chili leaves. In battle, the soldiers under his command all feared him. But as soon as they were behind the lines, they fawned on him, pleading with him to cook for them . . .

A cracking sound. A dead branch fell, grazing the nape of my neck. I shuddered at the thought: *To die from a broken branch, or the beam of a collapsing house.* The humidity and the cold seeped into my body. I started to walk. About a hundred feet on, strange, dull, thumping sounds. No doubt about it: the chopping of an ax. They were felling trees around here. I listened again. Each time the ax stopped, a deep, regular murmur rose from the jungle. *Strange—I've already gone at least 500 yards and there's still no camp . . . What is that weird noise? Could they have posted the sign to throw people off the track?*

I set off again, watchful. There couldn't be any spies here. Nobody would want to lay ambushes in this place. When

I was at Base F they had taken great pains to brief me about the region. Still lost in my thoughts, I saw a wooden gate: SPECIAL UNIT M.035. It had begun to rot and the wood was split by long cracks. I took a deep breath, relieved. I had finally found it, and it was still daylight. I stepped gingerly through the gate. About fifty yards on I found three rows of sheds made out of slats of wood.

A few poppies in the empty courtyard. There were rows of mint, Chinese parsley, cactus. For us, these were exotic, luxuries almost impossible to find during the war. *It was Huc, after all.* I smiled to myself as I crossed the courtyard and walked up to the central building. All the doors were boarded up. The last one had even been bound with iron wire. I headed toward the building to the left, where I had seen a door ajar. "Anyone there?" An echo. I called a second time. Again, just an echo. I pushed the door open: two rows of beds covered with dust. A bed at the very back of the room, with an ugly bedcover the color of dead grass, littered with pieces of white paper, school notebooks, an American ballpoint pen. There was even a dark piece of wood that had been sanded down and polished smooth as a buffalo horn. Probably the headrest. A knapsack hung from one of the rafters in the roof.

They've really gone. There's nobody but a guard here. I really don't have much luck. I put my rucksack down on the low table. I sat down on the steps and stretched out my legs.

From the west a ray of sun stung my eyes, blinding but warm. I closed them, tilting my head back against the door. I savored this moment of happiness in nature—a nature I had always known to be cruel and deceitful. The dusk smelled of flowers, the smell that had haunted me as an adolescent, kindling in me a yearning to love. My rebel stomach had calmed, as if hunger had receded. My mind wandered . . .

Heavy plodding footsteps. I opened my eyes. An old man, bald and green as a cadaver, walked painfully toward me. *How was it that there were old people around here?* The old man nodded his head, as if to greet me, and smiled faintly.

"Hello, comrade," I said, rising to my feet.

"Hello, comrade," grumbled the ghostlike man.

"I've come to see sergeant Ta Van Huc."

The old man nodded and pointed in the direction of the mountains behind the camp, the place where the strange, rumbling sound continued to come from. "The chief and the whole unit are out working in the field. I'm the only one here, elder brother."

"Where were you just now, before you came over here?"

"In the fields. I've got dysentery." His forehead had tightened and he held his stomach in his hands. A spasm, no doubt. Only then did I notice his white teeth, the unwrinkled skin around his eyes, his smooth nose. This was no old man, only a very sick one who had probably been so for many years. Nevertheless his bald head perplexed me, and I asked: "Have you had dysentery for a long time?"

"Four years and seven months. I got it just a year and a half after my enlistment."

"You've only been mobilized for six years?"

"Yes. I'll be twenty-four next month."

Incredulous, I stared at his baldness, the wizened skin on his neck, his almost translucent body, as if, instead of flesh and blood, he was made of rock and moss.

"Why weren't you treated at the very beginning?"

His eyes met mine, and I shuddered. He had such bright, clear eyes, the eyes of a young man still living his dreams.

"I've taken medication, elder brother. But the sickness kept coming back. Every time. This time it's serious."

"Why not ask for a transfer behind the lines?"

"I don't want to. I'll be okay, with a bit of willpower."

"Sickness is cured with medication."

"Of course. But we don't have any more. The special unit is deep in the jungle. Maintaining supply lines is difficult. Huc was waiting for a chance to send me to the military hospital. But no mission has passed through for a long time now. What's more, I've got malaria. I lost all my hair in two months."

"Who feeds you? When will the special unit come back through here?"

"I eat rice gruel. Huc is really worried about me. Whenever he can find game, he gives me a piece. I guess you know Commander Huc?"

"We fought in the same unit right after our enlistment."

"Well, go right ahead to the worksite. He'll be happy to see you again."

"Are you all alone here, comrade?" I asked hesitantly.

"Don't worry. I'm used to it. Always keep my AK on me!"

And he laughed. He had a beautiful mouth, but with lips as white as parchment. His teeth glinted in the sun. He wagged a finger at me jokingly: "Don't you worry. I've still got enough strength left to pull a trigger. Bang, bang, bang."

His voice was feeble, almost inaudible.

"You come in and rest now. Can I do anything for you?" I said.

"Thanks, but you'd better leave before nightfall. There's a shortcut this way. You'll be there in a quarter of an hour."

I took the path he indicated. It followed a dried-out stream. Just about ten minutes later I arrived at the worksite. A huge tree fell in a deafening crash, sending a tremor through the air, as if to salute my arrival. Echoes broke out all around me. Someone shouted. Another voice burst out: "Bravo! Now we can rest a bit."

More voices were lost in the commotion. I crossed a space covered with tree trunks about three feet tall, trampling over a mixture of grass and sawdust. Night had fallen, and I couldn't make out the tree roots anymore. I kept getting caught in them, stumbling and falling several times.

I made out a campfire. From time to time, I tripped over a tree stump. They were all over. All sizes. Here and there, huge saws had been left on the ground. The air was thick with the musty odor of wood. *This must be a woodcutters' unit. The strange sound that had intrigued me: sawing. It wasn't surprising that I hadn't recognized it.* The men ran in circles around the fire. Hidden in shadow, I advanced slowly, seeing them without being seen. *If I was a commando, none of them would get out of here alive.* How careless of them. And yet Huc was known for being so cautious. I stepped around a huge tree to look for Huc and found him stretched out on a pile of planks near the fire. He looked exhausted but contented.

"Who goes there? Hands up in the air!" I felt the barrel of a rifle thrust between my ribs. I lifted my hands over my head. Huc sat up. His men, who had been wandering around, gathered behind him. Huc looked like an elephant at the head of his herd. The rifle barrel thrust more brutally into my back. "Move it!"

I walked anxiously toward Huc. The guy behind me was capable of inadvertently pulling the trigger. This was war, a prisoner's life was cheap . . . Huc got up. He stared at me. I stared back. Suddenly I burst out laughing. The stern look on his face was so comical. "Quan, elder brother!" He exploded joyfully and bounded over, grabbing me in a bear hug. "Quan, elder brother, it's been so long!" Huc stammered. He had always stammered when he was emotional.

"I played spy to scare you. But then I'm the one who gets caught! Your guy there, he butted his rifle into my back all the way down the path. Here I am, your prisoner!"

The sentinel laughed, letting his rifle drop to the ground. Flattered, Huc exclaimed: "You really don't take me seriously, do you? I'm Huc, remember? I still remember the lessons you gave me, and now, on top of all that I've got my combat experience."

He took my hand and pulled me toward the fire. His bare chest glinted in its light like a coppery statue.

"How did you get so tanned?" I asked.

"We roast away the whole damned day on these bare hills. You'll see for yourself tomorrow."

"Where's Bien? Is he better?"

"He'll bring the rice over soon. A real Hercules, that guy, and he always wears his heart on his sleeve. Yes, Bien is worth his weight in gold. A real gift you gave me. And you know, we're the same age, too. We're already sworn to be friends for life."

"I'm glad."

"He often talks about you."

"We're from the same village. Old schoolmates."

I was covered with sweat and dust. Huc led me to a

stream. The night was starless, pitch-black. We groped for our way along the path. As we reached the pebbly bank, Huc said: "The kitchen is about sixty yards off. Bien is probably there now, packing the baskets with food for the road."

"But there's no light."

"It's a precaution. Against spies. Even though they tried to tell us at Base F that this region isn't targeted, I'm worried. Not so much about being attacked, but that they'll come steal salt. It's more precious than blood here. Last season I lost ten men to beriberi. For a long time we ate ash instead of salt. Some of the guys started peeing a funny, murky kind of urine, like muddy water. Without salt, even game makes you nauseous."

Huc jumped in the water first: "Come over here. The bottom is a gentle slope."

I peeled off my clothes and slid into the water. The waves undulated like serpents. My eyes had gotten used to darkness. I could just make out the surrounding countryside in the phosphorescent light that rose from the rotting leaves. The water was cool, pleasant.

"We'll wash your clothes tomorrow. Stay here with Bien and me for a few days," said Huc.

"I'd like to," I said. "Only Luong won't be very happy about it."

Still, I handed him my dirty clothes. He hung them on a branch. My stomach was starting to cry out from hunger.

We returned to camp. The men had huddled around a bonfire that rose up in a shaft from the middle of the forest, illuminating the night.

"Hurry up, Chief, we're starving!" someone cried out.

"Why didn't you start?" Huc grumbled.

Bien suddenly rose and bounded toward me. Silently, I patted him on the shoulder. We sat down. It was one of the best meals of my life. Sautéed papayas and wild chilies marinated in shrimp sauce. The warm rice was redolent of bran. The fragrance of my childhood, at harvest time. I had found it again, here, in the depths of the jungle.

"Stay on with us a few days, elder brother. I'll go hunting for deer. We'll have a barbecue."

"I've been gone for a long time. The division will make me pay for—"

"A few more days? What difference will that make? I could have left this evening with my rifle. Unfortunately, I have to deliver the goods soon."

"The goods? What are all these trees and planks used for, anyway?"

"You'll see, later. Special merchandise for the front."

One of the soldiers laughed hysterically: "Didn't you see the sign? SPECIAL PRODUCTION UNIT FOR THE FRONT."

"Every lettuce has its worm!" I said. "You're all alike, with your mysterious airs, from the chief right down to the privates!"

Huc laughed. Wild laughter rippled through the troop. Huc bent toward my ear and whispered: "Eat up. We have a rule here: During meals you only talk about food and sex. It's forbidden to talk about anything else."

Bien brought over a pot of sweet black-bean pudding for dessert. Huc told the story of how Bien had walked twenty-five miles to trade with the Montagnards bartering freeze-dried rice for normal rice and buying tea. Without Bien, the special unit would have come down with beriberi, because the freeze-dried rice, which had been stocked for years, was brittle and had no more bran. He added that the Van Kieu girls had been captivated by Bien. One of the girls followed him for thirty-five miles, all the way to the edge of the jungle, just to watch him.

The soldiers burst out laughing. Bien lowered his head for a moment. "You and your wild stories."

I laughed heartily and thumped Bien on the shoulder. "The hero of the special unit!"

The glow of the flames danced on these youthful, happy faces. Tongues of fire soared, roaring up, twisting and winding around the campfire. In this ancient, mysterious light it seemed possible to conjure up every imaginable image; the fluid, shifting images of the future, and those of the past, already so murky, so far away.

A flame in the night; one of the few pleasures of our long resistance. In the glow of the hearth, faces ravaged by dysentery appeared radiant. The green, ashen pallor of skin pinched by rheumatism and hunger somehow looked fresh, luminous. Eyes danced in this light. Tomorrow the sun would reveal the cruel truth. But this beauty intoxicated me. I didn't understand myself anymore—all at once sad, anxious, enraptured.

Conversation flowed, interrupted by sudden bursts of laughter, like firecrackers. Huc told me that visitors were rare, so everyone had been allowed to stay up late. The rest of the time, the men all went to sleep right after the evening meal. After such hard work, they dropped off immediately. But all joy must come to an end. At exactly nine o'clock Huc ordered everyone to go to bed. "Remember, tomorrow is the last day we have. The day after that, they're coming for the goods. Get ready to give it one last shot. We're still short fifteen of them."

"Okay, okay, we understand." The soldiers all got up. I glanced around me: Where did they all sleep? All around was empty space, nothing but fog and the distant mountains. The soldiers didn't seem to care. They moved toward a huge plank of wood where they had laid out their clothes, their hammocks, and other belongings. Each man collected his own.

Huc turned to Bien. "Tonight, Quan can sleep next to you. That way you'll be able to hear your fill of all the news of your village."

"Good."

"Give Quan my cover. I'll use your jacket instead."

Bien moved toward the unit's warehouse. He came back a few minutes later. Meanwhile, the soldiers had scattered. Bien turned to me: "Let's go."

"See you tomorrow," said Huc. "Sleep as long as you want, elder brother. But we've got to get up early."

Bien handed his jacket to Huc, who took it and left. Bien and I set off in another direction. As we walked away from the fire, I saw shadows dart about in the forest, weaving in and out of the tree trunks and fallen timber. My feet sank into the sawdust. All of a sudden, Huc's voice echoed: "Who's standing guard tonight?"

"Me. Quang."

"Careful. The tigers are out again."

"Don't worry, Chief."

Bien stopped. "We're here." He took my hand, gesturing toward a long, white rectangular object at my feet that gave off the smell of freshly cut wood. "You'll sleep here. I'm going to lift the cover. You get in and I'll close it over you," Bien instructed me.

I felt my neck muscles tense: "It's a coffin, isn't it?"

"Yes. Our unit's special product. Huc didn't want us to tell you before you ate. He was afraid it would spoil your appetite. We're used to it."

I just stood there, speechless, empty. All I could feel was a kind of paralysis, a numbness from head to toe. "In the beginning we built the coffins in the fields and then came back to camp to sleep. Later on there weren't any more trees. We had to move farther and farther into the mountains. We lost time going back and forth. So Huc decided to set up the kitchen here. Each of us gets into a coffin to sleep. It's clean, and it protects you from the wind and fog."

Bien knelt down and lifted the lid. "Lie down. You'll get used to it." I climbed into the coffin and lay down. Bien spread the cover over me. It was scouting fabric, as clean and as light as cotton. Bien closed the lid over me. He sat down on the grass, groping around for something. A moment later, he slid a piece of wood between the coffin and the lid, just enough space for air. Bien admired his handiwork. "There should be enough air like that. If I open it any more, you'll catch cold. Also, the smell of your skin might attract the tigers."

"Are there so many in this region?"

"Yes. We're behind the lines here. There are fewer bombardments. The tigers chased out of other regions by the planes have all come here."

"Have they claimed any victims?"

"No, not yet, because we always have a sentinel. Mainly to spot tigers, but also enemy scouts. Whoever stands watch opens fire as soon as they smell a tiger. When I first got here, I saw a tiger drag the head of a young girl right in front of the camp gate. She was probably a liaison agent."

Bien lay down in his coffin, but he left the lid up. He raised his head and began to ask questions about our village. I whispered all the news to him through the crack. Above me, the sky was cloudy, turbulent. A thin crescent moon shone, the purple color of wilted violet. When I had finished talking, Bien said, "My poor father. I love him so much."

"I hate mine."

Bien tried to change the subject. "When do you think we're going to win?"

"I asked Luong. He refused to answer."

A long silence fell between us. Then Bien spoke: "Let's sleep, Quan. I've got to get up early tomorrow."

I pulled the covers right up to my nose. The smell of wood mixed with sweat was becoming familiar to me. I no longer felt uneasy: It seemed as if I had always slept in this kind of bed.

◆　　◆　　◆

Millions of bees swarm into a translucent emerald sky. I am lulled by the beating of wings . . . A field of violets swaying in the splendor of dawn, bent heavy with dew and honey. The bees plunge, trembling into the flowers.

A huge bee's nest of ivory wax blooms into the air. A silvery sun illuminates wisps of green smoke that float, like scarves, in the wind. A monotonous, lonely hum. The steady beating of millions of wings. This music washes over every-

thing in a tidal wave, engulfing all sound, swallowing all song, smothering the universe . . .

I reel in this strange music, careen through a field of violets. Feverish, I pursue the song. I walk, and walk, on and on, without stopping. I float in space, like the earth. I can see myself. I am in rags, white-haired, with a faded beard. I am running now, staggering through field after field. Thunder shatters the horizon. A flash of lightning. Terrified, I look up. The enormous bee's nest melts. From each comb falls a coffin. Millions and millions of coffins pile up on the ground . . .

"Quan . . . Why are you screaming?"

The light blinded me. I pulled the covers over my face.

"Wake up, elder brother, wake up."

I recognized Huc's voice. It took me a few minutes to get a grip on myself. I threw off the covers and sat up. Huc was in front of me, his fists on his thighs, grinning: "God, for you to scream like that, it must have been some nightmare."

I laughed and climbed out of the coffin. The sun was already high. It pounded down on us, hammer-like. I glanced around: more than a hundred soldiers were slaving away. Saws grated continuously. Sawdust flew in all directions. The air smelled of fresh wood. The soldiers handed one another planks, cutting and assembling them. The sicklier soldiers pulled the ropes taut, measured the dimensions. With their ink-stained hands and pencils stuffed behind their ears, they looked like the apprentice carpenters you saw in the villages.

The hammering and the hum of saws echoed in the silence, the vast, empty space. Huc pointed to the barren mountains with their stubble of tree stumps and ferns. "As you can see, we've felled a few trees."

"It's frightening," I agreed.

Huc continued: "The demands of the front. We kill ourselves and we still can't meet their quotas. I've asked for reinforcements, a platoon of healthy men. The commander agreed, but they can't find an available unit. Right now, we're attempting the impossible. Look—" Huc gestured toward a sign that hung from a branch. "That's the slogan I came up with. See if it sounds good."

Then he shouted at one of the men: "Hey, Lam, fix that sign for me. It's got to show our enthusiasm. So I see one of you borrowed the wire yesterday, is that it?"

"It was the tree-felling group," replied Lam. "But it's no problem, Chief. I've found something to replace the wire." He put the sign back in place.

The letters had been painstakingly written in soot-black ink: THE SPECIAL UNIT IS DETERMINED TO SURPASS TARGET. EACH COMBATANT IS AN INVENTOR. CENTRALIZE COLLECTIVE INTELLIGENCE. REVITALIZE THE WORK EFFORT. RAISE PRODUCTIVITY. KEEP UP THE STRUGGLE TO DELIVER QUALITY GOODS TO THE FRONT.

"It's good," I said.

"Writing has never been my forte . . . But I've got to try and motivate the soldiers somehow. What do you expect?

We've been sent off to this godforsaken hole in the jungle. No newspapers. No letters from home for years on end. Terrible food. No medicine. Luckily for us, Bien is resourceful, hard-working. Otherwise things would be much worse."

"But you're a skilled hunter. Why don't you teach the others?"

"Hunting is an art. You can't just give lessons. In my company, only Lam has what it takes. I'm not going to hide anything from you: If we didn't know how to find our own food, we would all be on our knees by now. The water here is green as a cat's eye. Over there, near the springs, there's only ironwood. Here's some lunch. I've got to go and have a look at the assembly workshop."

Huc handed me some provisions and walked off toward the bald mountain. I sat down on a tree stump and opened the banana-leaf packet: a ball of rice the size of a large oyster with a bit of shrimp sauce. A piece of boiled manioc. I chewed it in small mouthfuls, savoring it.

There was a time when I couldn't stand shrimp sauce, when the smell of rotting fish revolted me. I had even hated women who ate it, the way they squatted down around a winnowing basket of steamed rice-flour pâté and shrimp sauce, sticking out their tongues to lick the cake. It was so vulgar . . . Since my enlistment, I had grown accustomed to it. Now I adored it. Its odd smell awakened memories of fishing hamlets, of the sea, of the bonfires we used to build on sand beaches, of wind whistling through the *filao* trees—the tortured landscapes of Quang Binh. I had lived there for almost three years, had once felt linked to those simple, generous people who lived on manioc all year round so they could send every last grain of rice to the soldiers. They had probably forgotten me, but I would never forget them.

All around me the gnashing and screeching of saws, the thud of hatchets, the dull, halting pounding of hammers.

"Finished, Huan? Hurry up, it's already noon."

"We've only got one afternoon left. Please, gentlemen, hurry."

"Hey, Quat, go get a bandage for Toan. He just gashed his arm with that saw."

A soldier hurried past me, grinning. "You don't have much luck, do you, elder brother? You arrived right when we were in full swing of things! Tomorrow, the Van Kieu will be here before dawn to pick up the goods."

"No problem. Just let me finish eating and I'll give you a hand."

He hesitated: "No, Huc will be furious with me."

"So what? If he is, I'm the one he should get mad at."

Still hesitant, the soldier said, "I'm over at the assembly workshop. It's very technical work. You wouldn't be of much help there. Go help Khoa's transport group carry the planks instead."

I agreed and went off to join the transport soldiers, offering them a hand with small odd jobs. They were all very brawny men. Everyone worked in shorts, bare-chested, drenched in sweat. Huc reappeared just as Bien brought lunch. After I had eaten, I went down to the stream to bathe and wash my clothes. I had to soak them for a while; they had dried and stiffened since I had left them hanging on the branch for so long.

Bien took me on a tour of the kitchen, his private kingdom. He made me take a nap and then forced me to taste a wild rooster he had trapped at dawn. The rooster seemed to still be young; its flesh was extraordinarily tender and savory.

"Watch it," Bien warned me. "Wild-rooster bones are really tough." I nodded.

"When will we see each other again?" he asked.

I tossed the bones on the ground outside and gazed at the banks of the stream. "Who knows. This war . . . I've done what I could for you. If you still need anything, just say the word. I'll do what I can."

Bien stared at his shoes, his nostrils quivering. Underneath it all, this huge man was so tender; I knew he cried easily.

"Before I get back to my unit," I added, "I'm definitely going to go see Luong at division headquarters. He really cares about you."

Two tears streamed down Bien's cheeks. "I'm a burden for everyone. And I'm not even happier for it."

"If you keep thinking like that, you *will* go crazy. Come on, let's go, the soldiers have been calling you from the stream for a while now."

Bien wiped away his tears. He raised himself heavily to his feet and began to lumber toward the stream. I watched his huge back disappear into the sunlight-dappled underbrush. I had seen this man's back so often, but never watched it with such a feeling of regret. Back then, we used to fly kites together. Bien was the strongest, so he was always the one who held the string, who launched the kites into the air. He would run ahead across the fields, the rest of us scampering behind him. The kites would dance and whistle in the blue expanse of the sky; the sight of it stirred our restless young souls, awakening countless desires in us.

That evening Huc was ecstatic; he had met his production target ten days ahead of schedule. He even had a surplus: one extra coffin. "Was this one for me?" I joked with him.

Huc laughed, and turned to the soldiers: "Recreation time. Tomorrow's a day off." They yelped with joy and applauded him. That night a huge bonfire lit the forest, and our souls. After dinner we took turns telling dirty stories. If you couldn't think of one, you'd get pummeled. Then the men started playing cards. The company only had four sets of cards, so dozens of spectators gathered around each game, commenting noisily. The losers had to roll out a Van Kieu tobacco leaf or they got their faces smeared with soot. The forest vibrated with laughter and shouts. Huc turned to me: "A party like this is rare. Stay awhile. Tomorrow I'll go hunting. Tonight I've got to rest a bit. I'm totally beat."

"Of course. Go take a bath. Get some sleep," I said.

I didn't want to upset him, but I planned to leave before dawn. I had run out of time.

The next morning, three rifle shots woke me up. Men running. A shout. Voices. I lifted the lid of the coffin and sat up. Bien was already awake. The day had just begun to break, but we still couldn't make out faces. "What is it?" I asked.

"A tiger. It got one of the men."

"Who?"

Bien pointed in the direction of the camp. "San. He had a bad case of dysentery. Huc put him in charge of guarding the camp. I don't know how he could have gotten caught like that. This morning a guy from the lumberjack group went off to pee in the jungle. He saw the tiger drag him off. The guy shouted. Then the guard fired three shots into the air. Then they went in after him . . ."

We waited side-by-side. The eastern sky looked like lacquer that had shattered. Greenness shot through with streaks of whiteness and ice. A desolate landscape. Above the forest, fog floated by in drifts, writhing. The bald mountains, stubbly with tree stumps, looked forlorn, threatening. Less than three hundred feet away, the newly built coffins had been piled up in well-ordered stacks. Hanging above them was the slogan: THE SPECIAL UNIT IS DETERMINED TO SURPASS THE TARGET.

"I'm leaving," I said to Bien. "As soon as Huc gets back."

"I've already packed some food for you."

Just then Huc returned with a group of soldiers who lumbered over to us, sweating and panting.

"Well?" asked Bien.

"That imbecile! I should have slapped him a few times. I told him a hundred times to block that door before going to sleep. He forgot! We found the door wide open!"

"That can't be the reason," said Bien.

"Don't look for excuses for him. In any case, he's dead."

"I'm not looking for excuses. San told me just the other day that tigers had already come at least three times to prowl around the shack. Every time they came, San rubbed two pieces of bamboo together to scare them away. In the forest, only sharpened bamboo can hurt a tiger. When they lick the wounds, they infect themselves; they can die from it. San was very careful. This time, he must just have been so sick that—"

"Oh, god, it's my fault," wailed Huc, his face ashen.

"Calm down," I said. "What's happened has happened."

"But it's my fault. What carelessness! I went to see him last week. He kept telling me not to worry. 'I'll feel better, Chief, I feel better. Don't you worry about me.' "

Huc gnashed his teeth, clenching and unclenching his jaw. "Who would have thought that, who . . ."

Another group of soldiers arrived. They were even paler. "Chief, we've found the body," one of them panted.

"Where?"

"Up on Black Rock. Near the stream bend. The tiger ate both his thighs and a piece of his liver."

"That's enough!" shouted Huc. "Shut up! Bring him back to camp and bury him." He turned away from them.

Everyone stood silent. Nothing moved. Suddenly, a bird cried out. It was dawn. A soldier came up behind me. "Reporting, Chief. The Van Kieu are here to pick up the goods."

Huc turned around, still flushed. "Coming, Bien."

"Who would have thought . . . that the extra coffin would have been for him." Then he turned to me. "Wait. Just a moment. I've got to deliver the goods."

"And I've got to go. I've got a hundred guys waiting for me, just like you," I said, reaching for his hand. He bit his lip.

"I've been through this," I said. "I understand. You've just got to take it, accept it. We've never had any other choice."

He took me in his arms. We stood there, holding each other like that for a long time, while the Van Kieu scaled the mountain. It was Huc who let go of me. "Have a good trip, elder brother."

"Thanks. We'll see each other again."

Bien brought me to the kitchen and gave me the provisions for the road. A heavy package wrapped in a banana leaf. Three packets of dehydrated food and two cans of meat.

"Where did you dig all this up?"

"Oh, you know me, I always find things."

He lifted my knapsack and accompanied me for part of the route. When we arrived in the valley, I spotted the Van Kieu; they were walking Indian file, each man shouldering a coffin. Backs hunched over, dwarfed by their burdens, they looked like peasants carrying a huge bamboo boat.

"How can they bear the weight?" I asked Bien.

"Well, they'd better get used to it. It's impossible to bring trucks in here. The only way to get the coffins over the mountain is on the backs of those men."

I nodded dreamily. *He's right. You just have to . . . we human beings have to get used to everything.*

The sun had risen. To the east, the sky had shed its cracked lacquer shell; the clouds sparkled. Ferns, tree trunks: Everything was drenched in the sun's rosy glow.

In the dawn, coffins on their shoulders, the Van Kieu men traced a snaking line up the mountain slope. Their silhouettes moved slowly, patiently, stubbornly. An unswerving trajectory. These men would persevere until exhaustion to carry these gifts to the front. *Who knows? Perhaps one of them is for me.* Like the other soldiers, I was prepared to accept this strange gift. Fighting and dying; two acts, the same indescribable beauty of the war.

Suddenly I remembered my mother's savage, heartrending cry, her face bathed in sweat, the horrible spasm that had disfigured her, and then, on that same, horribly twisted face, the radiance of the smile born with a child's cry, when she saw his tiny red legs beat the air . . . Barbaric beauty of life, of creation. It had slipped away, dissolved in the myriad memories of childhood.

I was seized with terror. No one can bathe in two different streams at the same time. Me, my friends, we had lived this war for too long, steeped ourselves for too long in the beauty of all its moments of fire and blood. Would it still be possible, one day, for us to go back, to rediscover our roots, the beauty of creation, the rapture of a peaceful life? I stopped and turned to Bien. "It's time for you to go back to camp."

"Be careful," said Bien.

I laughed and swore at him. "I don't give a fuck. The bombs will just have to miss us. Who can dodge a bomb? Come on, get going. Don't worry about me. Worry about yourself."

"Oh, please!" he grumbled.

I shook his hand and turned away. I hated poignant good-byes. They can stay with you for months. For years.

❖   ❖   ❖

I see my mother seated on the landing of our house, her legs spread apart, offering her breast to a skull. I see her breasts, so familiar, taut and round, soft, with their tiny, rosy nipples.

She presses a nipple between the rows of the skeleton's white teeth.

She sings. "Bong bong. Bong bong. Bong bong . . ."

I hear her lullaby float up into the sky. I watch the sky drip a golden light.

My brother is dead. Why is she nursing him? She pushes the nipple between the dried-out teeth. She weeps. Her tears fall into the black sockets. The skeleton keeps its teeth clenched.

"Bong, bong. Bong, bong. Bong bong . . ."

◆　　◆　　◆

I woke up and found myself propped up against a tree at the edge of the road. My rucksack and half of my rice ball lay at my side. A colony of ants had climbed my knee and was moving toward the rice. I closed the packet, chased away the ants, knotted it to my knapsack, and then took to the road. The sun pounded down on my skull.

◆　　◆　　◆

The front. A violet horizon, shattered banana groves. Broken shafts of bamboo. A recent bombardment, no doubt. Everything had been pulverized, upended. A woman dressed all in black ran toward me, screaming, "What are you doing here?"

"Hello," I called back, but she didn't seem to hear me.

"What are you doing here?" she cried out again.

I moved closer. "I'm looking for an old man and a little girl—"

She cut me off: "A bomb fell on their shelter. Get out of here, quickly," she said, pulling me by the hand.

I ran after her toward the mouth of the bunker. She stopped, panting, and explained: "The bombings just started. They always come just about this time. The B-52s are always on time."

Just at that moment, four little heads popped out of the bunker. "Mama, mama . . ."

The woman pulled me by the hand again. "Climb down."

The bunker stank of gasoline, dust, and fleas. Nauseating. My eyes started to get used to the dark. She didn't just have four kids; she had six. They were all skinny, about the same size. Like a flock of ducks. "Hello, uncle bo doi!"

I didn't have time to answer. The biggest kid grabbed me around the neck, screaming: "They're coming!"

The children immediately scurried off and hid under a plank of wood perched on trestles in the middle of the bunker. Just their bottoms poked out. Their mother cried out to them: "Are you all under there?"

"Yes, yes," they shouted back in unison.

The bombs exploded in a long rumble of thunder. The woman put her hands over her ears and cried: "Plug your ears or your brain will explode."

I felt like laughing: This woman bossed me around as if I were one of her kids. I put my hands on my temples just to please her. There were three waves of bombing. Probably three B-52s. The earth buckled and reared up in violent tremors. Sand and gravel cascaded over the bamboo roof, sifting down on my head and the wood plank. Twenty minutes later, silence had returned. The children crawled out from under the plank, shaking the dust off their heads, tipping their ears to the side to get the sand out.

"Be still, will you? Let the uncle rest. Understand?" their mother scolded. Then she turned to me. "You rest. You're all white. Sleep. I'll wake you up for lunch." I went to the stock, scooped out a bowl of uncooked rice and handed it to her. Then I stretched out on the wooden plank; it felt as cool as marble. I fell instantly into a dreamless, peaceful sleep . . . I awoke to little cries in my ear. "Uncle soldier, bo doi, wake up, we're ready to eat."

"Uncle, Mama told me to wake you."

"Hey, uncle, get up, quickly!"

I opened my eyes. Six little pairs of eyes stared back at me. Six tiny mouths pouted in my direction. I laughed. The eldest daughter, who looked about eight or nine, helped her mother serve. I heard her say. "They've left. Let's go up above to eat."

The woman scolded her. "No arguing. We're eating here."

"Why are you scolding me?"

The woman shouted now. "Well, don't you have a sharp tongue! Okay, bring the rice outside." The little girl laughed and carried the tray outside the bunker. The little ones were delighted. "We're going out, we're going out!" They grabbed at my shirt. "Come on, uncle, we're going out. Mama said it's okay."

The daughter set the tray down at the foot of a jackfruit tree. It was made of wood, square, and it stood on legs about four inches high. There was manioc, the same variety I had eaten during the entire rainy season in Quang Binh; a few crushed chilies in a bit of salt, and a bit of shrimp sauce served on a jackfruit leaf. The children gathered around, waiting. The sun beat down. The children squinted, their tiny, hungry nostrils pulsating. "Calm down. We're waiting for Mother. I'll break your fingers if you keep clowning around like that," said the eldest in her most imperious voice. She had the arching eyebrows of a young girl. The woman appeared, in one hand a bowl brimming with rice, and in the other a bowl of soup. "Here you are, it's ready."

She set the bowls down on a free corner of the tray and handed me a bowl and a pair of chopsticks. "Eat. There's not much left here. Just a few shrimp for the tamarind soup."

She weighed out the manioc into big and small pieces and divided them into six equal portions. "Here you are, Hoa, and you, Hac, and you, Hoang."

The little ones stretched out their hands. I saw them furtively glance at the rice and lower their eyes. I grabbed the woman's hand as she served me. "Divide up the rice for them. I'll take the manioc."

She shook her head.

"Then I won't eat anything."

"You have to eat. How will you find the strength to climb the mountains, to go fight the Americans? The little ones are still growing. They'll grow no matter what they eat."

The littlest one suddenly saw a ball of rice fall on the ground. He picked it up and popped it in his mouth. The eldest girl snapped at him. "That's not nice. You're taking uncle bo doi's rice? Who's going to go and fight the Americans for you? Huh? Huh?" She slapped him hard. The little guy, he couldn't have been more than two and a half years old, burst into tears. I grabbed the woman's hand again.

"Don't do this. I lived through a whole rainy season in Quang Binh on just manioc. Anyway, it doesn't matter whether it's rice or manioc, we'll never get tired of it."

She frowned, irritated. "I'm not going to bargain for a few grains of rice with you. My barn used to be brimming with paddy. With my baskets of shrimp, we weren't exactly poor. Now it's war. How are we going to beat the invaders if everyone doesn't bear a share of the burden?"

I shook my head. "No."

Her voice was soft, supplicating. "Please. You're not being reasonable. You need to eat to fight. It's your duty."

"Listen, elder sister, let's drop the logical discussion. If you don't, I'm leaving. Immediately." I got up. I pretended to go down into the bunker to look for my knapsack. The woman gave in. She grabbed my shirt. "Okay. It's okay. Whatever you want."

She served the rice to the kids. But she forced me to accept a bowlful. As for her, she didn't eat a bite of it. She was about thirty-six years old. I looked at the wrinkles around her mouth.

Who is she, really? What has her life been like?

She laughed, seeming to guess my thoughts. "Don't worry about me. I used to have a house, two buildings made out of a wood as red as lacquer. My husband tore them down to fill the road for the gun carriers. What he said was, as long as those vehicles can get by, no regrets for the house. That house was the fruit of a whole lifetime of hard work. During the Land Reform Campaign my father-in-law was branded a reactionary. They handcuffed him and took him off to the firing squad. Fortunately, while they were en route there was a counter-order. They took him into the town. From the town, they took him to a prison in the forest. Well, he escaped and managed to survive in the forest for a whole year, until the Campaign for the Rectification of Errors. The Party rehabilitated him and he came back. When I was married, we lived together, the three of us, father and son in a hut. Seven years later, my father-in-law built the biggest brick house in the village."

"Is your husband enlisted?" I asked.

"He's dead. Last December. He was commanding a marine supply company."

"What do you mean, marine?"

"Oh, we're seaside people. But ever since the war, about half the village migrated over here." She mussed the hair of her youngest child and murmured to him: "Someday, you'll go back there. You'll go on a big boat. And your brothers will go and find some wood in the forest and build me a nice new house."

She paused and then said, "When those American bastards leave." She gazed dreamily into the distance. I realized she thought it was the direction of the sea. One day there would be a boat waiting for a tiny sailor who liked to lick the last grains of rice from the bottoms of bowls. As long as we're still alive . . .

I said good-bye to them and left for the front. The horizon was as purple as a field of violets.

✦   ✦   ✦

My luck hadn't deserted me. As I was walking along the road a supply convoy appeared. I stepped into the middle of the road. The head truck stopped about two yards away from me.

"Are you crazy?"

The driver jumped out of the truck. "We don't have any

brakes left! Just a bit farther and you would have gone to hell and sent me to a court-martial!"

I laughed awkwardly.

"Sorry, elder brother, you understand . . ."

He grumbled. "Come on, get in."

I said nothing and climbed into the truck. After a moment he turned toward me and asked, "What's your name?"

"Quan."

"My name is Vu. Twenty-five years old. Hung Khoi village. And you? You must be about thirty?"

"Only twenty-eight. The white hair, that's from the sorrow of life. Dong Tien village."

"Ha, ha—your district is right next to mine! We're from the same province. So, shall we swear to eternal brotherhood in the peach garden? Our little club already has about twenty-three members, and that's just in my division. You want to sign up?"

"Sure." A shock threw me forward. I almost went right into the dashboard window. Vu bit his lip and clutched the steering wheel.

"Watch out. The road is terrible around here. You stop paying attention for a second and you lose your teeth!"

I grabbed the window casing and leaned out. In the twilight, the golden bushes of *lac tien* flowers seemed to gild the slopes. On top of them, jade-colored ferns, and vines, endless vines. I shuddered when I glanced into the distance: an immense valley unfurled toward the horizon. Vu said to me: "The Valley of the Seven Innocents. Surely you must have already come through here? It's hell—probably a breeding ground for termites."

I said nothing. I tried to place this part of the forest, the giant ferns, the vines, the forest of colocassias where I had gotten lost, where the bleached-out skeleton of a young man had laughed.

"Companion, you can't reproach me. I carried your sack all the way to Em Mo village and returned it to your mother. I couldn't stay long with her because the guy who brought me had a bad temper and I didn't want to annoy him," I murmured to myself.

I had gone to Em Mo and asked for a certain Madame Dai Thi Ly. They pointed to a tiny old woman with gray hair seated behind a food stall under the temple banyan tree. She chatted gaily with two other women, fanning her stall with a bamboo fan. I greeted her and set down my knapsack. When she saw me she paled and cried out, "My child!" She collapsed. They rubbed her feet with a balm and carried her home. One of the women stayed behind to watch over the stall. "He was all she had," she told me. "The husband died while she was pregnant. The child was born three months after the funeral. He was a gentle boy, especially gifted at playing the monochord, the recorder, and the flute. All the village girls were madly in love with him, but he didn't even look at them; he always clung to his mother's skirts. It's been eight years since he left. Ever since, the old woman gets up at dawn, in the fog, to prepare her goods. She saved every coin for her son's marriage. She sells everything: crab soup, steamed rice noodles, rice pancakes with grilled sesame seeds. She even has flour-and-sesame candies shaped like colored balls."

Suddenly Vu asked me, "What are you doing standing there, staring like that? Thinking of your mama or your sweetheart?"

"No, I was—" But a sudden sharp bump interrupted me. Vu shouted: "I warned you . . . It's frightening, this road follows the Valley of Seven Innocents to the west. You must have been here before?"

"Yes, it's a nice place. Except over there, the daisy-colored part."

"That's a soldier's nightmare. That's the forest they named this valley after . . . Take a good look. From the east to the south, it's another color, green: There are jungles of ferns, brambles, and, in the gullies, forests of colocassias. From the east to the northwest it's nothing but *khop* trees. The *khop* forest stretches out all the way to the chain of mountains on the other side. Anyone who loses his way there is as lost as if he were in the ocean. The trees all look exactly the same, like bricks cast in the same mold. It's impossible to get your bearings. I got lost once, right at the spot you just pointed to."

"Were you a liaison agent or in a special unit?" I asked him.

Vu shook his head. "Neither. I went into the forest to take a leak. Then I couldn't find the path. It doesn't matter what direction you go in; it all looks the same. It's like dreaming. That's what it's like when you plunge into a forest. You can call and scream all you like; no one can hear you. I hadn't even brought my rifle, so I couldn't alert my buddies. After I had shouted myself hoarse, I got up my courage and started walking. The farther I walked, the more I lost myself in the trees. And then, there was nothing to eat. I had nothing. Not a knife, not a bowl, not a cup—not even my lighter, which I had left in the truck. I wandered for five days like a ghost. On the sixth, when I couldn't even crawl, I lay down under a tree to wait for death. Just about that time, the unit started to search for me. The guys liked me; after they had delivered our load, they asked for reinforcements and split up into three groups to go look for me. They shot their guns into the air to keep their bearings. They found me in a coma under that tree, put me on a stretcher, and brought me back. Along the way, I was delirious. When I recovered, they told me they had stumbled across a cave with seven skeletons lying at its mouth. Termites had eaten everything—flesh, clothes, papers, knapsacks. All that was left were seven skeletons and their seven rusted rifles. Huge termite mounds everywhere. Since then we've called it the Valley of the Seven Innocents."

I said nothing. I thought of the eighth, the ninth, the tenth . . . Who would ever know the exact number of innocents in this war?

Vu asked me something: "After the war, will they come back and look for all the soldiers' bones?"

"I don't know . . . But for the missing in action like that, it's unlikely."

Vu clucked his tongue. "My god, by that time there'll be nothing left but mud!"

I didn't respond. The truck's motor purred. Vu said: "Later, at dinner, I'll introduce you to the other 'club' members. They'll be delighted."

✦   ✦   ✦

I will always remember the woman of my dreams. She walks across the horizon. Her face is radiant in the starlight, in the middle of those golden fields. *"When will we get married?"* Her waist is so small. The paleness of her face the day of my enlistment. Her eyes that watched me on the long marches, along the dusty roads, through the muddy, rutted footpaths overgrown with trees and grass, clotted with decomposing corpses. I'll always remember that woman. The woman afar. My woman. It was a face that dreamed, a face sometimes gaunt, sometimes radiant, youthful. It was the face that had once belonged to my mother, to her clear laughter, to the infinite openness of her gaze. And always, her tenderness, an innocent, soothing lullaby . . . again and again, neverending: *Bong, bong. Bong, bong. Bong, bong . . .*

◆　　◆　　◆

Dripping from the sky into the fields, a golden light.

◆　　◆　　◆

Back at division headquarters, I learned from Luong that during my absence my friend Luy had gone mad. He had remained prostrated in silence for an entire week. Khue had done all he could, alternately threatening and consoling him, but to no avail; they couldn't get a word out of him. On the eighth day he had refused all food and locked himself in his room, huddled up in a corner, his face in his hands. Whenever anyone tried to get near him, he screamed bloody murder. On the tenth day he wasn't just afraid of men, but of light. He hid under the covers and refused to come out. In the end, he was emaciated and stank. His eyes had the scared look of a wounded animal. They transferred him to the regional military hospital. No one has heard a word about him since. Luong consoled me, then told me to rejoin the company and to prepare myself; we were gearing up for a major battle.

He listened in silence as I told him about Bien and relayed the news of his own family, the events in the village.

All of this touched me. But our childhood was dead. He was a colonel now, the deputy commander of the division. Glory and honor were knocking at his door. For me, he could no longer be the friend he had once been. He had chosen another destiny, one that had begun with the betrayal of his roots. Sickened, I said good-bye, picked up my knapsack, and left to rejoin my company.

The battle was a triumph. "Waves of the Red River"— that was its code name—had ended in victory, glorious proof of the efficiency of our military techniques. We had annihilated one enemy regiment and decimated two others. Then we received orders to withdraw behind the lines to rest and gather our strength.

During the march back, a noncommissioned officer stepped on a mine. The reports said he had gone off into the jungle to relieve himself. But when they opened his knapsack, they found more than thirty spoons, knives, and forks, all stainless steel, all American-made. I almost ordered them to throw everything away. I clenched my jaw. *What use was it, the suffering of the poor?* My comrades were stupefied to see me furious like that, for no apparent reason, and they were silent around me. I went by myself to the stream. I smoked cigarette after cigarette, watching the smoke dance and evaporate. *You bastard, I should have straightened you out, given you a few slaps. Risking your life for lousy trophies.* I cursed the dead man. I cursed myself. And I looked out over the vast

fields teeming with white storks. Wretched creatures; they
were scraping for food in the mud. The bamboo hedges
twisted in the wind, and a flock of gaunt, sodden storks advanced, staggering, across the marshes.

◆　　　◆　　　◆

*I dream again. The same dream. For more than a year, it
haunts me, pursuing me on every road, like a creditor after a
debt. A desperate, dark horizon. A train derailed. Empty wag-
ons jostling and clattering along the tracks. A murky light
flickers in front of the locomotive. From time to time a siren
lets out a long, painful howl through the unnameable sadness
of the countryside. The wind whistles through the vacant
train, wagon by wagon, chasing bits of paper, schoolchil-
dren's notebooks half gnawed by moths, pages covered with
neatly drawn images and signatures. It sweeps aside stubs of
chalk, dried-out inkwells, the white caps we wore at vacation
time. All these objects roll along, laughing gaily in the howl
of the train siren.*

"Reporting for duty, Chief."

*I recognize the voice. It is far away. The siren howls
again, a long howl. The train starts up with a crash and
disappears behind the mournful horizon. I watch as the silhouettes of birds rise over the tips of the sodden marsh grass.
They don't fly, they walk, dragging their wings. They advance, threatening, moving closer and closer. I stare at them,*

terrified; these are not storks, nor herons, nor wild geese; they are vultures, the garbage collectors of the battlefield, the obsessive fear that haunts our daydreams, the unconscious flashes that rise from soldiers' souls. They move closer to me, switching their dirty feathers, their heads thrust forward, their beaks agape, streaked with blood.

For anyone who had lived in the jungle, in these mountains, this was the most horrific vision, the one that reminded us of the villages razed to ash, strewn with swollen corpses, of the gorges that swam with blood and rotting flesh; of the stench of death, the buzzing of flies. A scene congealed by the sun, seared into our brains.

"Chief, Chief . . ." It was no longer just one voice. Two hands shook me roughly. I jumped to my feet. Sergeant Mao stood at the foot of my bed. "Chief, Comrade Hung just stabbed Comrade Teu."

"Why?"

"They were kidding around and Hung got mad."

"Is Teu badly hurt?"

"The medic says the wound is four inches wide and two to three inches deep. It definitely touched the spleen."

"Get him to the hospital immediately."

"Yes, I've already prepared everything. The medic is bandaging him up right now."

"And Hung?"

"Um . . ."

"What do you mean, 'um'? You know what must be done, don't you?"

"Yes . . . yes." Mao was white-faced, probably terrified.

I just snorted. "This happened in *your* unit. You should have arrested him on the spot. And if you aren't capable of that, then you should take his place."

Mao stepped to one side, stammering. It was painful to look at him.

"Arrest the guilty man immediately," I snapped. "Take the wounded to the hospital, and then come back and give me a report."

"Yes, sir."

I felt dispirited. I had looked forward to a calm, restful day. For a long time we hadn't had anything like this. What's more, after years of eating bamboo and wild vegetables, we had just received three weeks' worth of supplies, and in huge quantities. The route that linked the Valley of the Funnel and the B5 military region was open. Supply unit 559 had brought us everything: rice, canned meat, fish, lard, Hai-Chau candies, dehydrated food BA70, and dried patties of shrimp sauce. And, the height of luxury, there was concentrated milk from the Soviet Union and powdered eggs from China. The day before, I had gathered all the platoon chiefs and ordered them to double the rations in celebration of the victory. I had also asked them to let me sleep. I had stayed up four nights running to write my report on the campaign and get it to the regiment's liaison agent in time. The respite hadn't lasted long when blood began to flow again.

I put on my shoes and went to wash my face. Mao was waiting for me when I got back. He was seated, his arms crossed. I sat down facing him and tossed him a cigarette. He lit it, hands shaking. He was a kind, simple boy. I tried not to add more tension to the atmosphere; if I did he would get scared and not say anything. I inhaled calmly before speaking: "What bad luck, and right on a day of celebration."

Mao sighed, relieved. "Yes, it would have been a real celebration, too." I took another drag on my cigarette, blew a smoke ring; I watched it float off. Mao followed it with his gaze. "Have you eaten lunch?"

"Not yet, it happened before we could even start. What a tragedy."

"What did they cook up for us today?"

"All kinds of things: canned meat fried with bamboo shoots, a salad made from wild banana trunk, vegetables in MSG . . ."

"How did it happen?"

"Teu was in charge of cooking today. He made deep-fried frogs with a batter of egg powder."

"We've got plenty of egg powder, but where did he find the frogs?"

"That was the start of the whole drama. Teu traded half a case of egg powder for a hindquarter of pork from the Van

Kieu. Everyone had congratulated him on the idea. He steamed the pork and shredded it into strips to imitate frog meat. Then he dipped them in the egg powder. The only thing was, before he fried them he chewed them up and sucked all the juice out. It takes away the flavor."

"What a jerk. And then?"

"That's not all. He took a piece of—" Mao stammered. I could see he was genuinely embarrassed and trying not to lie to me.

"Tell me everything," I said.

Mao looked confused, then smiled and lowered his voice. "Then he took a piece of the pig's vagina and stuffed a chili pepper into it. He dipped the whole thing in the egg powder and started frying it . . ."

I almost burst out laughing. I would never have imagined such a trick. Mao winced. "Teu had barely finished when Hung showed up to have a taste. He's always doing that. So Teu lets him taste six or seven pieces before asking him, 'Hey, Hung, kinda bland, don't you think?' Hung suddenly sees the light. Two years ago, in the Choi jungle, he himself had done the same thing to a piece of beef before he served it for a feast day."

"Is that all?"

"Oh, no. Just as Hung was about to jump on Teu, someone grabbed his sleeve. 'Why fight with this idiot? Eat the best pieces, the biggest ones. Later, when the other guys start eating, they'll have his hide.' So Hung said: 'Okay, that's a good solution.' He grabbed the biggest piece. That was the—"

"I know. He didn't realize until he had eaten it?"

"No, that damn thing was really leathery . . . No one has ever been able to finish it. Hung struggled, trying to chew it for a few minutes. But it was so tough and peppery that he had to spit it out. Everyone was in stitches. that's when Hung realized what had happened. He pulled out his dagger and jumped on Teu. It happened so quickly that no one had the time to step in.''

Mao crossed his arm again and waited. Judging by his face, I wouldn't get anything more out of him. "Bring Hung to me," I said.

Mao got up and walked away determinedly. Then I realized that there was something else behind Hung and Teu's quarrel, and I stopped Mao as he walked out the door. I ordered him to watch Hung carefully and to send him to regimental headquarters the following morning.

A mournful silence had fallen over the huts. After the incident the soldiers, dejected, had eaten and gone back to their huts in silence. There were no card parties, no shouts tonight. At this hour they usually played cards on bamboo mats, betting for tobacco, mint candies, chewing gum, parachute nets, stainless-steel knives, and photos of naked women. They played even during the times of great famine, and the losers were made to pay by having their faces smeared with soot or being forced to do a handstand. Nevertheless, they were touching moments. A thirst for peace and joy that burst out of nowhere like a mountain spring, sometimes flowing into a river, sometimes evaporating on the rocks. It was a question of luck. Bad luck came in all shapes and sizes, but I had never imagined this particular guise. Dying for a smoke, I fumbled in my knapsack for a pack of cigarettes we had taken from the enemy. One of the men, a gofer type, brought me some dinner. "Everyone has eaten. Have something before it gets cold."

"Just put it on the table and go get some rest."

"Chief, you look real pale."

"Thanks, I can take care of myself. Go on."

I watched him leave, as watchful as a mouse, his eyes darting about, surveying the surroundings. I didn't like this type. It was impossible to know what desires lurked behind his obsequious attitude: A promotion? Home leave? A posting as an officer up north? That wasn't even counting the possibility of desertion. There were quite a few men of his ilk. That was inevitable. And when it had been suggested that he become a liaison agent, I had immediately accepted. I had to tolerate those under my command, a duty that bore a vague resemblance to torture.

What was Hung thinking now? Those who had tied him down, the men who were guarding him now, had all been his comrades in battle. Stretched out side by side, they had faced enemy fire, had laughed over a card game on the same bamboo mat . . . I got a few pieces of paper out of my knapsack. It was up to me to write a detailed report of the incident before they took him to regimental headquarters at dawn. From there they would take him to a military court two forests away from headquarters. That was where the prisons were. I had heard about them, but had never been there.

The pen felt heavy in my hand. I bent over the blank page, and then almost immediately turned away from it. I saw myself an officer carrying out his duty—the horrible duty of a buffalo pulling the plow to dig up tombs.

> *Lai Phi Hung*
> *Age: 25*
> *Native Village: unknown*
> *Residence: Mai Dong village*
> *District of the Two Trung Sisters*

Hung was one of the braver soldiers in my company. He never ran away from danger, never panicked. It was as if he had been born to kill. He was the perfect illustration of the classic Chinese treatise on military strategy: The best soldiers were bandits, robbers, and vagabonds, followed by homeless orphans. These types hurtled toward death with no regrets. Physically they all had the same sharp, sullen look, the pointy, hooked nose, the prominent chin that jutted out under their flat cheekbones, the beady eyes, the eyebrows that curled back. And the same fixed, snakelike gaze. The type of men who could stroll along, lighthearted, and then suddenly transform themselves, like lynxes stalking their prey. And then just as quickly regain their peace of mind, their nonchalance.

In hand-to-hand combat Hung liked to invent new ways to kill. And he delighted in recounting his exploits: bayonet stabs through the mouth to the heart, or right through the groin, or ripping from the abdomen up to the waist. He was particularly proud of a certain surprise attack: he had slipped into the bedroom of a Vietnamese puppet officer, waited until the man was glued to his wife, skin glistening with sweat, and then plunged his bayonet through them both. ("Two pearls on one string—you should have seen it.")

One day, without thinking, I asked him something: "The day of your enlistment, who cried on your shoulder?" He had stared at me, his face contorted, his eyes filled with hatred, thinking that I was making fun of him. Then he realized that I was sincere, and he said to me: "No one has ever shed any tears for me. They just laugh. They laughed when I was beaten up by a bigger guy. They snickered when the police dragged me handcuffed through the marketplace. Chief, in my village we make a living slaughtering stolen water buffalo. Killing and stealing; those are the opposite sides of the dice. I make my living off these two professions. When I have money, I gamble. Nine times out of ten, I lose. But when I win, I win big. So when my pockets are full, I keep a dagger to protect myself."

And Hung had laughed. I still remembered that laugh. From then on, I had kept an eye on him. Without that confession I would have reacted to all his exploits without batting an eyelid. He had a thousand little talents. He could prepare every variety of meat to perfection: deer, wild goat, orangutan, water buffalo, pork—all that, of course, but also elephant meat. He even wove baskets with skill. They said he had lived in Mai Dong village for several years before he began to hang around its marketplace. He could fix rifles faster than the best armaments worker. Sometimes, when inspired, he would sing. But he set the warmth of his voice to some horrific lyrics:

> *O fuzzy dog sleeping in a corner*
> *One blow will send you right to heaven*
> *Hello barbecue, pudding, stew—*
> *Seven dishes I'll make of you*
> *And then I'll put out your skull to dry . . .*

For seven years he sang the same old melody over and over again. Perhaps he would sing in prison.

In a certain way, I liked him. At least he was more interesting than sycophants like the liaison agent. But he also repulsed me. He had no home, no family, knew nothing about his parents. The one-eyed woman he considered his adopted mother, who sold his stolen goods in the market and let him sleep on her stall, was only a temporary accomplice in his delinquent existence. Free of all attachments, he undoubtedly found the soldier's lot to be the perfect way of life.

One memory of Hung lingered with me. It was 1968, the terrible autumn of the year of the Monkey, almost seven years ago. Death stalked us every passing second, hour by hour, day after day. Every night, through a twilight swirling with ash, smoke, and dust, we dragged the corpses of our comrades away from the battlefield, from an earth soaked in blood, strewn with human flesh—that of the day's combat, the putrid shreds of the previous day, and the rotting debris of a whole week shrouded in fog. No words will ever be able to describe the stench. In the flickering light of dusk, bats crisscrossed the sky; crows cawed raucously. Cries dripping with blood and flesh. Caked in dried blood and sweat, we dragged our rifles and our dead on our backs. Some bodies were intact, some truncated, missing a head or a leg, others had their stomachs ripped open, their intestines dangling. The blood of our comrades mingled with our sweat and soaked into our clothes. We marched, stunned by exhaustion and despair. We threw our last remaining energy into each retreat, not in the hope of saving our lives, but with the feverish desire to participate in the next day's butchery. We wanted to live so that in twenty-four or forty-eight or seventy-two hours we could spit fire on the enemy, watch the bodies tumble, the blood spurt forth, the brains shatter . . . We would have done anything to see this magnificent spectacle, because we knew from experience that we had to redress the balance, tip the scales in the opposite direction. Annihilation had to be evenly distributed. This insane thirst had taken hold of everyone without exception.

That night, the yapping of bats and crows followed us to the edge of the jungle. Their black wings beat at the air, which was motionless, unruffled by even the slightest breeze. I felt my heart implode. I had told my comrades to rest, to catch their breath before the final stage. Each man had staggered toward a tree and laid down his arms and corpse. Some of them just leaned against the trees; others collapsed on the grass, gasping for breath. It was night. We couldn't see one another very well, but we could each feel it inside, and in one another: the venom, the shame, the hatred.

I ran my fingers through the hair of a corpse, that of my youngest soldier, Hoang. He had been the purest soul in the company. Barely eighteen years old, Hoang was the son of an intellectual couple; the father a doctor, the mother a schoolteacher of the third rank. There were two sisters. He had taken first place in the math competition that selected students for study abroad. But he had volunteered for the army instead. "No, the college classrooms aren't as important as the battlefield. There have been and there always will be classrooms for those who want them. Only the war gives me a chance to participate in our country's historic mission. I've heard the sacred call. Good-bye, beloved high school, beautiful Hanoi sky flaming red, good-bye, West Lake, Quang Ba Lake, flowering gardens, sweet memories. We'll meet again one day." His diary was delirious with enthusiasm.

Hoang's face had been finely drawn, with white skin, rosy lips, and clear eyes. He had always been clean and well groomed. He liked to gather wildflowers to decorate the barracks. Hoang had cultivated all the city customs and manners that seemed so distant, so alien to this war.

I had been attached to Hoang, but had always tried to hide my affection; if I hadn't, he would have become a scapegoat for the whole company. Discreetly, I tried to keep an eye out for him, tried to protect him from certain things in our soldier's life, from the common snares that had been laid for this sensitive idealist. How many times had I watched, helpless, as men like him were snuffed out by the violence, the deprivation. A shell had ripped off one of his arms and a leg. The corpse had gone cold, begun to stiffen. His blood had run dry and hardened on my shirt. I caressed his hair, his shoulders. The night shielded me; no one could have seen my gestures. The little one was dead! From now on I had the right to express my affection, my regret, my hatred. I had restrained myself for so long. It had finally come, the moment I had feared; I hadn't been able to protect him. Death was a whore; she always chose the fragile ones. And at that moment I imagined the day I would go back, if ever I did. What would I say to his young mother, his sisters? He had lived near Lake Haller. I had gone by there when I was young. A calm, blue lake. Nguyen Du Avenue, a street of cool shadows and flowers whose poetry had seduced so many innocent souls.

Suddenly, birds shrieked. The soldier next to me had jumped and whispered: "They're here."

"Shh!"

"Those dogs."

"Spread the word. Make sure you get the comrades who are still sleeping."

We crawled toward the others, alerted them in whispers. Quite a few of them were still asleep, exhausted. But everyone was immediately on their guard. The footsteps grew nearer. We didn't have time to consult, to prepare a battle plan. We found one another by smell. Fanning out into the underbrush, we opened fire like madmen, aiming at menacing shadows, toward the place where the wind carried a foreign scent, the smell of the enemy . . .

Cries, shouts. Explosions. Flashes ripped through the night. Those dogs! We could just make out their silhouettes. No doubt it was an independent squad with orders to track us down, perhaps acting in concert with regular forces. Or were they reinforcements that had arrived late? In any case, one thing was clear: they were a bunch of rookies. We could tell by their frightened howls, their clumsiness, the way they scattered.

Survivors of a horrible massacre, crushed by our own pain and hatred, we all felt a yearning for revenge burn inside of us, felt it rise like a thirst. Hunger, fatigue, pain—that had all subsided; now every soldier was alert to the slightest movement. The eye found the target even through the shadows. The nose could whiff out the slightest movement. We shot like madmen, to cleanse ourselves of the pain, the despair.

Slowly the cries subsided. The shooting stopped. Silence became total . . . We could hear the distinct, lone cry of a stray bird. Then Hung's voice: "You had enough, son? Papa'll put you out of your misery." Hung had snickered, fell silent for a moment, and then shouted: "I'm warning you, no bush is gonna hide you from me." I heard him brace a submachine gun against his thigh.

"Comrade Hung," I said. "It's against the law to kill prisoners. We're bringing them back to base." I had barely finished my sentence when I saw a trembling shadow advance toward me. "I beg you, please . . ." The unlucky enemy platoon had been decimated. Hung took three prisoners. We hauled the corpses of our comrades on our backs for the last stage of our retreat. Suddenly I remembered something and called out: "Comrade Hung, who were you carrying before?"

"No one. I was carrying Comrade De Tham's rifle."

Later I learned that Hung refused to carry the dead and

wounded. One time he had laughed and said: "I'll give you as much killing as you like. But as for carrying dead and wounded, you won't get much from me."

That night we all wandered like lost souls. Our warriors' madness had been spent; our limbs were paralyzed by hunger and fatigue. Hoang's corpse stiffened, and since it was missing a leg I was constantly knocked off balance. My soldiers were on the verge of collapse. "Just a little longer, brothers, just a little farther and we'll be there." I encouraged my buddies from time to time. But I knew it was no use. I too was totally exhausted. I saw stars and felt my back go limp.

We crossed the Khan Gorge. It was deep, dark. Sinister echos and sounds rose in the night. We were only about half an hour from the base. Suddenly Hung shouted, "Faster!"

"I beg you . . . I'm in pain," moaned the prisoner.

"Stand up. I'm giving you one minute," Hung snapped.

"Okay, okay."

Bang. A sharp crack. Before I realized what had happened, the jungle resounded with the poor man's howling. A mass of flesh had fallen into the ravine. We heard the echo of the stones rolling. The two remaining prisoners yelled like madmen. They had just witnessed the death of their companion. They ran off.

Bang. Another dry crack. Then another two. Two corpses had fallen into the ravine. The echo repeated itself, over and over . . . . I bounded over to Hung. I could hear his breathing and my own. His was regular, peaceful, mine was panting, frantic. I should have disciplined him severely and in front of everyone, cited prisoners' rights, the War Charter, the dignity and humanity of the combatants . . . But my tongue went numb. Was I somehow complicit, a party to this? Because of Hoang's death, because of all the pain, the disinherited, the hopelessness, the massacres? Perhaps for all that . . . or perhaps because of nothing at all.

We stared at each other, motionless, mute. The other soldiers stayed silent, as if paralyzed. After a moment Hung spoke up, listlessly, but with an assured voice: "Let's go. We're almost there." And he was off. He only carried two rifles. Of all of us he had the lightest burden, and yet he was the real chief here! My blood flowed back, choking me. The shame was as brutal as the defeat I had just suffered on the battlefield.

Now this memory overwhelmed me. My face burned with the shame of a truth I had never admitted to myself. I hadn't just been an accomplice. Hung had dared to commit an act that I had contemplated and I didn't want to reprimand him.

I wrote hastily, summarizing the simple facts. I concluded as follows: "May the relevant authorities decide." Then I called Mao in and gave him the report. "Have whoever carries this accompanied by three men we can trust. And watch that Hung doesn't kill them and go desert on us."

"Don't worry, Chief, I'd already thought of that."

He left. Weary, I turned to my dinner, which had gone cold. I was ashamed, but I had to admit to relief when I thought of the next day: that fiend would be gone!

A cheerful voice spoke up behind me. "Chief, I hope you've got something for me, since I've got some mail for you." The little fellow pulled a letter out of his pocket. I said lightly: "Next time. All I've got left is chewing gum."

It was a letter from Hoa. The woman who haunted my brain. A yellowed, moldy envelope whose edges had been gnawed by insects. The postal stamp had completely faded.

Quan, dearest,

I've sent you sixteen letters and you haven't replied. Every month, Sister Soan and Miss Lien drag me to the post office in the city to ask for your news. They say they've received nothing. We come home empty-handed. The road is long. It's very cold. We cry as we walk. Darling, are you dead or alive?

Why don't you answer? It's been fourteen months since your last letter. Everything is fine in the village. Nothing has changed. It looks like the harvest won't be very good this season. We started October without any ceremony, without chicken or sticky rice. All we have is a few pieces of fruit and

rice wine for the ancestors' altars. It's so sad com-
pared to the festivals we used to have, when we all
used to go to the pagoda together.

Quan, darling, you know how I miss you, how
I need you. Eight years and two months have gone
by since you left. I've gotten thinner. I'm not as
beautiful as I once was. The day that I went to
town, I only weighed ninety-two pounds. Do you
still love me? As for me, I'll love you till I die . . .

The signature was splotchy. Had it been tears or the
work of time? The letter was dated; it had been sent one year,
seven months, and thirteen days before my return to the
village.

◆   ◆   ◆

It was a calm evening. We were drinking some black tea that
friends in the high plateaux had given me as a gift. I liked to
drink it with a spoonful of honey or raw sugar. To me its
sweetness was imbued with the perfume of a nostalgia for
something unnameable, a longing that haunted our soldiers'
souls. Two men kept me company: my deputy, Thai, and one
of the infantrymen, Tao. Thai had brought half a ration's
worth of food and Tao had two ripe mangosteens. With my
sweetened tea, it all made a magnificent banquet.

The jungle sank into the softness of dusk. It was so

beautiful that Tao even interrupted his elegy on the art of preparing green tea to admire it. We sipped in silence, watching the leaves quiver and sway.

All of a sudden, a lynx mewed. A sharp, tortured wail. We looked at one another. The anguished wailing rose again. The lynx appeared. Thai let out a cry. We all stepped back in the same movement. By the time we realized what was happening, the lynx had bounded onto the bamboo table where we had been drinking tea. It crouched low on all fours, back arched, as if preparing to leap. But it didn't. It glanced about, its icy green eyes sweeping the space around us. I reached toward my hip, but Thai whispered to me: "Don't shoot it!"

The lynx flicked a tea cup over with its tail, its hackles suddenly raised, its eyes dilated diabolically. And again it stared at us, one after the other—a wild, possessed look. But it didn't seem scared. Its translucent green eyes sent off flashes that paralyzed us. Trembling, Thai stammered: "Don't shoot, don't anyone shoot." He was ashen. Tao stepped back to load his revolver. The lynx stared at us, contemptuous, and began to mew again. Then it bounded out the door. We stood there for a moment, without moving, transfixed.

Thai was still in shock. He swallowed a mouthful of tea, as if to get a grip on himself. Tao exclaimed: "My god, I've never seen such a terrifying lynx!" I added, "That's the first time I've seen that damn animal since I've been in the army."

Thai said nothing.

"I thought lynxes avoided us. They're only aggressive when they protect their young," I mused.

Thai shot me a look and then told us this: "I have an uncle who got married in the high plateaux. He was a carpenter, and sometimes he would accompany the hunters. He said that lynxes never prowl near fields, rice paddies, or villages. You set traps for tigers that come to hunt pigs and cows, for the wild boar that ravage the crops, for the monkeys that come to eat the corn, for the bears that steal honeycomb—but never for lynxes. When you see one, it's always a sign of disaster. They appear maybe once every three generations. But when they do, you can be sure that a storm will wipe out a village, that a fire will raze a whole region, or that there will be some deadly epidemic . . . My uncle used to say that if someone shot a lynx—the messenger—the misfortune would be eternal. If it were an epidemic, it would pass from generation to generation, decade after decade. If it was a fire or a flood, it would come back every year . . . And don't think I'm superstitious. My uncle is a simple, honest man. He has never told a lie in his life. I have to believe him . . ."

Tao grabbed my shirt, panicky. "That's horrible, eerie."

"Don't tell anyone about this," I said.

Thai agreed. "Yes, not a word."

We all fell silent. The evening was over. The memory of

it was to haunt me for a long time. A month and a half later, the omen was fulfilled.

◆　　◆　　◆

Campaign "Lightning Arrow" had begun. It was the dry season. And yet the sky had abruptly clouded over. The morning fog lingered for a long time before burning off. A heavy, suffocating odor, like fumes from a chemical factory, suffused the air. And everywhere, all through the valleys and ravines, drifted a weird, oppressive, green vapor. It seeped slowly, carrying with it shattered, mutilated mirages. Lights merged and flickered out, etching strange patterns in space. Citadels ringed with spears. Sometimes smiling faces slashed into threes and fours, each chasing the other, each evanescent, like soap bubbles ready to burst.

We had received orders to camouflage ourselves, to preserve our strength, to prepare rations for the final battle. We had always planned our movements so as not to leave a single trace. Like cats, we erased all signs of our presence. Cooking fires were carefully covered over, our footprints meticulously swept away, our excrement buried. The previous year the enemy had detected an entire unit just because instead of pissing into the bushes one guy had done it into a wildflower that camouflaged an American sensor.

Ordinarily the march began at nightfall. The guide wore a mask. Passwords changed every week. Soldiers didn't have the right to ask questions, express opinions, or joke around. When you arrived at the rallying point, you hung up your hammock, ate, and went to sleep. Everyone understood; there was a battle coming . . . One night when we were at the rallying point Thai led me into the jungle. I had thought it was going to be one of our routine meetings and I asked him where the others were.

Thai had shaken his head. "It doesn't matter. I want to talk to you alone." He turned and led me into the jungle. We descended into a gorge thick with ancient trees and strewn with huge boulders. The moon shone. We sat down under a tree, shaded by its huge, earthly shadow. Above us, chill moonlight danced on the leaves that swayed in the wind, a drunken wind only found here on West Mountain. Thai had said, "Quan, you know, my brother's dead."

"Thang?"

"Yes. He was all I had. I told you that . . ."

"I know. He was in the company that defended B-41."

I remembered the company well. One day Thai had come down with malaria. He thought he was going to die. In a moment of lucidity he told me about his family, and had asked me to look after his aging father and younger brother. Altogether there were seven children, but Thai and Thang were the only males. Thai's mother had died in childbirth with the youngest. His father grew tobacco. He had decided to remain a widower and raise his children alone. Thai's voice quavered: "Quan, do you know Huu, the regiment's political officer?"

"Of course."

"The captain was off on some mission. That bastard Huu wanted to impress division headquarters, so he decided to launch an operation. Since the colonel was also gone, Huu's subordinates approved his plan. Huu was secretary of the regimental Party cell. The comrades voted unanimously in favor of the operation. Half to please him, half out of negligence, the scout platoon concocted some fantastic report about the situation. All false. That's how the B-41 platoon got the order to annihilate the enemy, why they launched battle F.E. 18. They crawled all the way to the front. And they'd barely begun to dig when the massacre began. The terrain was nothing like the loamy earth and sand that had been described to them; it was all granite and old stone. Their shovels sent sparks flying at the slightest contact. And the enemy shot mortars point-blank everywhere they saw sparks. The platoon was totally exposed under the rain of fire. The next day it took three platoons to retaliate and remove the corpses. What's more, there were fifty dead . . . All that's left of the B-41 platoon is some poor guy from Quang Binh. They brought him back to the hospital, gasping for breath. His spleen and liver had been cut out. We don't know what became of him."

"A whole platoon eliminated? Did they find all the corpses?"

"You really think that's possible?"

"Did he have a girlfriend?"

"No . . . not yet. Even I didn't have the time to fall in love; how could he? He's dead. The whole platoon—they were all kids, like him." And Thai sobbed. "He's dead, Quan—for nothing, because of some idiot's ambition. They're *all* dead because of that bastard . . ."

I fell silent. I saw two legs kicking in an earthenware bowl, twilight dancing on the quivering surface of the water. Men: They were born so full of life; they left for the front so full of ardor.

Thai sobbed in the darkness. I said nothing, waiting for him to calm down, and then spoke. "Be calm, try to think of morale, of the other comrades."

"I know. But I needed to tell you."

"I'm afraid there's going to come a time when no one will want to say anything to anyone anymore . . ."

We went back. I knew Thai was thinking about the lynx because I myself was thinking about it, as I would a curse. The next morning, the medic informed me that an entire platoon had been striken with malaria. The other guys were all mumbling about how a few bastards had gone off on their own and had stuffed their faces with poison fruit. Three days later, one by one, all the platoons had succumbed to the onslaught of the jungle. By the eighth day, the sickness had struck a third of the company. No one was laughing anymore. Every face was pale. The hardiest men ministered to the sickest. The sick ones howled, ran naked into the jungle, as if flames were licking at their guts, their skin, as if the terror had overcome them, engulfed them like the jungle that surrounded us, torturing them with a strange, unnameable yearning . . .

Ten days later, when the orders came to take to the road no matter what, I wrote a report to the commander. The messenger watched me through his mask and said in a calm voice: "Tonight. Without fail."

"But a third of my men are sick."

"That's the final order. This is the last regrouping before the battle."

That night the fog was thicker than ever. The company advanced single-file, a fierce, icy wind at our backs. Two ablebodied combatants carried each of the sick men and the weapons.

We walked down a path crawling with roots and vines. The guide was just a few steps ahead of me, his back straight as a board. Thai brought up the rear. Khue, the strongest of us all, walked back and forth, tending to the sick, lending a hand when they had to be carried. No one spoke. We were so tired that everyone concentrated on preserving what little strength he had left to go on.

March, march, march! Suddenly I remembered it: the chant we had sung ten years ago, in 1965, when we began the march to liberate the south. Our clamor had shaken the jungle. At the time, I had been eighteen years old.

Bang! A shot rang through my ears. The guide stopped in his tracks and shouted "Halt!" A second shot echoed. I bounded ahead, flashlight in hand, running after a shadow. The guide followed close behind. A few minutes later, we stopped a kid with scorched skin, totally bald. He had collapsed onto a pile of rotten leaves, his neck sunk back between his shoulders, hands raised, pleading: "Please, brothers, mercy . . ."

I recognized the accent of Ha Tay province. On his back he carried a dirty knapsack, like a beggar's bag. He wrung his hands, stammering, "Pity, brothers, I beg you." His breath was short. He probably hadn't eaten for a long time.

"Are you a deserter?" I asked him. "Show me your papers!"

He pulled a soldier's ID card and a ragged mission order from his pocket. "I'm not a deserter. I got lost . . ."

I took a quick look at his papers: "What do you take me for, a fool? This mission order dates back to June of last year. What are you doing now?"

"Chief, I lost my way. I was sick . . . malaria. I stayed back with the Van Kieu." He pointed with his finger. It was night out. I couldn't tell which direction he was pointing in.

The guide's lantern lit up his ravaged, emaciated face. He pulled a rag out of his pocket and handed it to me. "Here, here's the certificate from our Van Kieu brothers."

"But if you aren't a deserter, why haven't you gone back to your unit?"

He winced and suddenly began to weep. "Chief . . . I miss my mother . . . I'm all she has. And my unit is so far away now, in B9, how would I find them?"

At that moment Khue ran over. "What's going on?"

"We caught a little deserter," I said.

Khue said, "Okay, let's take him with us. Hurry, the men are falling into a trance."

I agreed. The soldiers who carried the sick men had picked up their stretchers again after the unexpected pause. "Follow me," I said to the kid.

The guide found the path again. The march continued. We arrived at a mountain path. Thanks to the moonlight, the path was more visible. The deserter followed me, often tripping up against me. Each time, he would bump into my leg or step on my heels. I finally turned around. "What's the matter with you? Are you hungry?" He said nothing. I got out the dried rations Thai had given me at noon and handed them to him. "Have this." He took them without a word. And from then on he stopped tripping and falling. From time to time I turned around and saw him following in my steps, like my shadow.

Who was his mother? Probably a woman who lived in misery in Ha Tay province. Perhaps I had met her among the women hunched over by their burdens, who lugged baskets of snails, cabbage, vegetables, bananas, and potatoes dozens of miles to the city in the hope of earning a bit of cash. Or was she one of the women who ran barefoot after the trucks, hawking cups of green tea, who waded through the mud of the rice paddies all year long for a few lousy baskets of paddy rice, who smiled proudly when she was invited to pose for a photo at harvest time with the provincial Party secretary? Who was his mother? The thought tortured me. The moon shone cruel, icy. Just ahead of us, the dark mountains were crouched low, like seated monsters. I could hear my soldiers breathing in the chill air. Turning, I saw the little guy still plodding determinedly behind me. I remembered how one time the soldiers had chanted our march, twisting the words:

> *I'm my daddy and my mama's child*
> *Come home when I feel like it*
> *Don't need no knapsack*
> *Don't need no rations*
> *Don't need no car*
> *'Cause I'm comin' back home for Tet*
> *One day, I'll come back to you.*

The little guy was probably one of the ones who made up the words. These were chants no historian would ever record.

When we arrived at the rallying point, half of my troops were sick. Fortunately, the medication arrived in time. Barely recovered, the soldiers went into battle. Campaign Lightning Arrow had entered the third phase, and our unit had played a key role. The campaign wasn't as successful as Campaign Waves of the Red River. Out of my hundred-strong company, only Thai, myself, and seventeen soldiers survived. Khue was killed in the first engagement. We were decorated as a "Heroic Company" and given immediate reinforcements. In spite of it all, we were the victors.

Before withdrawing from the battlefield, we, the nineteen survivors, had organized the backbone of the new company and a farewell ceremony for our dead comrades. We knelt before an altar of bamboo covered with white gauze. I gave the order to light the pyre. It would take an inferno to conjure up the faces of more than a hundred dead. They would never leave us, those faces: ashen, drained of blood, twisted in pain, accusatory, demanding justice . . .

◆　　◆　　◆

I dream of a blue ao dai. A woman wears it, a woman who appears out of the blue of the sky. She is both the woman I once loved and not her at all. This one doesn't have a gaunt

*face, the bloated belly of a woman ready to give birth. Her
face is handsome, delicate, with long eyebrows. I am dying of
love for her, enough to die with no regrets, having loved, having been loved.*

◆   ◆   ◆

I awoke, alone in my hammock, bathed in sweat and filth.
You imbecile. Dreaming again. Nothing but illusions . . . I see
myself: this man who talks to himself, swears aloud, who
gnashes his teeth. This man who goes calmly, wearily, to wash
his clothes in the stream, who eats dinner every night and
then discusses the next move in the plan with Thai.

That evening, when the liaison agent came, we were
drinking tea. He handed me orders from divisional headquarters. We were to lead four prisoners to the base and hand
them over to the security forces. The order was firm: Don't
lose them; don't let them escape, fall sick, or die under any
circumstances. Luong himself had signed the order in the
name of the commander-in-chief.

◆   ◆   ◆

The rain had fallen suddenly, like fate, like an accident, like
love. For half a month it pounded down in torrential, blinding
sheets, completely masking the sun, weaving a dense, white
woof through space. The streams and rivers swelled into
cataracts.

It was impossible to advance. We had decided to set up camp at Base X3-57. Day after day I watched the flood, the shuddering leaves battered by the rain. Night after night I watched the gas lanterns give off a thick smoke, cast their reddish light on the ruddy faces of my men as they bent over their card games. I became irascible. I often thought of my brother, saw his little red feet again, fighting like fish caught in a net. It came upon me unawares, sometimes during a meager meal, or even in the middle of conversation, as we sipped an infusion made from leaves. Sometimes it no longer seemed to be a dream. The sadness, the weariness would overcome me. And then I would see myself wriggling like a fish in a net, crushed by the weight of my past . . .

One rainy morning, I got up and walked toward hut No. 2, crossing a long veranda to keep out of the rain. Uniforms hung all over, suspended there to drip-dry. Then they would have to be strung up by the cooking fire all night to dry completely. That was how it was during the rainy season. Suddenly I saw prisoner No. 4, standing all alone in front of the hut. He was gathering rainwater as it fell from the roof into his hands, splashing all around. In profile, he bore an eerie resemblance to Hien, the little sister of the woman I loved. The ridge of his nose, the shape of his mouth, that chin . . . It all evoked the sweet face of a monk. He didn't see me as he played in the rain, happy, as natural as a schoolboy. If Hung had seen him, he would have laughed and spat out his contempt: "Bags of fat, chickens who lounge around with their guitars and flutes, their diaries and poems, the dried flower petals . . . Stupid hobbies for effeminate souls, drawing-room soldiers. May the bombs reduce them to jelly, may the mortars—"

A branch snapped. The puppet soldier jumped, startled, flushed red with confusion. "Sir, sir . . ." I wanted to reassure him, but that seemed ridiculous. He continued to stammer.

All of a sudden he looked terribly like Hien. He must have been Hoang's age. Did he also record glorious dreams in his diary? Had he also left the university in search of an ideal? I spoke to him: "Prisoner Number Four, follow me."

I turned to go back to my room, heard him following behind me. I lived in a separate room reserved for the commander. It was made out of carefully arranged planks of wood. A few faded calendars hung on the wall. There was quite a bit of furniture: a bed, a cabinet for documents, a table, a few chairs. Everything was made of wood.

"Come in."

He entered hesitantly, lowered his head, and wiped his hair with his shirtsleeve. I gestured to the chair facing me. "Have a seat."

He seated himself and placed his hands over his stomach. He had lovely hands, with long, thin fingers, the hands of a woman. I poured tea. "Drink to warm yourself up."

The tea steamed. He took a tiny sip and then sat motionless, anxious. When he lowered his gaze, his thick, black lashes half covered his eyes. A few stray hairs here and there over his mouth.

I didn't move. He gave me an alarmed look. Seeing the fear in his eyes, I said: "Calm down. I'm not going to kill you on a whim."

He lowered his eyes again in silence.

"Anyway, here we practically pay you not to escape, don't we?"

"Lieutenant Huyen already told us."

I laughed to myself. He was truly naive. I had never met a puppet soldier who behaved like this. "Huyen, that's the man with gray hair, prisoner Number One, isn't it?"

"Yes, sir, the lieutenant said that if we try to escape, we'll fall into the hands of other units, and that nine chances out of ten times we'll get to taste a copper candy or a bayonet blade."

I laughed. "That's right. But you and the others, you're no angels. No man is forgiving enough to share his ration of rice with men who fire mortars on him. You are the enemy. The least we can do is to give you a few pieces of copper candy."

He remained silent, I continued: "You're safe here. I've got orders to deliver you to the security services. I must feed and protect you."

I had lit a cigarette. I glanced distractedly into the white space of the rain, my mind wandered. Suddenly, I missed my mother.

A deserted cemetery: Here and there, tombstones, choked with bloody vines, rise above the spiny pineapple bushes. One by one, I gather the crushed fake gold paper, scattered on the damp earth. I walk along rotted planks . . . My mother . . . The joss sticks flare violently. She must have heard me.

"Careful!" the prisoner cried, pointing toward my hand. The cigarette was burning my skin. I tossed it outside into the rain, and turned to him. "Your name?"

"Huynh Hoai An. Eighteen years old."

"Your village?"

"Gia Dinh. Saigon."

"Profession?"

"My father is a schoolteacher there, my mother runs a clothes shop."

"She's a tailor?"

"Yeah, specialized in women's clothes."

"Why did you enlist?"

"I . . . I . . ." He shot me an anxious look and lowered his eyes.

"Why?"

"Out of . . . duty."

"What?"

"For . . . for the nationalist ideal."

I remembered the man in the gold-rimmed glasses, with the white skin of a cricket kept too long in its box: "That ideal, well, the kids need it. And it's all we need to turn them into monks, soldiers or cops." The little man had laughed with the admirable insolence of those who hold power. All things considered, I should have thanked him for it . . . The prisoner looked at me, tense, waiting for the interrogation. I smiled: "For an ideal?"

"Yes . . ."

"To defend the beloved motherland?"

"Yes."

"To fulfill the patriot's duties, to prove yourself worthy of the Lac Hong?"

"Yes, sir . . ."

"To serve the country, swearing to spill the last drop of your blood?"

"Yes," he said, echoing each of my phrases, becoming paler and paler. I saw his hands shake violently; his legs had begun to tremble. He was obviously trying to guess what kind of trap this Vietcong was laying for him, how I planned to drag him in front of the firing squad or the gallows. His eyes had a wild, distraught look.

"What god do you worship?"

He stammered, "Sir? My family is atheist . . . My mother just prays to Buddha and eats vegetarian the first and fifteenth day of the month . . ."

I shook my head. "I asked you who your god was."

He wrung his hands. "I beg you . . . spare me."

"Don't sniffle. No one's going to eat you alive. Listen now. We worship a theory. But you enemy soldiers are all the same. Our god's name is Marx. He's got a pug nose, blue eyes, and a shaggy beard. So, who's your god? Is he bald or hairy? Does he have a high forehead or a low one? Does he wear a goatee or a mustache?"

Only then did he become calmer. He drew his breath sharply. "No, sir, we don't have a—"

I grimaced. "What do you mean, *'No'*? So you mean your nationalist ideal is a sham? You mean you can't even find yourselves a god?"

"I don't follow you," he stammered.

"Don't play dumb. There is one, that's for sure."

"Yes, sir, when I was in secondary school, they spoke to me about Mr. Marx, Mr. Hegel, Mr. Kant, Mr. Nietzsche . . . There were a lot of them. But philosophy never attracted me, so I didn't really try to pursue all that."

I laughed. "So many gods? Well, then, you're a polytheist. Why, your ideal is quite impressive! Why did you give it up?"

"We fell into an ambush. I was Lieutenant Huyen's orderly."

"The little guy with the gray hair? That's your chief?"

"Yes."

"How many battles did you take part in?"

"Two."

"In the first one, how many Vietcong did you kill?"

"I . . . I . . ."

"You know, I might have been facing you that day. Maybe you were the one who ripped off a piece of my ear. Here, look, you see?" I said, gesturing to the ragged edge of my ear. He paled, tears gathering.

"It's impossible, I couldn't have shot at you!"

"And why not?"

"Because . . . that time . . . I heard shooting from everywhere. There were lots of men dying all around me. I was so scared that I lay down on the ground to hide. I didn't even dare raise my head."

"You didn't dare? Indeed. But the second time, the third time, you'll raise it, and the fourth time you'll aim for my face, and you won't even flinch—right?"

"Sir . . ." he said, trembling.

I smiled. Again he was stupefied. He was the spitting image of little Hien. He must have thought I had come out of hell. I saw the muscles on his face tense up. I could imagine the tumult of his mind at that moment, as he desperately tried to understand. It amused me. "Don't be afraid. In war, everyone kills. I'd also shoot at you like I'd shoot at an animal, without even thinking about it. Perhaps all this misery comes from worshipping different gods. Why don't you ask your lieutenant to advise his government to worship the god Marx?"

The prisoner stared at me fixedly, his mouth agape. He must have thought I was crazy, unless he was the one who had gone mad. I continued: "Or we could all just agree to choose any old god. Take, for example, the god Tho Dia, who lounges around with his big belly in the corner of the kitchen . . . Nobody would even think of going and killing someone over such a lousy god."

The prisoner was mute for a long time before he could stammer out, "Oh, please, spare me . . . I don't understand a thing you're saying . . . Please."

I burst out laughing: "Don't worry, it's just a joke . . . Go on, go back to your room."

He got up, clasped his hands together, and said, "With your permission, sir . . ." He took a few steps backward, and once he was in front of the door, he turned around and suddenly darted off like a mouse. He had looked at me with the terrified eyes of a young girl confronted with a dirty old man! It was still raining in torrents. Drops of icy water flew in through the window, spattering me. I watched the white rain, the mountains, the endless forests, battlefield after battlefield, stretched out all the way to the horizon. This vast space swarming with soldiers, armies of black ants, red ants, winged ants, fire ants, bee ants, termites, all paddling about in the mud, running through scorched, desolate fields . . .

On both sides you screamed, you killed in mad, frenzied bursts, shrieking for joy when the blood gushed, the brains shattered; you went at one another like savages under the dense rain of machine-gun fire. Then the survivors limped off the battlefields to swell the reserves, to join the ranks of future combatants. The dead offered their bodies to carnivorous birds and worms.

On both sides you died believing that you had attained your ideal. We had forgotten everything: mother Au Co, father Lac Long Quan, the shared womb from which we had sprung. A more beautiful legend had never been told . . .

✦　　✦　　✦

The fever knocked me out for a week. I couldn't eat anything. The medic fed me glucose syrup through an IV. On the eighth day the fever broke. I just managed to swallow some rice gruel. The rain had stopped. It was evening; the air was humid. Supporting myself with a stick, I went out and stood in the doorway.

There was a poignant beauty about the jungle. Happy to have survived, I let my mind wander back to my village, let it follow the length of the dikes, through the fields. Wild ducks honked their way across the sky. I had gathered my lost fragments of life, had drank a bit of blue sky from the bottom of a cup . . . Perhaps I could grow again like a strand of paddy spared the harvest, bent by hatred and storms but still able to flower, to bear fruit.

"Chief, you get inside this instant." The medic dragged me toward the bed, forcing me to lie down under the covers. My body had barely started to warm when I sank into a chilling dream.

◆　　◆　　◆

I see Hoa. She makes love with a huge, hairy man. He is monstrous, like a monkey. She moans, her face as white as a drowned person's. The man fondles her with bony, hairy hands. His hair stands on end. His body wriggles painfully, oddly, like a large ape. He looks at me and laughs broadly, arrogant, gloating over his conquest . . .

My heart twists. The desire for vengeance tears me apart. I want to scream, but my burning throat chokes me. I melt. Strange sensation of sliding, of slowly dissolving in water to cross the fields of grass, winding between two stands of old reeds, yielding, merging with the river that flows, softly, silently, near my village.

◆　　◆　　◆

The previous night a guy from the regiment had come to see us. He was quite elegant. He had brought a letter from Luong, a box of Chinese apples, and half a package of tobacco. Luong had learned that I had been stricken with malaria. Unable to come himself, he had sent this messenger. His envoy was eleven years my senior and higher in rank than I was. He was a smooth talker. After dinner, we all chatted together. He boasted of having wounded a guy in the knee. I asked, "Was he an enemy spy?"

"No, a deserter. Serves him right. With two shots I got both knees. He's going to lose the legs, that's for sure. I haven't shot that accurately since I enlisted."

"What did he look like?"

"He has a Ha Tay accent. A little guy . . . He must be about the age of my eldest son. What a jerk. Instead of stopping in his tracks when he heard my warning, he kept running." He laughed. "Hey, this lighter's great. Even the puppet soldiers couldn't afford such a luxury! Will you give it to me as a souvenir?"

"No problem." I tossed him the lighter and his face lit up.

◆   ◆   ◆

One day we called a conference for all officers ranking captain and above. The meeting place was kept secret. Liaison agents guided us from one stage to the next.

I was recovering from sickness. I had proposed that they send Thai in my place, but headquarters refused. "I have no choice," I told him. "Stay and keep an eye on the company. Monitor the quality of the meals. Hanging around idle like this, the soldiers will probably chase after women and get into trouble."

Thai looked worried and said: "I don't like seeing you go off so far."

I laughed. "Well, you're going to have to face the fact that I'm going to die one of these days."

"Don't say that."

"Don't be an idiot. Nothing could be more natural. It's already happened to a hundred thirty-seven people in this unit alone."

"But it's not going to happen to the nineteen who are left."

"Why not?"

"Because that's what I believe. The heavens aren't blind, after all."

"Oh, yeah? Then why do men kill one another like this?"

Thai dropped his head and, in a choked voice, said, "Tell me, Quan, what are we going to do for a living when the war's over? Take me, for example: my brother's dead. At home there are only girls left . . . Who are we going to marry them to? They're going to be chasing after me the whole blasted day."

"You think too much! Try to concentrate on your nerves and muscles instead so you can get out of this war alive. After that, we'll see about the rest."

Thai handed me a pack of Vinh Bao cigarettes that a peasant had given him; it had came from the north and had molded along the way. Thai must have washed the tobacco and then dried it. Anyway, it was better than papaya leaves.

I left at dawn. The liaison agent guided me to the first rallying point, where I spent the night with fifty other officers. The next morning a truck came to pick us up and take us through the forest. A tarpaulin sealed the truck. After two days and one night on the road, we reached the second rallying point. We found ourselves in a dense forest.

Shacks were crowded under the foliage of the trees. The smoke from the kitchens had been channeled underground through pipes that emptied into a deep ravine. Men came and went, clanking their bowls and spoons, chatting in loud voices . . .

Here you could fraternize with clubs of people from the same province. People struck up friendships easily, gave spontaneous artistic performances for days and nights on end. Poems were recited in a central accent; the northern accents blended chanting Quin Ho songs. There were only men, and yet we managed to have a good time.

The next morning the liaison agent arrived: "Hey, comrades, look at the beauty they've given us for a guide." The men bolted out of their shacks. A woman! Shouts and yelps from all directions. Some jumped up and down; others ran in all directions. Pandemonium. Moved by all this, I crouched in the middle of the crowd. It was only a long time afterward that I saw her. She was worth waiting for. Attractive, though not really beautiful. Pale skin, jet-black eyes, ebony hair. Petite, almost fragile. All the men rushed toward her, trying to get in a word with her. She greeted all of them, smiled at every man, calmly, patiently. She must have been used to the madness that came over men who had spent too long in the jungle.

Guided by this lovely fairy, we moved toward the river. Small boats were waiting for us. We crossed the forest toward the rapids on translucent, emerald-colored water. Twelve boats, twelve men in each; an entire company. We had all been completely organized into groups according to rank.

The girl had gotten in the head boat with the commander. I hadn't been selected. But I felt lucky, since this way I could watch from a distance, her silhouette etched against the sky. How graceful, how beautiful she looked in the black silk pajamas of a peasant woman! Like a beckoning, a call. I heard sighs rise from the boats that followed.

A voice rang out: "It's really worth belonging to headquarters!"

"Blessed are those in the head boat. Just a whiff of her is enough to soothe your homesickness."

"O wind, share her perfume with us!"

"Hey, what is this, some kind of modern theater?"

"Theater of my ass, yeah! That's what you had in mind, wasn't it?"

Peals of laughter rose. Then, only silence. They stared at her, their faces rapt.

On the banks the lush green foliage gently rippled. The paddles lapped monotonously at the water, in cadence. We took turns every hour. The pilot only took charge in the dangerous parts, near the rockiest shoals. We leaned against one another, sleeping while the boats glided slowly toward the plain. I woke up that evening. The sun at our backs scattered in a thousand sparkles on the waves. In front, as far as you could see, were beaches of red sand . . .

This was the land of the Cham . . . I had crossed on the way to Zone K. The young Van Kieu, Te Chieng, drifted back to my memory, how he had urinated noisily, right next to me. Thinking about him chased away the darker thoughts in my brain. We were in the land of red sands . . . I sat up and gazed at the shore, awestruck. Dunes flowed the length of the river, infinite red waves flecked with a few tufts of gray-green grass, as far as the eye could see. When twilight fell, the sand turned to purple, the color of marsh-flowers.

I gazed at the sand. It no longer stirred the ghosts of the past in me, but rather an unfathomable sadness. It had gotten chilly. The sun's furnace had died down; all the agitated desires, the passions, had flown away. Grasses vanished slowly behind the earth's steady breathing. I was no longer in pain.

I didn't expect anything anymore. I heard something like a
sob. Was it just the rush of the waves?

◆   ◆   ◆

*Sad, far-off music. Perhaps it is just the night. Somewhere,
at the foot of a spiral citadel, the flickering of a flame. Seated
in front of it, mute, secretive, is a wraith. He leans on his
lance, a tear glints in the glow of the hearth.*

"*Who is it?*" *I ask.*

"*It is I.*"

"*Who are you?*"

"*Your ancestor, from the seventieth generation.*"

"*I don't know you.*"

"*Of course not. No one can know their own ancestors.*"

*The wraith raises his head. Tears trace a furrow on his
cheek. It seems to me I have already seen this face somewhere
along my peregrinations. It is a face at once familiar and
strange. The curve of the eyebrows, the wrinkled brow.*

"*What do you want?*"

"*To see you, my child.*"

"*What for?*"

"*Your hatred has raised me from the tomb.*"

"*Perhaps . . .*"

"*You have already passed through here. It was here that
you fled from the ghosts of the Cham. You were afraid. You
cursed us.*"

"True."

"You must not."

"The crime has been committed. You can bury it under seven layers of the blackest earth; the truth is the truth."

"Of course."

"So there is nothing more to say."

"Oh yes, there is."

The wraith watches me, tears brimming in his eyes. A shiver runs up my spine. I refuse to be intimidated by a spirit. And yet this sad, pained regard touches me as irresistibly as love. The wraith smiles, his gaze vanishing in the distance, through my eyes.

"There is another truth."

"Then speak," I snap at him, furious.

The wraith laughs a sad laugh: *"There was a distant lake, a distant river, a distant forest . . ."*

"Get to the point. I don't understand you!"

The wraith laughs softly. *"You will. Back there, far up north, there is an emerald lake, a river, a forest, good rice paddies. That is my native land, and yours. My ancestors of the seventieth generation were born there, married there, gave birth to their children. It was there that they constructed their homes. Then the Chinese barbarians invaded the north; they killed, pillaged, chased my ancestors from their land. So my ancestors had to leave . . ."*

"I know. The barbarians from the north hunted you

down. You bore arms against those who lived in the south. It was an unending circle of crimes."

"History is enmired in crime," says the wraith.

"Why didn't you resist?"

"No one can resist his fate."

"And yet it was you who taught us: There is no absolute fatality. Even man has his word to say about fate."

The wraith laughs: "That's exactly what I wanted to say to you."

"You would have done better to do it rather than just say it."

"In my time, we killed each other with sabers and lances. A letter took a week to reach its destination. Humanity was fragmented, cloistered in small, savage warrens. We lived in ignorance, isolated, like wild beasts, incapable of seeing over the bamboo hedgerow ringed with thorns. There was no promised land."

"You left us with an empty sack."

"And yet there was something," the wraith answers.

"What?"

"The triumphal arches."

I almost choke with laughter. "Ours far surpass anything you ever knew."

"Pride is the naiveté of children. Look at me: I have neither sandals nor hat nor rifle. I walk barefoot, a sack of roast corn on my shoulder. My lance was forged in one of the village hearths. We were almost naked. But yet we left you *the triumphal arches, left them with our flesh, our blood."*

"I don't give a damn about your triumphal arches, or you. Stop bothering me. I've had enough."

The wraith answers: "You are a drop of my blood. However many generations it has been, you belong to me. Don't be angry. Don't betray me. Once, before dying of sickness on this merciless earth, I too, I cursed my ancestors. Poor child. No one can choose his own history."

I feel as if I will suffocate, as if I will weep. I shout: "I don't give a damn!"

The wraith continues to watch me, without anger, without the slightest gesture of consolation. "It is better not to enter life with an empty sack. But neither should you dip into the sack you have inherited without hoping to fill another. Woe to he who inherits nothing. But even more wretched is he who leaves nothing to his descendants."

Disoriented, I stare into the vacant eyes of the wraith. "What do you mean? What do you still want from us?"

"We left you our triumphal arches. Why don't you build your own?"

I think to myself: He's lost it, the old man. Doesn't he see what we're doing? Hasn't he seen all the young people who've left for the front, who died with a song on their lips? And what about all those who're still advancing toward the wondrous half-circle of the horizon? But my tongue is frozen. I am incapable of pronouncing a single word.

The wraith gazes at me, tenderly, deeply, for a long

time. A gaze full of generosity and expectancy, intense, de-fying time, generations, dynasties, and cultures. I look at his dusty feet, his filthy, miserable pants, his lance, his sack of roast corn. My poor ancestors. Wretched architects of glory.

◆　◆　◆

"Hey, you're really snoozing soundly!"

I started and wheeled around. It was no flickering flame at the foot of a citadel I saw but the face of a tiny man coming out of Zone B9. "What were you dreaming about like that?" He chuckled. "Better off looking over there . . ." And he pointed to the boat that carried the leading team. The young guide was asleep, her head resting on the commander's shoulder. He was probably both flattered and scared, because he stood speechless, staring in front of him. My neighbor laughed, his mouth spreading into a toothy grin. "I bet you'd like to trade places with the commander, eh?"

"No," I responded brutally.

He turned up his nose. "My, you're touchy."

I fell silent. I didn't feel like talking.

◆　◆　◆

The sun had plummeted. Only a crescent still lingered, red as a painted fingernail. The river shimmered. Clouds had gathered on the distant banks; the sandbars turned to violet. I imagined an identical evening lost through the ages, the strains of a solitary flute drifting over battlefields littered with the bodies of horses and men.

❖　❖　❖

Luong was waiting for me. He had been there for a week already, preparing his ideological-education course. The hair at his temples had become even whiter. The first night we saw quite an amazing play. No one had the heart to talk about anything. As for myself, I forgot all about Luong the moment the red curtains rose in front of the sunken stage they had dug out of the earth. From behind the set the sounds of an out-of-tune piano, a halting accordion. You would almost have thought it was the croaking of frogs. And yet my heart froze. Schoolboy memories mixed with half-bloomed dreams of childhood washed over me, rekindling hopes long dead. I stood motionless, transfixed, listening to the artists tune their instruments in a jumble of chords. I lay in wait for the ring of a woman's laughter. Every time I heard it, I felt a wild longing to meet her. But fear held me back. Someone tugged at my shoulder: "Let's go in quickly, it's going to start."

I followed obediently, like a raft borne by the current. Dance after dance. I remember nothing, except that I watched, spellbound, the faces shimmering with beauty and joy, the lithe, bewitching bodies of the men and women on stage. My mind emptied. With all my soul, I watched. Like a man wandering in the jungle at night follows a beacon, I was hypnotized by the beauty that had deserted us, that I only barely remembered. A radiant smile, a tantalizing, liquid gaze, an invitation to dream, a romance full of love and youth, the legendary seductress, Thi Mau, with her long, glistening hair, her curves beguiling beneath a wispy, flowered tunic. The audience exploded in wave after wave of applause. Someone grabbed my sleeve: "Have you lost your wits?"

I didn't answer, just looked at him, dazed. He laughed in my face. "Do I hear your blood rumbling?"

"Yeah, it's rumbling all right," I agreed.

"Well, keep the lid on your hormones. The ideological rectification sessions are coming up. Watch out for low blows."

I just grumbled and shook my head. He did the same. "Bitch of life. A guy isn't even allowed to fantasize a bit."

I was just about to say something when Luong appeared. As always, his head held straight and high, his neck rigid, his face grave. "Let's go to my room," he said.

I said good-bye to my carefree companion and followed Luong down a crazy welter of paths. It was as complicated as a labyrinth, like an enormous spider's web spread out on the ground, among the rotting, phosphorescent leaves. Groups of men came and went, the beams of their flashlights sweeping over the ground. They consulted our camp map, asked directions, joked, laughed, whispered. A real nocturnal hive of activity. Luong asked: "How did you like the performers?"

"They're very good."

He made some black tea and served me a cup of it with two spoonfuls of sugar. "Drink this."

He waited until I had drained the cup: "I didn't want to tell you. But you would have learned about it anyway."

I looked at him. And he lowered his eyes. I realized it was serious. "You want to transfer me to another unit?"

"No."

"Is the division in danger?"

"No."

I stopped and waited. A long moment passed. His gaze lost in the distance, Luong sighed and said softly: "Bien is dead."

I didn't move. Slowly, he continued: "He had mobilized some guys to raise vegetables, some corn. One day he stepped on a piece of shrapnel. The wound got infected. It was tetanus that killed him."

I got up. "Take me to see Huc. I want to know how he died."

"Huc isn't here. The special unit was exempted from the ideological education course; they got some urgent production quotas. Look, we're going to launch a big campaign. We've sent Huc two companies as reinforcement. He's just been promoted to captain."

"New quotas? How many? Ten thousand coffins? A hundred thousand?" I asked.

Luong didn't move. I watched his rigid head set on his rigid neck. I realized he wasn't going to say anything more, that he would never tell me anything ever again. Men came and went in my brain; I saw the Van Kieu carrying the coffins on their backs, their shadows against the mountain in the dazzling greenness of the dawn. I saw the convoys of trucks covered with canvas, tightly sealed, jolting through the forest with their funereal cargo. Coffins, empty eyes, empty sacks. This was what awaited me.

Luong kept silent, motionless.

Suddenly I feared him. "Luong, don't you have anything to say to me?" He didn't answer. I shouted at him: "Luong!"

"I'm very sad, Quan. But war is war. The historic mission that has fallen to our people . . ."

"I've heard that on the radio a hundred times. Thousands of times." I turned and left. He looked as if he had wanted to see me out, but I left too quickly for that. I hadn't even looked at him, this man, my childhood friend.

◆　　　◆　　　◆

We used to dive together into the same river, splashing the sun into a million shards on the surface of the water. Once we had measured our penises with blades of grass to see who had the longest. Luong, Bien, and I—we all had penises the size of chili peppers. Childhood. Time of friendship, time of equality.

Lovesick doves cooed all day in the bamboo. Grasshoppers flew in the grass on the edge of the dikes. Women laughed, teasing and chasing one another, rolling in the rice fields. They made us laugh . . . There was once a kite that dipped and swayed in the blue of the sky, our dreams reeling in the same space . . . And there is this earth, this mud where the flesh rots, where eyes decompose. These arms, these legs that crunch in the jaws of the boars. The souls ulcerated and foul from killing, the bodies so starved for tenderness that they haunt stables in search of pleasure. There is this gangrene that eats at the heart . . .

You fool. You should have listened to me. I remembered the morning that Bien saw me off; if only he had listened to me, if only he had gone back to the village, gone back to breathe life into the young man who had once carried a hundred loads of paddy a day!

If only . . .

Words. These were only words. You throw them like a bridge between regret and despair. *If only . . .*

✦   ✦   ✦

An evening in springtime, on the riverbanks. It is cool outside. We hear the fish flick at the surface of the water, wind murmuring in the grass. The sky seems too near the earth, pressing down on us; three country boys are sprawled on the ground, hands folded behind their heads, dreaming. Dreams teeming like tadpoles, then suddenly swallowed up by a huge

*jaw. Grandiose dream of the masses. A dream of sainthood
on earth for all of humanity.*

"I left you the triumphal arches."

*The wraith's voice wanders through the forests, merging
with the rustle of leaves, the rushing of waterfalls. I sit down
under the spiral-shaped citadel. I listen to the sad whistle of
the flute. The wraith sits at my side, lays down his lance. The
stench of rotting flesh rises from his feet; green tears gather
in his eyes; ancient mosses sprout from his temples, his ears.
I ask him: "Why do you weep all the time? We've had more
than enough of that, we don't know what to do with all these
ghost tears."*

"I am lamenting for you."

*"Better to lament your feet, your lance, your sack of
rotten corn."*

*The wraith nodded in agreement: "And yet it was we
who expelled the army of Genghis Khan."*

*"Your triumphal arch is outdated. It'll rot just like the
old temple roofs from those days."*

*"Keep the faith. Without this old altar, your knees would
be like cotton before today's invaders."*

*"But in the old days, humanity didn't even know the
name of this country."*

*His green tears glint in the night, fall one by one. The
wraith lowers his head: "A drop of my blood, wandering until
now . . . Poor child."*

I fall silent. I listen to his sobs echo through the night. The wraith raises his head and stares at me with sad, doleful eyes. "We fought to defend the altar of the ancestors, the future of the country, we never fought for the cheers and applause of others."

A long sigh is carried off in the wind. The swollen feet lurch from path to path. The odor of stale sweat rushes back to me. The jungle slowly engulfs the shadow of times past. All that remained before me was a vacillating flame, a strange green glow, translucent, frigid.

◆   ◆   ◆

That night, the man who slept next to me was incontinent. In the morning I found one corner of my bedcovers wet, stinking of urine. He didn't even apologize, he just grumbled: "My machine is all screwed up. Anyway, by the time I go home to the village, there won't be a bitch left to enjoy it."

I carried my bedsheet off to the stream in silence. He joined me with his own covers and dirty clothes. It was cold; the fog swirled about in the wind. The icy water stung my hands, the fog grazed my face. The man had slipped in the water, wetting the legs of his pants. He trembled as he finished his washing. He turned abruptly toward me and tried to start a quarrel: "So, you're above speaking to me, eh? Are you trying to humiliate me or something?"

I threw the bedcovers on the ground. In one glance I

took stock of the situation. *Just three steps, and then, in the scuffle, a quick kick. He'll fall right into the water. That'll refresh him.*

He was livid. A huge bump rose on his forehead, right in the middle of his eyebrows. Like an old rooster, he stretched his neck over his threadbare pea jacket. I shivered. *With that face, he's not going to be with us for long. He won't come out of the next battle alive.* Judging from the content of Luong's ideological courses, I could imagine the atrocities they expected in the upcoming battle. One day soon . . . I suddenly saw his face gone white, lifeless, two eye sockets filled with rotting mud. I dropped my hands and began to wash my bedcover again. He continued to glare at me, mumbling: "So, you're not looking for any more trouble?"

❖   ❖   ❖

"North Star." Any battle baptized with that name could of course only be crowned with success. North Star had been dazzling and our battalion ceased to exist. Of the company, twelve soldiers survived. I received reinforcements within forty-eight hours. The north poured them out in torrents. Like a tide, the sons of Lac Hong swarmed toward the front.

❖   ❖   ❖

We advanced toward the south, toward a horizon ablaze.

❖   ❖   ❖

I was startled. *Bang, bang, bang.* I asked, "Who's shooting wildly like that?"

Tao got up. "I'll go see, Chief."

He vanished into the darkness. I stayed back, alone with the medic. The electric bulb blinded me. Never had I been bathed in so much light! The room was intact with its red leather armchairs, its curtains in white nylon, its telephone, its piles of stationery printed with violets. Accustomed to such luxury, how had the enemy been able to resist us? And what good were these pads of paper with little violets in the middle of a war?

"Don't move, Chief, I haven't finished yet." He was still changing my bandage. The wound looked like it was infected; it itched as if it were covered with ants. I heard another burst of gunfire.

"Weird. Who's the nut shooting like that? I've got to go. Haven't you finished?"

"Almost. Wait a minute." He finished winding up the roll of gauze, then gently but firmly secured it. *He's really ugly, but what hands of gold! He would be a marvelous sculptor.* Then the medic turned to me and said, "Let me come along with you."

"Okay."

We left the room, crossed a huge cement courtyard, moved in the direction of the shooting. It was coming from a warehouse. An odd, murky light lit the dark construction cranes, white sheets, pieces of parachute cloth hung from stiff

threads. The smell of gunpowder mingled with smoke and the
stench of wounds and blood suffused the night air, filtering
into my brain. I listened to the odd clacking of my footsteps
on the cold, hard cement. Up until now I was accustomed to
having the noise of my steps lost in the rustle of grass and
underbrush, sucked up by the mud, drowned out by the
crunch of empty shells underfoot, by the clattering of guns.
This was the first time we had entered a city.

"Hurry up," I said. We hurried toward a group of huts
that we could make out in the pallid light of a lantern. Tao
rushed up to me: "Chief, they won't stop shooting. I can't
stop them . . ."

"Shooting at who?"

"No one. They're just shooting at anything they can
find."

"Lead me there, quickly."

Tao ran ahead. We entered the warehouse. The roof
must have been eleven yards high; it was supported by a wire
framework that was at once simple and bizarre. Crates of
merchandise were piled right up to the roof, leaving only
enough space for little rectilinear alleyways between them.
Bursts of submachine-gun fire. Laughter rang out, chanting
mixed with grumbling, drunken voices.

"Who are they?" I asked.

"That's Lanh's patrol," answered Tao.

"Are they all drunk?"

"Some of them. Not all." Then Tao stopped me. "Chief, let's go over there."

We entered another warehouse. The alleyways were larger there. Rows of bare light bulbs lit the roof. The ceiling shone. Suddenly I saw a trickle of red liquid spread, slowly dripping down onto my shoes. Before I could react, another translucent stream, like grenadine, glistened and oozed across the roof.

"What the hell is this?"

"Medicine, Chief!"

"What kind?"

"Vitamin B12 serum. It's American, really good quality. They've already smashed four other containers in the other warehouse. We were in it up to our ankles, and it still hasn't stopped . . ."

I felt moisture on my feet and looked down to see a sticky, red substance spreading across the alleyway. We walked through the stream.

Another burst of gunfire. The echoes rebounded violently inside the warehouse, hurting my eyes. Tao rushed forward and shouted: "The chief is here—cease fire!" His voice was drowned out by the reports. They were still shouting when we arrived, the medic and I.

Two steps away from Tao a little guy, his skin blackened by sun, shot like a madman into a crate. It was Tuan, who was from Ha Tinh. He stood on his bowed legs, as skinny as two branches, and shot with his teeth clenched. He had the red eyes of a drunkard. Tao thumped him hard on the shoulder and he turned around and saw us. He looked at me, distraught, then burst out laughing.

"Who gave you the order to shoot?"

He planted his submachine gun between his legs. "Chief, this stuff is American, so I'm destroying it."

"Are you blind? Do you know what this is?"

"I don't know anything. All I know is that it's American."

"This is medicine, energy food. The stuff they inject you with when you're in the army hospital."

"No, Chief, you've got it wrong," Tuan shrieked. "They . . . they injected me with Soviet medicine." He fell silent, teetered for a moment, unsteady on his feet, and stepped aside. I saw a vein on his neck pulse.

"Where's Lanh?" I asked the guys standing behind Tuan. "Sleeping, Chief. He's totally smashed."

"Well, this is a fine mess! Where the hell did you find the booze?"

"In the headquarters' kitchen," said one of the soldiers, pointing. "There's lots of it. All kinds." They all had the faces of whipped dogs. I realized that the instigator was somewhere else; these men were totally incapable of planning a ransacking like this. "Who put you up to this? Who? Or do you all want to be court-martialed?"

Tuan stepped forward, still reeling. "Chief, forgive us. We didn't do anything bad."

"Who brought you here?" I barked imperiously.

He raised his head, stammering: "It was Kha. He said—"

"Oh so it was him, that little fool! Bring him to me!" I shouted. But even before the soldiers had had a chance to go look for him, Kha suddenly appeared behind me. "Here I am, Chief."

Undoubtedly he had hidden between two rows of crates. He was white with fear, but still calm. "So it was you!" I said.

Kha said nothing.

"How much have you had to drink?"

I sniffed his breath. Not the slightest scent of alcohol. "Oh so that's it; you stay sober so you can mastermind the whole operation." He lowered his eyes in silence. "Follow me," I said.

Tao led Tuan and the other drunkards back to their huts. Kha followed me, the medic bringing up the rear.

As we crossed the airstrip, a huge fire broke out to the west. On the horizon, the arrow-shaped silhouette of a church in flames, gleaming like a bayonet pointed toward the sky. Next to it a few stars glowed weakly.

A clock chimed in the distance. "It's midnight, Chief," said the medic.

"You go get some sleep," I said. I took Kha to my office. It was open and the lights were on. The wind had overturned the crystal paperweight, scattering my letters. I ordered Kha to sit down, took a bottle of white wine out of the closet, and filled two glasses.

"Well, now it's our turn to drink. After that, if there's nothing left to shoot at, we can always shoot at each other."

Kha took the glass and looked at me. "Forgive me, Quan."

"Have a drink first." I emptied my glass. He did the same. His face showed no sign of fear. *The bastard: he knows I like him and he's taking advantage of it.* After Hoang's death, I had transferred my affections to Kha. He wasn't as pure as Hoang; he was a clever one, full of mischief, lazy, but good-hearted. When the situation required it, he knew how to fight to redress the balance, and didn't balk at sacrifice. In battle he always found the most efficient solution, the way to save our blood. He didn't run after women. He liked to dream. He could think of a thousand and one practical jokes.

"That's the way. You know how to drink, don't you? Let's empty the bottle."

"If you like."

"Now you're talking. You probably think I'm here to fortify your health, to listen to your exploits."

He lowered his head, fidgeted with his glass. In the transparence of the crystal, the ripple of waves, a luminous tide, endless and shoreless. Waves of my childhood in the middle of the marshes. Birds swoon and fall as hunters from town launch a volley of lead. Blood flows onto the weeds, the flowers, into the water; children paddle about in the mud and the marsh grass, stare at a horizon where nothing ever happens. Only the passing of an old steam train, spitting soot, tottering along like Don Quixote's old horse, lost in the centuries of this country. Little girls who straddle the water buffalo see their tiny breasts for the first time reflected in the water. Frightened by some ancestral terror, they hide them like stolen fruit, watch them anxiously as they swell and blossom. Later they will gaze at them with hatred as they wither and sag onto flattened chests, that no man would ever fondle, that no baby would ever suckle. A circle of light quivered . . . the marshes . . . crystal dreams. A huge fireworks display cascades down into ash over the remains of a thousand disemboweled firecrackers . . .

A gust of wind raised the curtain in the room, shattering my glass on the floor. The crystal shards scattered on the stone floor. Kha glanced at the debris, still waiting. I went and sat down next to him.

"Why?"

Kha spoke softly. "Forgive me, elder brother."

"But why did you do it?"

He said nothing. I pressed him: "What was in it for you?" Kha raised his eyes and looked me straight in the face. "In any case, it will all be the same for me."

"You're wrong. You ransacked public property, the people's property. Everything we've paid for with our blood belongs to the people."

Kha just laughed. "Ah, but do the people really exist?"

Suddenly I saw his weary smile, his discouraged eyes against his pale face. The little bastard that I had always protected was calling me a gullible fool. I swallowed my anger and smiled. "Go ahead; I'm listening. What did you destroy today?"

"Three types of containers. They had glass windows. The way the glass shattered, it was like a party. There were also the refrigerators in the headquarters' kitchen. As for this evening—"

"That's enough. What you've destroyed would have been enough to treat thousands of sick people. As for the containers with glass windows, those were big televisions, they could have provided entertainment for hundreds of viewers."

"Yes. But the ones who get to watch have nothing to do with the people . . . The people, that's my mother, my father, your parents, the soldiers. None of them will ever get a crumb."

"How dare you!"

Kha put his hand on my shoulder. "Quan, listen. When I was seventeen I lived in a little provincial town. We organized a big charity effort to build a cemetery for the men who died during the anticolonial resistance. By coincidence, I was at home when they came by. I watched as my mother gave them money. I noticed a thousand-dong bill that had a hole about the size of a sesame seed right on the picture of the stalk of rice. Five days later, a female classmate of mine invited me to go for a walk in town. The girl was younger than I was, with rosy skin, but she had a thick neck and was a bit cross-eyed. She was madly in love with me. She threw money to the wind, bought everything without even haggling, only the most expensive trinkets. Her father was president of the town. But in one day she could spend six times his monthly salary. Among one of the bills in her wallet I recognized the thousand-dong note with the hole in it the size of the sesame seed . . . No doubt about it, that was my mother's money."

I said nothing. Neither did Kha. We both listened to the wind whistle over the airstrip, the crackling of the fire in the distance. After a long moment I said, "You've confused me, Kha."

"I've thought a lot. I also listen to everything that's said. You see, the people, they do exist from time to time, but they're only a shadow. When they need rice, the people are the buffalo that pulls the plow. When they need soldiers, they cover the people with armor, put guns in the people's hands. When all is said and done, at the festivals, when it comes time for the banquets, they put the people on an altar, and feed them incense and ashes. But the real food, that's always for them."

I was dazed. I felt as if I were drowning, just like when

my cousin used to play at pushing me into the river. Kha continued: "You can court-martial me, but I can't change. It's too bad that I've learned the truth. I won't be able to see things in the same way anymore."

He lowered his head. The bastard. He had completely stunned me. I remembered the whiteness of his hands as he warmed them over the fire in Scorpion Cave. I remembered the piece of stringy, burned vulture he had given me on the murderous Route No. 9. I remembered his skinny, naked body, tortured by malaria, scampering along the edge of the stream. I remembered . . . and my body tensed, started to shake. I shouted at him: "Get out of here! You deserve a bullet from the firing squad. Go to sleep. And from now on, stop fucking around, and stop this mindless waste."

Kha rose. He left without a word.

✦   ✦   ✦

I stayed alone. The wind swept through the room, scattering my writing paper. I picked up the crystal paperweight and fondled it, passing it between my hands, watching the pieces of paper take flight like huge white butterflies. The room swirled with white wings. I was cold. It wasn't the wind; it was a cold that came from far off, as if it had been bred in my marrowless bones, in my own flesh and skin. A cold more intense than all the rainy seasons on the Truong Son mountain range, than all the water and jungle fog. It was as if the cold of all those years had suddenly frozen my heart, here, tonight . . . My whole body shook. I placed the paperweight on the floor and watched the wind scatter the white sheets around the room, out the door, toward the night.

✦   ✦   ✦

A rooster announced the dawn. I rose and went to look for it. I hadn't slept a wink all night. I felt washed out. My new liaison agent arrived: "You're quite an early riser, Chief."

"Make me some tea."

He actually looked genuinely enthusiastic. Eighteen years old, just enlisted, and he had already volunteered to liberate the plains. He had never known hunger, thirst, malaria, depression, the desire for a woman, homesickness for his village . . . They had given him to me to replace the liaison agent who died during the "North Star" campaign. I crossed the airstrip. The chill air braced me, made me lucid again.

A rooster crowed insistently behind the wall. I jumped over a pile of bricks littered with cartridges, empty cans, cotton, and bandages. I found the rooster, a white one, locked in a pretty little wire-mesh cage that was perched, miraculously, in the middle of these ruins. A half-empty bowl filled with rice fragments, another with crushed corn, and a bowl of water in which a spent shell floated. The feathered creature glared at me, clucking its tongue softly, as if calling for chickens. A thought crossed my mind: Would you be the evil rooster out of the legend of An Duong Vuong, to come here at dawn like this? He cocked his head to one side, stared fixedly at me, as if to say: "Why not? Whenever I crow, citadels crumble."

"Chief."

I started and wheeled around; it was the liaison agent. "Chief," he said, pointing to the rooster. "If you like, at noon . . ." I forced myself to hide the sensation of unease that had overcome me.

"What's the matter?" My voice was dry.

He sulked, scratching his head: "Chief, the tea is ready . . ."

"Well, come in then."

He stood in one corner of the room and I in the other, heavy-hearted. I always felt depressed when I drank tea with Thai. Deep down inside, I cursed Kha and yet, inexplicably, I knew he was right. His vague premonitions seemed to flutter about me like ravens above a cemetery.

"According to the commander's orders, the unit should take to the road at seven o'clock tonight. I'll give them fresh food at noon," Thai said.

"Very good. Let's eat early. Dinner at four-thirty. We'll be lighter for the march."

"Do you have any special instructions for the platoon leaders?"

"No."

Thai finished his tea and left. I remained alone, tortured by my doubts and fears. I heard the soldiers running back and forth in the courtyard. A feverish mood had taken hold of everyone. Eyes shone with excitement, mouths twitched impatiently, gestures were brusque. Everyone was enlisted to watch over the trucks. They all rushed toward the horizon, over there, where the triumphal arch soared up already from behind the curtain of blood and dust. I felt alone. Kha's story obsessed me. My cowardly heart couldn't bear the doubt. My own private was tougher than I. Kha had fought like the rest of us, put up with all the misery, the deprivation, and he had survived. He was one of the twelve men still left from my old company. And yet Kha had made the long march without ever dreaming of glory, without even hoping for a share of the spoils. In his numbed brain, beyond the rainbow of glory, he knew that there would come a day when he would go back to the mud of the rice paddies, to life as it had always been, from time immemorial.

◆　　◆　　◆

At noon, at the victory banquet, the champagne flowed. I pretended not to notice Kha, but I knew he was watching me. It must have been a pitying look. No doubt he discerned in my pale, troubled face the confusion of a kid who had just been left in the dark for the first time. *Son of a bitch. How dare he look at me like that? I let him off too easily. I should teach him a lesson* . . . I tried to control my fury, let my eyes wander over the gathering. When I looked at him, he smiled. A sad, comprehending smile, like a last ray of winter sun. He looked uneasy, like a man for whom time was running out, and who had just shifted his burden to another's back, a burden he had carried alone for too long, that he couldn't bear any longer.

Laughter and toasts rang out all around us. Their enthusiasm had reached its peak. Faces shone with hope. Outside, they were revving the motors of the trucks, getting ready to drive us away as soon as the sun set. I suddenly knew that we were alone, Kha and I, in the middle of this happy gathering. We were linked to each other by the same pain, for having shared the same secret . . .

It was dawn. The sun poured streams of red light onto the earth. Our vehicles advanced along a road littered with boots, shoes, uniforms, berets, sacks, and packages, sparkling cartridges, broken toothbrushes, bras, smashed sandwiches, headless dolls . . . The enemy's demise had just begun.

"Toward the Delta, ahead toward the Delta," someone shouted. Everyone echoed in chorus: "Toward the Delta, comrades, toward the Delta."

The wind blew in my face. Red dust swirled, drowning everything around us. Behind my back a guy laughed: "Ha ha . . . We've been buried like rats in the jungle for years. You bunch of bastards, here we come. Now it's your turn to dance!"

Laughter burst forth over the wind, over the rumble of the trucks. At an intersection we passed a convoy of trucks to our left. In front of the convoy stood a white jeep abandoned by the puppet army, its tires reduced to ashes. The driver was dead, slumped over the wheel. The soldiers cried out: "Hey, tank comrades, crush it for us!" The tank commanders seated on top of their tanks greeted us with a wave.

"Bravo, bravo!"

"Farewell!"

My soldiers, all excited, got up, waving about, shouting themselves hoarse: "Crush it, comrades!"

The tank commanders seemed to understand. One of them slipped back down inside his turret. We saw the tank turn slowly in the direction of the jeep and move to crush it. "Bravo, bravo!"

"You guys are great!"

I turned away. I caught Kha's gaze. He looked different; he was smiling. My soldiers continued to shout and gesticulate, waving at the tanks as they went on their way. And then we moved on. I fell asleep to the chanting of the young recruits. They were bursting with energy. They could have kept on shouting forever. Even in my sleep I felt as if I could imagine the impending battle; it was certain to be a hundred times less dangerous than all the previous battles. The enemy was in flight. A headlong retreat like that destroyed the possibility of even the slightest resistance. We would win. The triumphal arch flickered on the horizon. My heart brimmed over with a

poignant, painful joy. At the same time, my mind was etched
with a chilling image.

◆ ◆ ◆

*I see myself break away from the crowd. I grab onto red-and-
gold lacquered posts, grope my way out a door, through ru-
ined fields. Bits of fodder still lie about. In the distance the
marshes glisten. A flock of storks paddles about in the silt,
chasing tiny shrimp. I track them, silent as a shadow, my
bare feet plunging into the grass, into the mud.*

◆ ◆ ◆

The battle had unfolded as predictably as if it had been a
parade: assault, a rapid conclusion. We had never dreamed
of this outcome. Compared to the battles of the last ten years,
it almost seemed like a game. I don't know how many times
I sat alone in the immaculate enemy headquarters, listening
to the clock on the wall tick out the time. Every half hour I
heard a cuckoo bird call. In the drawers I found documents,
cards, bills, garishly colored photos of nude women. Suddenly
the liaison agent entered: "Chief, chief . . ."

"What is it?"

"There's an American among the prisoners. The guys
are asking what to do."

"That's strange. The Americans left two years ago. How
could there be any left here?"

"Chief, he's huge, and no one can understand what the hell he's saying."

"Bring him here."

He complied politely and left. I gazed absently at a window bathed in sunlight, my mind empty. A few minutes later they brought the American. At least four of my soldiers, all with their guns pointed at him. The prisoner had his arms tied behind him and he walked awkwardly. The soldiers pushed him brutally. He squinted in pain as he fell to his knees onto the floor. He raised his head and looked at me. An indescribable look.

"Does anyone in the company speak English?"

One of the guys spoke up: "Chief, when we first caught him, Thai asked around. Nobody here speaks English. Khiem tried to speak to him in Russian, but he just shook his head."

"Untie him," I said. "In the middle of this forest of guns, how could he escape?"

The soldiers untied him. The man said something, undoubtedly his thanks, relaxed, and stretched his purple fingers a few times. His skin was as white as soybean sprouts. He talked for a long time, gesticulating. Apparently he wanted to say that he wasn't a soldier but a journalist or a photographer. He kept thumping his chest and pointing his finger to it, mimicking that he was taking a picture. Blond, with clear blue eyes, he had pink skin and a hairy chest. These foreign features had long designated him as the target of our ancestral hatred. The foreign invader. Our fathers had felt the same hatred for the braided plaits of the Huns. They channeled their hatred into their arrows, their swords. The same force animated us when we launched our B-40 and B-41 rockets, when we thrust with our bayonets.

"We're wasting our time," said one of the soldiers.

"He's probably a spy. Throw him in prison," said another.

"In prison? Who's going to guard him? Give him a copper candy."

"Now that's a wise decision, Chief. The road is waiting. Let's get rid of this nuisance."

The prisoner looked at the soldiers who surrounded him, who discussed him, and he smiled. He had an engaging air. What an idiot—did he think we were discussing his dinner menu? He tossed his blond hair as he smiled. He shrugged his shoulders. It was at that moment that I realized how big he was. A real colossus. He had the same back and shoulders as Bien; a man who looked like he was born to carry a hundred loads of paddy a day . . . He kept smiling naively, watching me. My hatred suddenly subsided, like a tiger slipped from its cage, it wandered outside, somewhere in the jungle. Even the wild beast knew moments of weariness . . . Another time and I would have shot him on sight, without hesitation, with his rosy skin, his blond hair. A foreign invader! The object of our hatred! We had wedded our dignity to that hatred, confused survival with destruction.

"Chief." My soldiers were pressing me. "Chief, make up your mind."

One of them said in a low voice: "Chief, these Yankees only eat meat. Are we going to feed him and make our own comrades go hungry? Give me your consent. I'll take care of it. It'll be all over in a flash."

The prisoner looked at the soldier, blinking, pensive. I suddenly imagined a green hill, this young man embracing his lover, rolling in the grass. Perhaps she was a city girl, like the woman in the strange nude photos I had seen. Or maybe a country girl, like one of ours, with a name like Flower, Peace, Glory, Jasmine, Plum, or Apricot. Perhaps he too had stretched out beside a friend on some spring evening and dreamed of the gods and their lovemaking, just as Bien had dreamed about Goddess Nu Oa mating with Tu Tuong. Perhaps this man had left it all behind to put on a soldier's uniform, to defend freedom, to write passionate lines in his diary. He too must have been drunk on a vision of himself marching till dawn with medals across his chest against a horizon of fire and flames . . . I felt my back break out in a cold sweat.

"Chief, it's time to eat. We're hungry. Make a decision quickly."

"My god, you're simpleminded!" I said coldly. "The war's over. We're not in the jungle anymore. Anybody, including me, who doesn't respect the policy toward prisoners goes before a court-martial, is that clear?"

I turned and left. The guys were cowed. They led the American off in silence, gently, trying not to jostle him.

◆ ◆ ◆

I returned to my office. I thought about the spiderwebs that hung in the wind, about this strange game of hide-and-seek we called war. How many times had I seen corpses hanging from branches, eyes gouged out, men's bodies split into two, ligaments cut at the knee, legs folded back like those of grasshoppers? An endless settling of scores. Even as the cannons announced our victory, crows shriek in circles above our cemeteries, violating corpses we didn't have time to bury . . . A dizzying stench of carrion and gunpowder.

The sun set. All the lights in the town flickered on. By dusk the air was aglow with flashlights and candles. My soldiers had gotten their hands on a stock of candles. They lit them all over the place—in their rooms, in the courtyards. As the evening meal was served, night fell. The kitchen team discovered a cellar filled with wine and they emptied the bottles into a huge bathtub, marrying red and white wine, champagne, cognac. Everyone helped themselves to their fill, ladling it up with their mess tins. Faces multiplied in the glow of hundreds and hundreds of candles and lightbulbs. The men laughed and chattered, reeling, celebrating, singing . . . The table was piled with canned goods—ours and the enemy's.

American and Soviet fish, Chinese meat, American cookies, Chinese apples . . . The meal dragged on for a long time. Thai sat next to me. He seemed to have something to say, but he lowered his head, furtively wiping away a tear. He must have been thinking of his brother.

I wanted to console him, but I said nothing. I thought of my own brother. Then I don't think of anyone at all. I remember a face without a name, silent, still alive, a face that surfaces from the flood of my past. Fifteen years have gone by. He smiles at me.

Some of the soldiers staggered off. Others stayed and gathered to chat. Kha and Tao went by. I saw them go outside. I hear two cans clank against each other.

"Go ahead, Kha, piss."

"Why not?"

"I challenge you to fill these two cans."

"Oh, so this is a contest? All right."

The sound of piss spurting into the can. Kha says: "I think you've got the edge on me. I'm drunk, so a lot went to the side. Go on, bring the candle; let's see."

Tao bursts into the room, grabs the candle and bolts out. We hear him laugh: "It's a tie. You filled two American fish cans, and I filled half a Chinese meat can. We're even."

"Okay. So your bladder and mine are the same size. Good lord, I've never been this drunk. Your face is dancing. Let's go to sleep, Tao."

I hear their footsteps grow distant. The soldiers around

me also leave. There are only two of us left now. Thai asks me: "So when do we start marching again?"

"Let's wait for orders."

"All these years, our company was always at the front line of the key offensives," says Thai bitterly.

I laugh. "Everything changes. There are only twelve veterans now. The rest, they're rookies. What good is it to send them to the hot spots? To have a barbecue?"

"Of course. But it's sad, Quan."

"Yeah, glory only lasts so long."

"What happens afterward?"

"How do I know? We're all in the same herd of sheep."

Thai falls silent a moment, then says in a low voice: "Our company received the Heroes' Medal. We . . . you and I, we're going to climb the ranks quickly."

I don't answer. His voice pours into my ear, but all I hear now is the lapping of water at the foot of a bridge, the murmur of stalks of rice, a clear chant that rises from the fields, from the solitude of the countryside:

> *I'm climbing on Mount Quan Doc,*
> *I'm sitting at the foot of the banyan tree . . .*

A mournful chant we had wedded to the lament of a two-string guitar. Chant of the months, of the years spent in the Truong Son mountains. Soldier, the dawn is icy. You fall under the bullets. On the white of the parachute cloth, I see your blood spreading.

Hanoi, December 11, 1990
Twenty-fifth day of the tenth month
of the Year of the Horse

FOR THE BEST IN PAPERBACKS, LOOK FOR THE

In every corner of the world, on every subject under the sun, Penguin represents quality and variety—the very best in publishing today.

For complete information about books available from Penguin—including Penguin Classics, Penguin Compass, and Puffins—and how to order them, write to us at the appropriate address below. Please note that for copyright reasons the selection of books varies from country to country.

In the United States: Please write to *Penguin Group (USA), P.O. Box 12289 Dept. B, Newark, New Jersey 07101-5289* or call 1-800-788-6262.

In the United Kingdom: Please write to *Dept. EP, Penguin Books Ltd, Bath Road, Harmondsworth, West Drayton, Middlesex UB7 0DA.*

In Canada: Please write to *Penguin Books Canada Ltd, 90 Eglinton Avenue East, Suite 700, Toronto, Ontario M4P 2Y3.*

In Australia: Please write to *Penguin Books Australia Ltd, P.O. Box 257, Ringwood, Victoria 3134.*

In New Zealand: Please write to *Penguin Books (NZ) Ltd, Private Bag 102902, North Shore Mail Centre, Auckland 10.*

In India: Please write to *Penguin Books India Pvt Ltd, 11 Panchsheel Shopping Centre, Panchsheel Park, New Delhi 110 017.*

In the Netherlands: Please write to *Penguin Books Netherlands bv, Postbus 3507, NL-1001 AH Amsterdam.*

In Germany: Please write to *Penguin Books Deutschland GmbH, Metzlerstrasse 26, 60594 Frankfurt am Main.*

In Spain: Please write to *Penguin Books S. A., Bravo Murillo 19, 1° B, 28015 Madrid.*

In Italy: Please write to *Penguin Italia s.r.l., Via Benedetto Croce 2, 20094 Corsico, Milano.*

In France: Please write to *Penguin France, Le Carré Wilson, 62 rue Benjamin Baillaud, 31500 Toulouse.*

In Japan: Please write to *Penguin Books Japan Ltd, Kaneko Building, 2-3-25 Koraku, Bunkyo-Ku, Tokyo 112.*

In South Africa: Please write to *Penguin Books South Africa (Pty) Ltd, Private Bag X14, Parkview, 2122 Johannesburg.*